Praise for
THE
SCORCHED
EARTH

ALSO BY RACHAEL BLOK

Under the Ice

THE SCORCHED EARTH

RACHAEL BLOK

First published in the UK in 2019 by Head of Zeus Ltd
This paperback edition first published in the UK in 2020
by Head of Zeus Ltd

9 7 5 3 1 2 4 6 8

A catalogue record for this book is available from
the British Library.

ISBN (PB): 9781788548052
ISBN (E): 9781788548021

Typeset by Divaddict Publishing Solutions Ltd

Printed and bound in Great Britain by
CPI Group (UK) Ltd, Croydon CR0 4YY

Head of Zeus Ltd
5–8 Hardwick Street
London EC1R 4RG

WWW.HEADOFZEUS.COM

For Mum and Dad, with love

Prologue

Two Years Earlier

'Leo!' The scream catches the wind and flies eastwards, outwards, over the sea.

But he is nowhere.

'Leo!'

Thick, foetid, clogged blood; sticky, soaking.

'Leo! Leo!'

Ben is alone. Rainwater runs through a hole in the tent; the tarpaulin ripped, broken; and he lies drenched, red and wanting. His hands, shaking, fumble with the zip.

The horizon lies flat, hazy with morning mist.

Leo is gone.

Secrets swim. Even buried – beneath rocks, rubble, sand – they find their way. Minutes, weeks, years... burying them papers over the cracks, a temporary fix. At some point they float upwards, looking for the light. Once out, frying in the sun, their form changes, and they blossom.

They bloat.

1

ANA

The earth is hard. The garden parched; cracked and faded, its colours leached and bled.

Every morning, too early, the sun wakes her, burning in from the east. Will not be ignored. They're both thirsty from the run. Jam with her tongue hanging out. Ana feels like doing the same.

Bare feet on the yellow grass, it's barely 7 a.m. and already the ground burns like coals. The light is hot on Ana's face; she closes her eyes to it, turning towards it. So many hot days without a break. She's already singed.

There had been a storm last night. She was sure there would be some sign of it but it barely registers. The wind is the only force to leave a trace. The dry leaves have been knocked from their branches; the bins are tilted or fallen, rubbish splayed and rotting. A glass left out on the patio has smashed. Its shards catch the light of the morning sun. Their edges flash with the early heat; Ana shivers.

Jam barks at her feet, then runs to scratch at the compost heap. She's Ana's shadow on her morning run. The dogs all get their walks early now, their paws burning on the ground once it approaches midday. Jam has been shorn, like a sheep. Her golden coat is cropped close. Her tongue lolls and pants, and Ana imagines she can see the steam rising from it.

'Kettle on?'

The voice of her mother rattles through the windows Ana had opened on coming downstairs. The pub smell, with its morning belch, is too much for her first thing. Coming home, an unwanted surprise in itself, offers its familiar scent without request, telling of weariness, of one drink too many, like an uncle with bad breath in an unwashed jumper.

'Coffee? Here.' Her mother lands a mug on the bar as Ana ducks under the low stone doorway. Her mother is pushing up her sleeves in her faded tartan shirt. She's wearing Marigolds.

'Mum, the cleaner is starting this morning. You don't need to do in here.'

'Ana, love. I've cleaned this bar at 7 a.m. for thirty years, and a bit of—'

'Mum, look, she's here.' Ana opens the door, watching Jess arrive in flared jeans and rainbow T-shirt, smiling at the sixty-year-old; her hair catches the sun, the purple tinge from a dye grown out glinting, and the rest fading upwards into a soft grey.

Her mum looks nervous as she smiles, ready for Jess, who shouts, *'Bye, love,'* outside the open window, in answer to the male voice saying, *'See you later, Mum'*. The back doors of a white van are visible through the window.

It must be hard for her mum, handing the reins to someone else. But watching her mother wince when she stands after scrubbing, pull her shoulders with a grimace – well, Ana had insisted. She can see the cracks in her mother. She's grown brittle, like the earth.

Ana needs to be useful. Now she's here.

'I'll get started then. This for me? Ta.' Jess picks up Ana's coffee and takes a drink.

Ana catches her mother's eye and they smile.

'Got police out already I see, up at the temple graveyard.'

'Police?' Ana asks quickly.

'Yes, I got Charlie to stop the van and I asked on my way past. Anyway, the police are there for something to do with a body, I'm guessing. Sunny Atkinson was there. I know his mum. Said I wasn't to say anything as he's not supposed to talk about it. Got his police gear on and all that, but I've known him since nappies.'

'A body? What? Someone's died?'

'Well, that's the thing.' Jess leans in for a second,

hand on the wooden bar, cloths hung over the real ale handles, ice buckets empty and upended. 'It's not just someone's died. Seems someone's gone and been buried. In a new grave. Done it in the night. Not supposed to be there is what Sunny says. Someone's put a body in a grave what they've dug themselves. Must've been hard in that wind. I wouldn't have wanted to hang around a graveyard in that.' She leans out and reaches for the bucket, shuddering.

'Who is it?' Ana's mum leans over the bar, mug in hand. 'Who's dead?'

'Well, ain't that the thing. They don't know. Sunny tells me it's not a new body. Looks like it's been dead a while. No question, right queer affair.'

Ana leans back, thankful for the white stone wall, solid, behind her.

She sees her mother look over, the glee of gossip gone from her eyes.

'But is there any sign of who put it there? Of why they'd bury an old body?' There must be some betrayal of emotion in Ana's tone. She'd tried to keep it steady, but Jess glances her way.

Jess knows. The village knows. Everyone knows.

Changing tack, shifting the weight from hip to hip, Jess halts, stands, looking at Ana properly. She fingers the edge of the mop handle gently, dips her eyes down, and her volume. Her fingernails are short, with chipped dark-blue paint, and she wears a black Casio watch, the kind you can buy from the market in town. Ana watches the blink of the screen as the seconds flash by.

'Now, I know nothing else.' Jess's tone is softer. 'I shouldn't have spoken. I'm sure it's... Well, I'm sure whatever it is will clear itself up quickly.' She catches Ana's eye and smiles.

Fay Seabrook brings another mug of coffee and presses it into Ana's hands. 'Here, love. Sit down. I know what you're hoping for, but if there's anything to know, the police will call.'

'It's not just me. It's more if Ben sees it, if it's on the news before I know anything, and I'd want to be the first one to—'

'If there's anything to say,' her mum breaks in, 'then the police will say it.'

Ana's hands shake as she drinks.

'Another bit of news.' Jess's voice breaks in with cleaning, the beats of her speech landing with each sweep of the mop. 'Fabian Irvine is due back in the village. Flying in from *America*.' She breathes *America*, like it's made of gold.

Still thinking of the grave, of the body, that it might be... Ana doesn't feel her mother's fingers dig into her wrist until the nails meet her skin and the words follow, entering through the hairline indents.

Her mother sits next to her on the window seat, ready to bear her weight, her back straight.

'Fabian Irvine? Back in Ayot?' It's her mother who asks the question. Her grip remains like steel.

'Not yet. You're hosting his parents' anniversary party here, aren't you?'

Fay nods, slowly. 'Yes, in a few weeks. They didn't think Fabian could make it. He's busy over there, I hear. Got some new single out or something, his mum said. He produces a few big names now. The party is quite small.'

'Well, I've heard he's booked some tickets as a late surprise. Be good to have him back for a bit. Used to be a flame of yours, I remember?' This last bit comes with a wink, sent to Ana as an appeasement.

Her mother's grip is cold and firm. But it keeps her in the room. Keeps her from crying out.

'It was a while ago, nothing serious.' Her mother answers for her. Answers lightly.

The heat of the room creeps in, tying its knots.

Lying back, Ana rests her head on the window and allows her eyes to close. Jam comes up and licks her leg. Her dry tongue rasps, warm. And she reaches out, stroking what remains of Jam's silky blonde hair.

The coffee sits untouched as she thinks of Fabian Irvine in one sharp breath and of Ben in the other, waking to the news of an unidentified body discovered in an unmarked grave.

The heat of the dry sun has made its way into the bar. Its blanket smothers her.

2

MAARTEN

'Here's the water you asked for, sir.'

Sunny is by Maarten's side, passing out paper cups to an already overheated team. Adrika kneels in the dirt. It's brittle and crumbling, despite the storm.

The graveyard lies in an arc in front of the Palladian church. Nicknamed 'the temple' by the locals, its pillars maintain their cold against the burn of the sun; surrounded by the flurry of the crime scene, already sweating. Fingers hot in plastic gloves; equipment slippery to oily hands.

'Adrika, drink. It's hot. Only getting hotter.' The heat has crawled under his skin and it's barely 9.30 a.m.; the call centre had received a 101 call around 5 a.m., from a runner who had seen the grave. He was on the committee for the temple and graves here are fought for tooth and nail. His tone had been outraged rather than concerned: '...and they think they can just bury anyone they like...'

Niamh had been in charge of the call centre and had set in motion the crime scene. She'd called him personally. 'Sorry, Maarten, but so many are on holiday, and the SIO on call this morning has come down with food poisoning after last night's curry. Is there someone else I should call?'

Adrika, newly promoted to DI, could have run it. But it would have been her first one. He's planned to begin and then step back; she's assisted as SIO previously and is ready for the step up.

She steps forward, just off the phone. 'Forensics are set up and have finished the area sweep. They're going to start the body evacuation now.'

Maarten nods, wincing. The runner had kicked back some of the fresh dirt that morning when he'd seen the mound of earth. Part of a skeleton had appeared. It had been the size of the mound and the length of bone that had led the PC, first on site, to raise the status to SOCO. It's not unheard of for some people to bury their pets in graveyards. But the unearthed suspected human bone had killed that theory.

'Let me know when the pathologist is doing the first look,' he says.

'Only a skeleton, so it'll be tricky to tell much. Takes a month, doesn't it, for the flesh to start to decay?' Adrika looks over to where the ground has been divided into grids. A tent has been set up. 'They seem to be taking longer today.'

'No immediate threat of rain, so the DNA is fairly stable. And it's even hotter. Come on, I can see Robyn. She must be on today.' He heads over to the grave, swallowing bile. Decomposition: autolysis, bloat, active decay, skeletonization. He knows the stages, but discussing the disintegration of once-warm flesh... The sense of death lies in the heat heavily, not dispersing. Decay is dense in the thick air.

It's buried quite deep, given the hardness of the ground. About half a foot.

Pausing, he hunkers down, prodding the earth with his fingers. 'It must have been a difficult job,' he says. He's far enough away from the site to avoid contamination, and he scratches the earth with his fingernail, feeling his nail pull back against the pink skin. His hands are raw with blisters from a bike ride at the weekend. The heat creates friction everywhere. 'Someone wanted it buried here, knowing we'd just dig it straight up. A lot of effort.'

'How long do you think it took them to dig the hole?' Adrika asks, only half aloud. 'Maybe there was more than one?'

'It's deep enough to have been carefully planned. Whoever dug this must have used more than a simple spade. And the body. Why bury a skeleton? It seems so pronounced,' he says, thinking the word is wrong but is halfway there. Maybe *announced* would be better. A body has been announced. But so much effort for a body so long dead...

'Maarten.' Robyn rises, wiping her brow with the back of her forearm, her American accent as thick as the heat. Her black hair, streaked with grey, is tightly braided and the tiny plaits curve in a sweep, caught up in a knot. Her arms move gently, like she's on stage, unassumingly elegant. She holds his attention by appearing to rebuff it.

'They've lifted all the dirt,' she says, gesturing in a sweep to the bags disappearing. 'Tell you something interesting, it's not dirt from round here. It's more dense – some texture in it, almost like clay. It will need looking into. Taj is CSM on this one, I spoke to him earlier – he said he'll prioritise the soil analysis. If this body has been somewhere else then you'll need to know where. Check with him once Forensics get going – oh, look, as if on cue.'

Maarten glances left, smiling at the tall man, head down, tapping on an iPad. He speaks to the team clearing the bags as he passes, gesturing left then right ahead of them.

'Let's start, y'all,' Robyn calls, bending her frame easily, as though practising yoga. She must be at least ten years older than Maarten, but he hears his knees crack as he bends. *It's the cycling*, he thinks, forgiving himself.

His jacket is off and the hairs on his forearms are bleached lighter by the sun. Next to him, Robyn's skin glistens like she wears crushed diamonds.

Maarten hunkers further, following her example as she leans over the body, his height making it hard to balance.

'A skeleton, and I can't begin to guess yet at when the death took place, but we can see from the broken bones around the chest area that there has been some trauma. I would say it's been a violent death, and I wouldn't be surprised if a knife was involved. Hair and teeth missing, trauma to the jawbone suggesting the teeth have been removed deliberately, and something else interesting – the distal phalanx, here – look at the tip.'

She indicates gently to a finger bone, quiet with reverence for the dead, and Maarten peers, tipping forward slightly as he leans. Anxious not to fall into the grave, he puts a finger down to steady himself in one of the marked grids of ground and Taj frowns.

Robyn continues, 'The bones at the end of the fingers have been damaged, some more clearly than others. Someone has made an effort to get rid of means of identifying the corpse. Bit obsolete now for the fingertips, but whoever has hidden this body has taken no chances. When this body was first killed, it doesn't look as though it was meant to be found.'

'How long will it take to get some form of ID?' Maarten asks, thinking that bodies which are meant to stay buried always surface at some point. Whoever did this has had to change their plan for some reason. There's no textbook murder.

Robyn smiles, sitting back easily on her heels, her legs folding beneath her. 'Always hopeful, aren't you? Well, I'll try for something – bones can often tell their own story. I won't know anything soon. We're busy at the moment, it's the holiday season. But I'll do my best.'

'We'll run the missing persons search. If we've got any leads, we'll let you know. But why bury it here? And where has the body been? We'll check any grave thefts in the last week.'

Adrika stands to his left, making notes.

'Sir!' There's a shout and he rises, looking over at a group of press pushing at the boundaries. They've been all over police alerts recently, looking for any story but the weather. 'Thanks, Robyn. Let me know when you know.'

She nods, turning back to the earth, grass thin on top as though it is entering middle age.

Sunny is dealing with the press as Maarten approaches, and they retreat, seeing his face. Maarten drinks from his bottle, his fingers cracking as he flexes. His throat aches and his mouth is sour.

'Cheeky buggers,' Sunny says, his blond hair tipping forward over his brow, which blooms with shades of plum and rose petals – Maarten had winced when he'd seen him that morning, and Sunny had shrugged. There had been a police cricket friendly early after work the day before and he'd not bothered with sun cream. Sun cream, apparently, was for wimps. Under the rose hue was a tinge of green. He'd been out for the curry too.

'Anything from the witness? Anyone else come forward?' Maarten asks.

'I've made an initial list. The local milk company were out early this morning and reported a white van seen in the village. Nothing suspicious, except it was so early, and it was moving quickly. The milk van is electric, and the van overtook him without waiting for the road to widen sufficiently.'

Flies land on Maarten's face. No matter how many times he swats them, they still return. He thinks of their feet, multiplying the bacteria of countryside waste, and wishes he could get back in the shower. There's not an inch of him that isn't sticky with heat.

'Great. Well, once we have a list of names we'll get started. The ground is almost too dry to expect any decent footprints. No tools left at the scene. It will likely rely on the body. Hopefully some fingerprints, a witness, CCTV from the village?'

'Makes no sense,' Adrika says. But her eyes show a gleam. A spark of ambition. 'But should be interesting. There's a lot of press gathering early.'

Maarten glances round. The press hold no glee for him.

'Graveyards are not the best way to start the day.' Adrika peels off the gloves, shaking her shoulders back after bending down. 'There's a girl over there, only sixteen years old. Caitlin Miller. She died on this day ten years ago. *Beloved daughter and sister*. Horrible.' Adrika shakes her head.

'The young ones are the worst,' Sunny says, then he turns with a shrug, his phone tucked up by his ear.

'Family grief.' Maarten glances at his watch. 'Bet they didn't get over that. Twists your heart.' Maarten thinks briefly of his parents, the car crash just outside of Rotterdam. Of the black hole, the pit, that had swallowed him when he'd heard the news. 'Grief is… Well, it's like nothing else. All the love you have, nowhere to put it.' No point trying to describe it. It's something felt. And you can't spit it out.

'Come on, we're almost done here. Want to run the meeting when we're back at the station? I'll stay for it. Let's compare notes first, but…' Maarten's phone vibrates. He has ignored it for the last five minutes. But they're pretty much done here and he pulls it out reluctantly. An unknown number. He sighs.

'Yes,' he says, answering, thinking that there's something about this case. That maybe the family holiday they've planned in a couple of weeks might be affected. He imagines Liv's face if he tells her he has a few calls to do, a few case notes to review. Won't be the first time. He can see the eye roll, feel the children pulling his hands towards the beach as the calls come in.

'Hello, is that Maarten Jansen?' The voice pronounces his surname with a hard English *J*.

'Yes.'

'I'm sorry to have to tell you, Maarten, but this is Staff Nurse Edwards at Lister Hospital, in Stevenage. There's been an accident. Your wife and children are here. They're being looked after. Your daughter unlocked your wife's phone to give us the number. Both girls are awake.'

'What? Are they... Are Nic and Sanne...'

'They're in good hands, Maarten. But you need to come in. I can't talk to you over the phone. You need to come in.'

Maarten can feel his foot is damp and he sees he's dropped the water. The flies land again; Taj calls his name from near the temple entrance.

He can think only of Liv, and Nic and Sanne. He stalls briefly, closing his eyes for just a fraction, then opens them again. Moving as he speaks.

'Liv and the girls are in hospital. Car accident. Adrika, keep me updated. Call if there are any problems.'

Adrika and Sunny are speaking as he leaves but he doesn't wait to hear the end of their statements. 'Anything I can do...' falls behind him as he leaves their faces stunned with the shock he feels. Others turn towards him, hearing their call, sensing alarm.

His blood heats and he quickens his pace, running towards the car. He jumps the police tape that cordons the crime scene and lengthens his stride once free of the forensic photography, the ringed pathways of investigation. The grass is brittle on his legs, more like straw now, and it spears him as he crosses to the edge of the field where the car is parked.

How the day can twist from one moment to the next. From calm to chaos. To heartbreak.

He brushes tears from his face as he reverses the car, swearing. The gears grind; his eyes blur, bright under the glare of the sun.

The flies follow him, but as the car powers forward, they fall backwards, returning to the sleeping dead and the stench of remains.

3

BEN

Ben wakes with a headache. Storms seem to churn the men up. *It's the wind*, he thinks. *It's the sound of the wind, flying in all directions, unpinned*. He doubts many slept last night.

As he waits for the cell to be opened for breakfast, there is shouting from down the wing. Swearing, words like currency, thrown around to mark status, to warn, to provoke. A porridge of *F*s and *C*s.

He wakes slowly, his eyes straining at the brightness of the strip lights, no curtains, the sun relentless. A fight breaks out somewhere. The noise rattles from cell to cell like a Mexican wave: catcalling, name-calling.

He dips his head. The base of the top bunk above seems lower today. His back aches. He rises slowly to stand, to stretch up and forward. He doesn't turn towards the door, or towards the top bunk. He keeps his eyes firmly fixed on the glimmer of the outside; it's strip bright. The sun is already hot.

Kiz is talking. The dream he had last night, how hungry he is, how noisy it was: '…hot, the bird was stonking, I was like "yeah, come get it" and then…'

The rattle of words like a hammer against a bin. Battering.

The door opens as Kiz winds up his story and the call for Ben arrives: a bark, but not unkind. Two guards stand outside, both with keys. Already agreeing with Kiz, whose noise is expected, they pacify him as Ben moves past him to stand outside the cell.

'…right good one, lad, honestly, I proper swear like, never thought, I was arsking him wasn't I…'

Kiz's stream of consciousness moves outwards, catching where it will somewhere in the guard who remains behind Ben, supervising inmates carrying boxes of breakfast to deliver: sachets of jam, sachets of tea. Cereal Ben eats because you need to eat.

The packets of food apportioned arrive like the packets of time in here. Everything is boxed. Half an hour for meds. Twenty minutes for breakfast. A nap can last an hour. Sleep is the goal. Lack of consciousness. Kiz is a fan of spice – enforced blackouts. The cost is big, in health and finance.

The relief of the quiet beyond his cell is physical.

He catches Tabs's eye as he walks past his cell; he is up against the window in the door. The thickset Scotsman nods at him.

A fight kicks off behind another door nearby and a

guard shouts to calm them: 'Don't kill each other before breakfast. I haven't had me coffee yet.'

The air is fresh outside. The stroll to the medical block, with its warm air like liquid and the chance to stretch his legs, is worth a chest infection.

'Morning. Feeling any better?' The nurse who delivers the controlled meds today is small. Much smaller than Ben. Black hairs run up his wiry arms, and an inked crab sits on his forearm. At the weekend it had been someone with softer flesh, a stomach that had strained against the uniform trousers, pulling tight into camel toe, pinned by the buttons and tight cuffs. Ben had felt a flash of pity that such soft abundance had to be forced into restraints. Even flesh should find freedom.

He nods, swallowing with a paper thimble of water.

'Right, wait an hour before eating. We'll see you again in about six hours. You keep coming down with this, don't you?' A sharp nod follows, and Ben turns, moving past the few men who line up outside the treatment centre.

Walking back to his wing, he swallows the clear air, stocking up. He ponders briefly again how bad things would have to get before they'd allow him out further. Hospital treatment was a real trip out, broken bones, or worse – a real excursion.

Fourteen months have passed. Only about ten and a half years remain. Might get out sooner.

'Right, Benny. Back in. You've got cleaning later, haven't you, mate? See you in a few hours. Judge Judy reruns on soon. That should shut Kiz up for a bit.' Mr Burke, this guard, is kind, and Ben likes him. It's not often he gets much sympathy. But Burke rolls his eyes as they approach the cell and Kiz is at the bars, already shouting: 'Not enough fucking sugar, I need sugar in me tea, tastes like...'

He winks at Ben. 'Get that telly on, mate. It's what I do with the kids when I need five minutes' peace.'

The same fight from earlier kicks off again behind them and two guards hammer on the door with the base of their fists. Like someone has pressed the rewind button.

It's settling as Ben sits on his bed, his breakfast on his lap. He checks the time to see when he can start eating, fingering the white plastic of the unbranded cereal, cupping the sachets of tea, throwing them up and back, as the TV begins. The morning news bulletin is finishing; Kiz will change channel soon. The smell from the toilet turns his stomach. The drainage in this heat is rank.

It's when he first sees the story. It's only on the local news. An item of interest rather than a lead story, following the recap of the headlines that ends the breakfast show.

You can't cry in here, not publicly at least. As the tears bubble, his nose feels tight and he's close to breaking down. He picks up his plastic fork and pushes the tips of the tines into the palm of his hand, waiting for the moment to pass.

Looking again, he blinks hard, to check he is reading properly. His eyes still ache from the long night, but no – it's still there. A body has been found. Police tape is marked out behind the reporter holding the microphone. A body has been found in Ayot, so close to Ana. Could it be him? Could it be Leo?

Kiz says something to him, leaning forward, repeating it over and over, but Ben can't hear, can't turn his head from the screen.

'Please, God,' he mutters. Sometimes his brother sits inside of him like a hole, a gap that has been dug out, mercilessly mined. At other times, the memory throbs like the beating of a second heart. Caught between two snapshots, he is both laughing, leaning back off the boat, spray from the sea catching the light like crystals, and then vanished, Ben's arms empty and blood-drenched.

Grief and guilt roll like a wave and a scream ignites inside of him, catching flame.

4

ANA

On the train, the pain of Ben rocks to shock of Fabian. The carriage bounces her between the two. Thoughts rattle around like peppercorns.

She had walked halfway to the graveyard. The scent of the flowers on the bushes that lined the road had been heady. Police cars were out, tape erected, and people stood in clusters, heads bent close, whispering. A few teenagers passed on bikes. The fancy cars of the village, on their way to the London commute, crawled past – heads crooked.

Then she'd paused... was it a profile she recognised? She had felt the creeping sensation of being watched.

She knows Fabian's not back yet. Jess had only mentioned the flight this morning. She is sure she's started to look for him, glancing left and right as though watching for speeding cars when you cross the road: Fabian Irvine, back in Ayot.

The figure hadn't been looking directly at her but had

been leaning on a wall watching the police, a cap pulled down low over his face. He hadn't turned around. But every hair on her body had stood up.

Sliding into the calm of the day, she stands as the train stops and commuters line up, passive-aggressively queueing, a collective tut as someone with a bike gets it stuck when turning before the doors, skin already slick with morning sweat.

The air in the station is like soup. Commuters on their way to work are in as much of a state of undress as the City will allow: vest tops, Birkenstocks, flip-flops – high heels stowed in bags, men with shirts already darkening under the arms.

The air conditioning of the office is a blast of welcome relief and she ducks in to wash her hands. Her reflection needs work. She arranges her hair, applies lipstick, making shapes with her mouth and checking her teeth. She finds two more lines, assesses the ones she's already spotted.

Deep breath. She remembers not to think of Ben, of his steadfast calm when she was upset, of his laugh, which let people in on a joke they hadn't heard; that he could do a backflip after a few beers when camping, his party piece by a campfire. She buries thoughts of Fabian – remembers that it might not have been his profile she saw at the graveyard. The cap was too low to see his face. And he was always too vain about his hair to wear hats.

I'm not being stalked, she thinks firmly, *not again*.

But her hands shake as she pushes the bathroom door, and she has to pause for a second to breathe.

'Morning!' she says, sitting in her chair. The door to the office she shares sits open. The huge window to her right is hot, its blinds already lowering to dim the City glare. She slips in easily, matches the polished environment, loses one self, finds another.

'You've a meeting in five,' Fran says, drinking coffee and staring at her computer.

'When did that happen?' Ana asks, logging in.

'Oh, The Leith stuck his head round here a minute ago. I told him you'd just nipped out. Who have you paid to land a deal with him?' She spins on her chair, voice humming, eyes smiling. 'Good night last night?'

'So-so. You? How was Jack812? Did he really have a GSOH?'

Fran laughs and pulls her chair forward, opening her eyes wide and clapping quickly. Her hair is long and smooth, and it swings forward as she tilts towards Ana, confiding. With it loose, she looks a bit like Meghan Markle, Ana thinks. More *Suits* than princess. It's a good look.

'Ana Seabrook, he did indeed! A bloody GSOH. Look, I took a photo of him for you when I was pretending to answer a text.' She lifts her phone and thrusts it in front of Ana's face. 'That. Face.' She wiggles the phone. 'I might love him.'

Laughing, Ana looks. The man has olive skin and large

brown eyes. He's clearly glancing elsewhere waiting for Fran to fake text, and Ana sees his eyes focused on a tall woman walking past.

'So, we love him, but do we trust him?' she says.

'We're not sure. But we're willing to find out. This Friday. I'll keep you posted!'

'Well, let me know if you need an exit route. And remember the rules. You call me from the loo every two hours until the third date.'

'Ana, the Round Room?' Leith's voice carries across the office.

She stands quickly, nodding.

'So I heard they were going to give it to Jon Tallon, but he's been called on to something else and pulled an all-nighter last night. Good luck. This could be your chance to get yourself noticed by The Leith himself.' Fran has already swung back, typing quickly. Her phone rings, and she lifts it with one hand, not taking her eyes off the screen. 'Fran Howland...'

Ana enters the room and there are six people sitting round the table. Everyone shakes hands, introductions, coffee is handed out; St Paul's rises high outside the window of the law firm.

Has Ben heard yet? Does he know? She forces herself to listen to the man who has just introduced himself as Dante. His jaw moves quickly.

Dante's top lip, the upper part of his jaw, remains strangely still as he speaks. It's like a cartoon jaw. Tilting her head a touch to reinforce her listening, she focuses on its stillness, calming her thoughts.

She hasn't done anything more than nod and smile to Leith. He radiates something. He's the partner at the table so they will all defer to him this morning anyway; Dante glances his way more frequently than hers. Writing notes, Ana catches his eye as she looks up.

There are two women on the clients' side. One is clearly the most senior, as they all check with her with their eyes before and after they speak, but she has said nothing. Dante is still running through their details by way of introduction: a pharmaceutical firm; they've developed a new weight-loss drug, an appetite suppressant. Early tests have been promising and an offer has been made by a bigger firm to buy them out. This wouldn't be one of the hardest mergers Ana has worked on, but the figures are large.

Has he heard? It's not as though there's anything concrete to know. There's been no mention of Leo Fenton, or of anything that happened two years ago. But it's so close to home. She knows Ben watches TV there. Has it been on the news?

Dante's jaw, locked and still, draws her back in. She's heard of the firm: PharmaCreate. She keeps nodding and smiling. Their main office is in London, their research facility positioned further out, north of the M25.

The technical terms she doesn't understand she jots down as she goes, to look them up later. Her pad fills with numbers, staff. She leans forward, speaking. 'Can we discuss the synergies...'

Has Ben heard?

Her work life has been separate until now, her safe space. Uncluttered by the trial, two years ago, that nearly broke her.

She just wants Ben back.

'Early results for the drug look promising. We're in phase two, the staff size will need to increase for the next round...' Dante is saying.

Leith taps the table with the end of his pen and smiles round at his team. Ana is included in this beam, like a headlight. She blinks. The main part is over.

'...absolutely, I feel confident about the deadline. Let us speak to the other side and hopefully we'll get this wrapped up quickly. Ana, can you make a start on this? Ana is one of our brightest lawyers.'

The woman who is in charge now speaks, suggesting a meeting time; her voice is deep and warm. Dates are scribbled. Dante, of the stilled top jaw, concludes a few points and Ana, jolted by Leith's praise, leans in to begin with her questions. 'I'd like to go over the timescale for the trial currently taking place...'

Has he heard? Has he heard?

'Well done in there,' Leith says, once the handshakes are finished and they are walking past indoor foliage and the small fountain in Reception, back to the lift and up to their floor.

Ana nods, struggles to think of a reply, as Leith walks into the lift first and they stand alongside each other. The door slides slowly.

'I'll head there first thing tomorrow,' Ana says. 'Research facility, then head office.'

'Great, it won't hurt to get a feel for it all.' His mild Australian accent softens the business tone. 'I'll come too. Email me the details when it's set up?'

He had been on her interviewing panel. He had been the friendliest, asking her about her hobbies, and she'd worried she'd talked too much, telling them of sailing with Ben, the race she'd been in with Leo. She hadn't realised he'd been the most important person in the room until later, but she'd got the job.

He smells like lemons and pepper. Not overpowering, but like an Italian meal outside, al fresco. Makes her think of rolling hills and olive groves.

'You're from Sydney?' she asks after a beat, the lift pausing at a floor, doors opening, but no one gets in. It's a scratchy silence. The doors glide shut.

'I worked at the Sydney office before coming over here.' He smiles at her quickly, glancing at his watch. His eyes are so blue they look like a child has coloured them with the brightest sky blue in the crayon pot.

The door slides back at their floor, and he leaves first, without comment. Rolling her eyes, she checks her reflection in the mirrored interior of the lift before exiting. Nothing in her teeth.

There's a package on her desk. It has been delivered by courier, with the usual stamp on the front. Fran has left for a meeting, but there's a Post-it Note on Ana's screen: *Text from Jack812!!! Buy a hat xxx*

Smiling, Ana checks her emails first, then rips the top of the package.

Her teeth clench. She feels her pulse quicken; her blood races as though in full flight.

It contains a photo, nothing else. Turning it face down quickly, she holds her breath. This is not a work package, and yet she's at work. She is not dressed for this, she is not ready. She touches her desk, something solid. Glancing round, she checks no one is looking her way.

Slowly, she turns it back over. The photo, stiff and sharp at the edges, is slightly blurry, but nevertheless, she is there. She traces the outline of her face with her finger. She is smiling. She can't drag her eyes away, or bring herself to look at the rest of the image. She knows what it contains.

And now someone else knows. But how...

Why has it come to her? Why now? And who...? How could they possibly have this photo?

There's a prickle on her skin, a metallic taste in her mouth.

The chair beneath her tilts back slightly and swings to the right. The windows before her still show the tip of St Paul's. The glare of the sun is bright, bouncing off the City windows in flashes.

There is no sign of the sender. No words on a note. No return address.

An anonymous package. Here at her place of work.

Her mind stalls, curls. Avenues of thought circle and loop.

What could anyone gain? It makes no sense.

The dread, like a sleeping beast awoken before its time, rises from the grave.

5

Wednesday 13th June

MAARTEN

Lister Hospital is always busy. But… His hands shake. He needs to park. His eyes stream tight, small, salty tears. They blur his vision, make his face itchy. Trying to read the signs explaining how the payment system works is a torture, cruel and slow.

Swinging the car right again, round and round. There is a multistorey but the sign says it's full. Cars are parked in bays all the way down the sides of the road that lead round the edge of the hospital. He circles the whole thing twice; there aren't many spaces. A car flies past him and he glares.

But reverse lights switch on nearby, and he holds his breath as he waits for the slow, careful exit ahead of him; willing them faster; willing himself inside.

Running into A & E, he finds a short queue for the reception desk, but his patience is gone. He can judge how badly he is behaving by the reaction of others. He attempts to curtail himself, to lower his voice, to calm his movements, but he is frantic. His height causes eyes to swivel. His voice, louder than he intends, makes a few step aside.

The blue plastic seats are filled with people. A mother with children seated nearby averts her gaze gently, and even he can hear the catch in his voice, the panic. Everyone is in shorts, T-shirts. Blood and scratches are out for all to see; tattoos, flesh in various hues of pink to brown. Bare skin peels off plastic chairs and sweat marks are left on seats recently vacated.

The woman sitting behind the desk stares patiently, tapping carefully on her computer, calming, organising as others in the queue step forward, anxious not to be ignored, that he shouldn't jump the queue; but an older nurse moves quickly towards him. His hair is thinning and he's tall and lean, coming up to Maarten's shoulder. His eyes are set quite far apart, and they're piercing blue. It gives him a striking quality: authority.

'Mr Jansen? Maarten? I'm Staff Nurse Edwards. We spoke on the phone. Please come with me.' The smile is steadying but still Maarten can't stop himself from grabbing the man's arm.

'Please, are they OK, is Liv... Is she alive?'

'Yes, they're all alive. But it's a complicated situation with your wife. Please, Maarten, follow me.'

The mother smiles at him as he passes and people move aside. His voice had cracked when he'd spoken. Life and death top and tail here.

They pass through a door, and the room balloons with colour. Children's A & E is a far brighter place to be. There is a Disney film playing to one side, and coloured tables covered with pens and paper.

They move into a curtained cubicle. Inside, the space is slightly darker.

Sanne lies on the bed in the centre, and Nic sits next to her, holding her hand. A nurse who has been sitting with them smiles as he enters, then slips out.

Maarten heads towards them, to sweep them up, to hold them.

Sanne's arm is held in a sling, immobile. Her face shines with sweat and tears.

Nic has a dressing on her head. Both of them cry, calling for him, like he's still miles away: *Papa, Papa*. The cries gain volume the closer he gets, and they sob as he strokes their hair, holds their hands.

He wants to cry too. He keeps it back only by swallowing the ball of panic stuck in his throat. He almost chokes on it.

'Nic, Sanne, you're OK. I was so worried, here, I'm here.' He's thankful for their tears, their realness – the proof of life.

'Papa,' Nic says, folding into his arm.

He strokes Sanne's face with the other hand, unwilling to disturb her sling, his eyes drawn to it, asking quietly if it hurts, how she feels.

His children, alive; their hair is soft under his

fingers, their faces dirtied with streaks of blood, tear-stained.

A moment of déjà vu: his face wet with tears, childish and raw. He had sat on a plastic seat. Doctors had taken him to where his parents had lain. He shakes his head. He hasn't thought of that for years. A confrontation with death, too early. He hadn't been twelve years old.

'Sanne needs a cast setting on her arm. We'd like to put her under a general anaesthetic. She's been very upset.' The nurse's voice is quiet but firm. 'If you'd like to step outside, the consultant is here. She's been very brave, they both have. You should be very proud of them. They looked after their mum, sat by her until the ambulance arrived.'

Maarten can feel Sanne trembling under his hand as she cries.

'Obviously, there are risks with the small operation here, and I'll talk to you about those in a minute. The consultant will explain it all to you.'

He nods. His tiny six-year-old, with a broken arm. He doesn't want to ask about Liv here, when the children can hear. But he asks with his eyes, and Edwards nods to outside the cubicle.

'Papa is just going to check on Mama. Can you both stay here? I'm not going anywhere. I'll be right outside.' He crouches so he looks into both their eyes, brushes tears with his thumb. 'I'm not going anywhere, girls. I'm staying right here.'

Nic looks all of her ten years as he smiles at them before letting the curtain fall. She's getting older but is still so fragile. She had sat with her mother senseless and her sister with a broken arm.

He had sat on his own, waiting to be told.

'She's unconscious, Maarten. She's being scanned at the moment, but she hasn't woken since the accident. She was unconscious at the scene.'

'What happened?' His mind buzzes with the imagined sound of a crash, of Liv's scream. He thinks of her hand flying to protect her face, of the windows on the car shattering. An image of the crumpled bonnet keeps appearing in front of his eyes, crushing Liv within it.

He needs the facts so that he can focus on them, understand what is happening. He just wants to hold her. But he knows they'd be taking him to her if they could.

'We don't know for certain. There was a jogger nearby at the scene who saw another car, but the vehicle didn't stop. The paramedics said a witness has given a statement to the police reporting they saw a car drive off. It was on one of the roads outside St Albans, leading to Redbourn. Your wife's car was found in a ditch. The girls were bumped in the back, but Olivia seems to have taken the force as the car nosedived. The airbag deployed, but even with that, she has taken quite a blow to the head. The witness called 999. A number of other cars stopped at the scene after the crash. Luckily, there was a doctor in one of them. Olivia has been looked after well.'

Maarten opens his mouth to speak, but there's nothing he can think of to say. His head echoes with the sound of a squeal of brakes, of tyres screaming on the road; the thud of the impact.

It's a sound he's often thought of. The last sound his parents heard – it's rung loudly in his head for years.

'Is there anyone else we can call? A parent? A friend?'

'Her parents. We need to call Liv's parents. Her father's away, I think... I'll do it now. And she has a sister who lives abroad – that's right, her father's staying there for a week. But what do I say? What do I tell them? What shall I tell her mum? Can I tell her she'll be OK?'

'Tell them she's in very good hands. But tell her, if she can, to come now. If she is able.'

The doctor is kind, and Maarten is ushered up towards the anaesthetic room with Sanne. She lies on the bed as they wheel her through the hospital.

'Look at the monkeys on the ceiling!' one of the nurses says.

Sanne's eyes are wide as she looks up, and the colours of the corridors on the children's ward whizz by. Maarten tries to stay in her view, tries to stay out of the way of the bed, tries not to bump into other patients walking slowly past them.

He wants to speak to Liv. They'd asked if anyone in their family had ever had a reaction to anaesthetic. He wants to check with her. He wants Liv to say it was the right thing that he'd agreed. He wants Liv.

'Papa!' she cries quickly as a tall doctor slips the cannula into her right hand. 'Ow, ow, ow!' Maarten bends his head low, kisses her hot brow, holds her other hand, whispers about milkshakes afterwards, chocolate when she wakes.

They secure the edges of the cannula with two plasters backed with teddy bears.

'Watch, the teddy bears are going to have their milk,' the nurse says quietly, smiling at Sanne.

Maarten smiles at her too and prays a silent thanks to the NHS and the kindness of its staff. Their strength is all that's holding him up right now.

White fluid, looking thick like glue, is pushed into her hand, and then a mask is slipped over Sanne's face.

'Now give her a kiss, Dad,' the anaesthesiologist says. 'We'll take her now and call you when she wakes.' She smiles at him, her voice urging him through the steps and pushing him into acting.

Bending to kiss Sanne's damp brow, warm under his lips, he wants to lift her and hold her close. Her eyes are falling closed as he stands up, and the anaesthesiologist smiles at him. 'We'll call you once she's out of theatre.'

'Won't be too long,' the nurse says, smiling. 'You did very well, Dad.'

He's led out of the room, and they wheel the bed forward, away from him.

He cracks, immobilised for a moment. She has never looked so small.

But Nic waits downstairs. She needs him too.

6

Two Years Earlier
June

LEO

In a million shades between white and black, clouds hang down over Blakeney Point, thick and bulbous. There is one patch of blue – it's luminous – and Leo can feel in his gut that the day will be good.

Leaning, he pushes on the tiller and then ducks as the boom swings quickly; the mainsail catches the wind and fills, taking shape and lifting the bow up to cut through the water. He races forward, the salt spray familiar. He's been coming here since he was a baby. Nowhere else on earth smells so close to home.

'Why so slow?' Ben shouts.

Leo laughs, watching his brother. They race out together, past the seals that lie slick and wet in shiny mounds on their islands. The tourist boats out to see the seals are turning, chugging their way back into harbour, and Leo leaves them behind, leaves it all behind.

Work has been crazy busy. But finally the deal is

closed and he has some vacation before he needs to head back. The new company owners have retained him on an advisory basis for the next two years, but only part-time. He wants to enjoy some of the proceeds. Fleeta moved out of his apartment a few months ago, and he still delights in waking to peace in the morning. The close of their relationship had been tense.

'Life in her yet!' Ben calls, tacking over towards him. The open sea lies ahead, offering an empty horizon, and the wind chases them. They'd had these two old Lasers moored up in Norfolk for years. They'd talked about trading them in, but Leo loves them. They are part of the family. Ben usually comes up with Ana every few weekends.

The sea opens up, as does the blue in the sky. The waves wash him as he bounces over the water.

It's June. Their race is traditional. And because it's June, he knows he also races against himself. If Fleeta had been on her way out, he'd known she'd be gone by June. It's when he finds relationships the hardest, when he's most likely to let women down. Like learned behaviour, his actions years ago had indented a groove into the year, in which he finds himself dipping.

Tucking his feet into the toe strap, he leans out and back over the sea, letting his weight fall back, the adrenaline lifting him; as the boat picks up speed, they race. Outrunning the memories. Drowning them before they drown him.

7

Wednesday 13ᵗʰ June

BEN

Ben fills his mind to block out the noise; noise like an attack. He fills it with whatever he can cling on to. And it's mainly Ana. Ana comes to him in gusts of air. This heat hangs and won't leave. Pushes the nerves of the guards, the inmates. Makes it harder to eat the food. It's usually a struggle. But in this heat...

He's thinner than ever. The nurse had looked sharply at him when his chest had been checked.

Ana arrives like a breeze.

The smell of her. Sometimes he panics he can't remember it, but then it comes back to him. And her skin – soft, groggy with sleep in the morning. He hasn't had a chance to have a private conversation with her since before he went camping with Leo. All he has of her is snippets of news, of the threads of who they were. So many things are unsaid. There are no private telephone rooms in here. Mobiles are banned. Each conversation over the phone is filled with echoes of shouts from inmates; echoes of what he hasn't told her; Leo's voice, what he'd said that last weekend.

He can't say only half of it. So he says nothing. He tells her of the cell, the food, the library, the heat. He protects himself, and her.

'How's it going, Benny?' It's Tabs. He's naked apart from a towel tied round his middle. He holds his bag with shampoo and shower gel. He's older than Ben, and he's been in longer. Lines are dug around his eyes.

'Come on, lads, we've not got all day,' one of the uniforms says, and they move forward.

The showers are open plan, cubicles with no doors, stainless steel and old. There are scratches down the sides, and a patina of soap, cleaning products, blood and dirt has faded the steel, carved its own history.

'So-so,' he says, but he knows there's something on his face, as Tabs raises his eyebrows.

'What gives, Benny?'

'I saw...'

'Stop the chatting,' the uniform says, calling from the back of the room. 'I've got B Wing in here next as there's a problem with their water. Come on, lads.'

Showering quickly, he speaks quietly to Tabs on the way out. 'The news bulletin. My brother. They've dug up a grave in Ayot, just outside of St Albans. It's so close to home. Ana practically lives next door. I wonder if... Well. You know.'

Tabs whistles, long and slow. 'Fuck, Benny. It's been newly buried? They never found the body, no? If it is your brother, then this could be your ticket out. I know Ayot. Used to teach near there.'

Ben nods, only half listening to Tabs, just focusing on the thing his brain has been going over since the news that morning. That it might be his route out. They might have found Leo's body. They might realise he didn't kill…

'So, what's next?' Tabs asks. 'I don't know many people, but I've been in here a few years. I could ask around. See if there's any word out? If it's your brother, must have taken some planning, to hide the body for that long. You got anyone in mind? Someone you think they might have missed?'

Shrugging, Ben starts saying, 'I need to think…' But then, too late, he sees a hand swing high and fall on Tabs's head. A shampoo bottle in a sock, landing with the weight of the swing, and blood pours quickly from the corner of Tabs's eye.

Ben stands back. Macca is laughing. 'Nonce,' he shouts, and the group around him titter like schoolboys, with adult aggression. Ben looks to the guards but there are only two of them. He sees one press his radio, but he knows they won't intervene. Not before the next blow. The guard shouts to warn them to stop, but that is all he'll do for now. They need three guards on each prisoner before they will step up. Safety of the guards comes first.

Tabs's eyes are still closed and he's hunched over. Macca is walking slowly, waiting to see if there's any response, but there won't be. He gets another kick in before a few more uniforms arrive. The sock with the shampoo is confiscated. He'll be nicked, but Macca is in for a long sentence. A few more days added on doesn't bother him.

They pick up their things. The blood from Tabs's head drips on the dirty floor, mingling with soiled water, and Ben steps back, keen not to get involved.

They dress. Lining up, eight of them walk back. The sun dries their hair. Ben's skin on his face is quickly tight with the rays, his neck beginning to burn just as they get to G Wing.

'Nonce,' Macca says again quietly as they enter, and they bend round, walking towards the cells.

Ben dips his head. Tabs's walk is slightly off; he tips into the wall before bouncing back out and making it to his pad with the arm of the guard.

'OK, mate?' the officer says, and Ben sees Macca's eyes narrow as Tabs lifts his head to answer. 'I can take you to medical?'

'Aye, just slipped in the shower. All good.'

The officer shrugs and carries on, putting them inside, each door locked from the jangle of keys that hang heavy and low from each belt.

Ben thinks of getting out. Allows himself to believe for a split second he could leave this all behind, but pulls himself back. That way madness lies.

The room. A shout down the hall.

It's hot in here, but not like a holiday. Not like an indulgence. Like a punishment. Hot like hell.

'…isn't, d'yer reckon…' Kiz is still going. The rattle against his brain like a tiny hammer. A bruise.

A fly buzzes in through the bars. The rattle of the trolley going past. A bucket spills somewhere and there is a shout. An alarm rings further up the wing.

He closes his eyes again as Kiz drifts back to the screen. Talking at the walls, the beds, the toilet that smells like piss.

Ana. He wills her to his mind. He wills her like a shield.

Leo and Ana, the three of them, before it broke.

8

ANA

The train rattles its way home. Her reflection is a ghost in the window. She'd finished late; starting a new deal always takes a bit of time, but she is happy to spend it. Since Ben has been in prison, time has had a price. She invests it at work, the pub, in her mum. She spends it where she will not feel the drag of days.

St Albans station is never empty. The trains run all night. Even now, just after midnight, there are still people falling out of the train, walking, striding. In this heat, even in the middle of the night people are in T-shirts, bare arms. The air is velvet.

She ducks left, exiting the main entrance towards the car park, passing two smokers, a few cars waiting to pick up.

Footsteps follow her. She slows for a second as her foot slips out of her heel, listening.

That glimpse of a profile returns behind her eyes, like a paper cut – whoever she had seen reminded her so much of someone, but was it Fabian? She can't be sure. There was a time when she'd seen that outline poking up when she'd least expected it; sometimes she'd been afraid to leave the flat. Even now, the thought of it sets her teeth on edge. Could it have been him who sent her that photo? Could he have her work address?

Is it in her mind? That the footsteps slow, too? That they follow her tread?

Stop it, she tells herself. *Stop allowing yourself to be spooked. Just because someone has tried to spook you.*

Instead of turning in to the first set of doors that lead into the car park, she walks on, to enter at the other doors further up. But still the footsteps follow her.

She thinks again of the anonymous envelope coming to her place of work. Of an unidentified body lying in a grave five minutes from the bed in which she sleeps.

The heavy doors scrape the floor in a screech, making her wince. She runs up the concrete steps on the balls of her feet. Jumping the last two in one stride. Her heel lands sharply.

The stench in here is putrid, the heat intensified. That car park smell is overpowering: urine, leaked oil.

Level 3. She checks behind her quickly: nothing.

The keys are in her hand already. She has taken them out of her bag on the train, years of knowing not to stand in a car park at midnight, fumbling for them, alone. Like most women, she learned these rules at an early age. As she approaches the car, the footsteps land: tap, tap.

Lengthening her stride, she unlocks the car. As the lights flash, she dives in, pulling the door behind her quickly.

Her breath still tight, she turns the key. She can hear her heart beating, her pulse hammering in her ear. The click of the central locking slotting into place calms her.

The figure passes behind and walks on. She can't see their face, but they're wearing a cap, with lettering unreadable in the dark.

There's a glimpse of something familiar. Her heart tugs and her mind screams. What is it?

She turns on the engine and takes a deep breath. Just someone on their way to their car. She mustn't lose it. A body has been found and Fabian Irvine is returning to Ayot. It's time for cool.

The larger roads of St Albans narrow to hedge-lined lanes as she approaches the village.

The pub lights are dark. Her mother closes prompt at 11.30 p.m. during the week. Ana finds an open ground-floor window and she closes it, checks the locked door. She checks all the locked doors.

The mattress of her teenage bed finds its familiar shape as she sits and lays her tote bag across her knees. The photograph burns inside, and she places a hesitant hand on the metal clasp that snaps the bag closed.

She is smiling in the photo. Even now, with all that has happened, there is a tiny pocket somewhere that smiles still: she feels composed of her memories, like flesh on bone, fragments of smells, colours. She had smiled and cried that night.

Should she phone the police? Pour wine? Wake her mum? But what would she say to the police? They will contact her soon if the body turns out to be Leo. And as for wine, she's nervous – Ben has years left inside. She can't medicate her way through this grief with alcohol. Running is her drug of choice, a defence against losing herself.

She doesn't pull the curtains. The night is cloudless, and she stares hard across the black ocean of space that lies between her and Ben. They are tiny dots in the vastness of the universe. And yet, sometimes, all she can feel is him. She had loved him for so long. For years, it had been like a distant goal – an island she was sailing towards. And then with him, she had realised what it was like to find her home, to know herself. There was no touch on earth that belonged on her skin more.

Flicking her bag's lock, she tugs at the edge of the package containing the photo. It's the first time she's thought of it for… She doesn't know.

She had tried to visit on Ben's birthday, but he hadn't wanted her inside. They speak on the phone, but he won't see her in there. Their calls are stilted, made in a corridor with other phones. At first it had been heartache. Now it sits with her beneath everything she does, like a blister underfoot.

The taste of toothpaste is sharp as she finally opens the envelope holding the A4 photo. Should she take it to the police tomorrow? It is difficult to decide. Someone is stirring up the past and carries knowledge like a weapon. If she is right, and the body *does* turn out to be Leo, then police involvement will be inevitable; it would be better to be upfront. But telling them means telling everyone...

She tries to hold the edges, thinking too late about fingerprints.

But why now? What possible reason could there be to stir this up now?

She should call Harper. She trusts Harper. But even as investigating officer, Harper couldn't save Ben.

She needs to think, to compose herself. She hopes Ben calls tomorrow. Her mother had been upset about the news of Fabian's return, but she had shaken her head gently when Ana had mentioned the body. 'Why, Ana?' she had said. 'Why would whoever killed Leo risk drawing attention to it? They've got away with it.'

And she is right. Ana can't think of a single reason why moving the body here might not be dangerous for the killer. But the body is here. And she has received the photo.

She stares across the night, through the empty sky, and thinks of Ben, sitting wilting on a bed in a cell in this heat. Dreaming of her. Of this air. Of being able to hold her.

Empty blackness.

9

Two Years Earlier
June

LEO

'Dinner at the White Horse?' Leo says as they shower off at the harbour.

'Rude not to,' Ben says. 'I've got the tent in the car. Ride down to the site and pitch it first?'

Nodding, Leo stretches back under the cold shower before upending his wet-boots and washing them out. The sea, the cold – he feels better.

The path around the harbour is rough and boggy at points. Standing on his pedals to ride over a coarse patch, Leo watches the sun dip lower in the sky. The horizon is clear blue now. Ben pulls alongside.

'How's Ana?' Leo asks.

'Good – she's looking forward to seeing you. You're still coming for dinner with us before you fly back?'

'Of course. It's her birthday soon. What you getting her?'

Ben goes over a bump and stands on his pedals, then

sits again. He says something but the words are lost in the wind as the track bends and the breeze flies at them.

'What?' Leo shouts.

'She's tricky to buy for,' Ben shouts. 'She hates the clothes I buy for her, she doesn't really wear much make-up, or much jewellery. I was thinking though…'

Leo cycles in front as they approach a couple with a dog. They ride single file to pass and stay like that for a few miles as the path narrows. People are out for late-afternoon walks, the sun bringing out the bodies.

The day begins to stretch into shadows as they approach. The path wends towards the sea, and the old house their parents owned sits behind their camping spot. They camped at the bottom of the big garden when they were kids. Now they come and pitch up just below the trees, on the flat ground off the coastal path that overlooks the sea and the small bay. The cliff isn't too high – they used to dive off it when they were young. There's not much beach here, but there's a little patch of shingle down from the cliff path. It's enough to moor a small boat if you sail there from further up the coast.

Riding faster, Leo jumps off, dropping the rucksack he's been carrying, and starts to pull the bike up the bank to the site, which is hidden from below.

'Here, throw me your gear,' he calls down to Ben.

Getting hot, he pulls off his T-shirt, then bends to start pegging the tent.

'What's that?' Ben says, laughing. 'When did you get a tattoo?'

'Oh that, a bit ago. Fancied a bit of a change once Fleeta moved out.' Leo glances down at his shoulder. 'Needed something new, and I can afford it now, since the deal. You know how much these things cost in New York?'

'Well, looks like you get to spend some money in the gym, too,' Ben says, throwing him the bag of pegs. 'Is that a nine-pack?'

'Fuck off,' Leo says, laughing. 'Yeah, I work out now. You know, eat well and all that. It's different over there. What were you saying earlier? You were thinking of getting Ana something for her birthday?'

Ben rubs his hand across his mouth, then sits, nodding. 'I wanted to tell you first. You ready for this, little bro?'

Falling back to the earth, Leo drops the mallet to the dirt and swivels to face Ben. The sun is in his eyes, and he pulls his shades off his head, slipping them down on his face. He knows what Ben is going to say. Preparing himself, his expression, he uses the last second of feigned ignorance to conjure a smile. There's a tiny bit of him, the hollow part that never gets filled, that starts to ache. It's not an unfamiliar feeling. It's the part of himself that he hates the most.

'Yeah?' he says. 'You have my full attention. Hit me.'

'I'm going to ask her to marry me. I've bought the ring and everything. I've been waiting to see you, to tell you. You're all I've got, apart from her. I need to know you're happy about it before I do anything else.' Ben's face is serious now. He looks at Leo.

For almost a second too long he sits, time stretching in the sun, Leo squinting up at his older brother, the smell of the sea... And then he does it. Stands, claps him on the back and hugs him.

'This is brilliant news! I'm so pleased for you both! What she sees in you, I've got no idea.'

They hug, standing under the sun. Leo feels the ache disappear. It was nothing.

It was nothing.

10

Thursday 14th June

MAARTEN

Liv lies still. Machines beep. There's a tube coming from her nose.

He's asked Nic to give him a minute, said that Sanne would need her until he could return. The operation has gone well and Sanne lies dozing with her cast.

'Papa!' she'd called as he'd gone up to the recovery ward, her voice drunk and soft. 'I feel dizzy,' she'd said, lying back on the bed. 'Do you want to write on it?'

They'd given her a certificate for being good in theatre, and she'd clutched it as they'd wheeled her back down to the ward, where Nic waited. Waving it when she'd arrived, a dot in a huge bed.

Liv is in a room on her own. And he needs this minute. He needs to fall apart before he has to put himself back together.

They have lowered the lights in the hospital. The staff have changed hands, speak in quiet voices. Someone had wheeled a machine that wouldn't stop beeping off the main ward floor and put it by the lift. The family room had been shown to him: it had biscuits and a hot water machine that hung from the wall. The fridge contained three pints of milk, all half-empty.

Liv.

Her hand feels warm. Still. Smooth.

His heart aches. It's heavy in his chest, and it pulls. The thought of losing her – it's a sharp pain, which makes him gasp, makes him reel backwards in the plastic chair. His heart is shooting stars, tiny fragments of anguish bursting out in flames, rocketing in his blood.

His phone buzzes in his pocket but he doesn't look, not for a minute. He needs just a minute.

'Liv, can you hear me? Can you hear me? It's me, it's Maarten.'

There's no response. Her lashes lie still on the top of her cheeks.

He hasn't let go of her hand. There is a knock at the door, and he knows that things wait outside. This minute is almost past. He leans close and whispers in her ear. She understands him. He knows that she will understand him.

'*Blijf bij mij.*'

Stay with me.

★★★

'Jane, thanks for coming.'

His mother-in-law is red-eyed. Her hair is a shade lighter than Liv's, the blonde fading with streaks of silver. She's roughly the same frame as Liv, but where Liv fills space with her energy, Jane sits now like a wisp on the chair, gripping the edge with her fingers. She looks crushed. Her handbag is on the floor by her pale deck shoes, tilted to one side. Everything wilts. It's still the middle of the night and the girls are asleep on the bed together. He sits in a chair.

'How is she?'

They move outside to the hospital corridor and stand beneath the strip light that is never turned off.

'She's holding her own. They can't find anything seriously wrong with her, but Jane, she hasn't woken up. Not since the accident. They—'

'Oh, Maarten!' Jane falls forward and he puts his arms around her.

'I'll take you to her.'

Visiting hours don't count in this room. They watch her, and Jane holds his hand. Her grip is tight, her face pale.

'They're hopeful, Jane. There's nothing they can find. They said sometimes the body just goes to sleep for a while to deal with the shock. We're still not at the first twenty-four hours.'

'Maarten, what can I do? How do I help?'

The relief at these words pulls his shoulders down and allows the tightness at the very top of his head to release itself ever so slightly.

'If you could take the girls home. Sanne has a broken arm, but she's fine to go home. Nic has a cut on her head, but they've watched her and it's been looked at. She's just got Steri-Strip on there so it needs to stay dry for the week. I've kept them here because I can't leave Liv, I felt we all needed to be here. But really, they need their own beds. They need some real food. I need to stay here, with Liv. She can't be alone. She—'

He stops. He can feel his voice cracking and there's no point because Jane knows what he wants to say. Her hand is still in his and she squeezes it.

'Of course. When they wake. And you'll let me know – the moment you hear. You'll call me the very moment you hear anything at all. I've phoned Pete. They can't get flights so I said I'd call tomorrow. When she wakes, we'll know more. But you let me know. The moment you hear. Anything.'

'Of course. Of course I will.'

Liv's dark blonde curls are slicked back on her head. Her hair looks peat brown. Her hairline is framed in tiny scabs of dried blood from scratches that are still fresh and bruises that mottle her brow. The thick dressing that covers her hair shrinks her face.

The hot night falls thickly. The windows are open in the room but no air comes through. He stagnates.

She will wake up.

Night's blackness sits with him.

11

Thursday 14th June

ANA

'Ms Seabrook?'

Ana is almost at the car when she hears her name. She is early for the commute and jolts with surprise at someone else being up at this hour.

'I wanted to catch you. I know you work in London so I thought the earlier the better. I'm DI Verma. I'm working on the discovery found yesterday in the Palladian church, the temple. I'm sure you heard about it.'

Ana nods. She places her hand on her car to steady herself. It's already hot to the touch. Whether it's the early heat or the presence of the police officer, she feels light-headed.

'I'm not here for an official interview; I'm in the area to speak to witnesses about the discovery.' The DI smiles at her. She lifts her sunglasses to the top of her head and takes a step forward, handing Ana her card. 'We have no idea of the identity of the body, but I'm aware that your brother-in-law's body was never recovered, and with all the press surrounding the case, there's already been some mention of him. I just wanted to check in with you. If you're bothered by the press, or if anything unusual does raise its head, then please give me a call.' She smiles, stepping back and glancing up the road. 'This way to the newsagent?' she asks.

She's giving Ana a chance to speak.

Ana nods and, finding her voice, manages, 'Yes, just up on your right. There hasn't been anything yet, but thanks for coming by. I did wonder, when I saw the news. I think until Leo's body is found, I'll always wonder when...' She stops, unsure how to finish. She thinks of the photo hidden beneath her pillow. The secret she has kept from Ben. She should tell the police, she knows that. But the DI is already smiling and waving a goodbye.

12

MAARTEN

'Go ahead, Sunny, what's the latest?' Maarten stands in the corridor, watching Liv through the glass. He kissed the girls goodbye an hour ago. His breakfast is untouched on the side. He hasn't slept. He can't take his eyes off Liv, can't leave her. But work is a distraction. He can check in with his team for five minutes; make sure it's all running smoothly.

'Well, bit of a turn-up really, sir. Taj pushed the soil testing to the top of the priorities and the soil site report came back. There was only a very small amount of soil so it's been hard, and also fragments of plastic sheeting. We've got a possible match. It's not infallible, but it's a great start. There's a lot of technical detail in the report – marine alluvium and chalk in the topsoil, loads of analysis in there. I'll send you the report, but cutting to the chase, it's looking like the North Norfolk coast. However, when we also ran a list of cases within the last ten years for any suspicious deaths missing a body, and cross-referenced those with a list of missing people from the St Albans area, one stood out – a male from St Albans who was killed up near Blakeney but his body was never recovered. It's not an exact science, but we need something to work with. His brother is currently serving time for his murder. And even more interesting, the partner of the brother who's in jail lives in Ayot, only five minutes from the Palladian church.'

'That's a result. Thank Taj for me, will you. He must have pushed the team hard to get the analysis so quickly.' Maarten glances through the glass. Liv looks asleep. Were it not for the machines and the hospital bed, he would find the picture of her resting comforting.

'Have you contacted Norfolk?' he asks.

'Yes. I called the officer who was involved with the original investigation two years ago, a DI Harper Carroll. She looked into Leo Fenton's murder. She's agreed to come down to hand over the file details. It's a bit of a pre-empt, as the identity isn't anywhere close to being confirmed. It could be anyone at the moment – we're just trying to cross lines and find a catch, as the post-mortem will take a while. She's on her way now.'

'Well done, Sunny. This is a great start. Whatever you do, don't speak to press. We'll be crucified if it turns out to be a dead end.'

'Yeah, and there's another thing. Adrika's... a bit upset. Took herself out to follow up on some CCTV after the meeting. Something I should be doing. She started early, visiting the female who lives in Ayot. She was here this morning but I haven't seen her since. Bloody good job we've got Taj here. You're best off out of it, I'm telling you.'

There's a pause. Sunny speaks again, and Maarten can hear the change of tone. 'Sorry. I didn't mean... How is she?'

'She's holding her own.' Liv lies, motionless since yesterday. But all vitals are strong. 'They're hoping she'll wake today. There's nothing else, really. Look, Sunny, I'm assuming you're doing witness interviews today, and when Adrika gets back from checking the CCTV, if she thinks there's anything this woman who lives in Ayot said that's of interest, make sure you bring her in for a statement. Find out if she's heard anything. If she lives in Ayot and she's involved with the brother who's convicted of murder, then she's one of the first people we need to speak to and I'm sure Adrika made a good start this morning, but probe. Keep an open mind – she could easily be involved if it's the same case. And when checking CCTV, I'm sure you've already got going on it, but there must be a vehicle involved to carry the body and equipment, there must be some trace of it at that time of night. This white van – can you make sure you check it through? And witness statements.'

'Will do, sir. Carroll's bringing the original file. Adrika started the board after the morning meeting. We're working through it all. And we're all rooting for you. Everyone sends their best. Don't worry about us, we've got this. With so many DIs around, it can't go too badly wrong.' Maarten can hear the smile back in Sunny's voice.

He leans his head up against the glass and gazes at Liv. The police are in later to speak to him about the road accident. He thinks of someone leaving her for dead and his fists clench. If anything happens to Liv, he knows he wouldn't rest. Couldn't rest.

13

Thursday 14th June

ANA

'Look, I don't know what's going on, but I've covered for you again. If The Leith asks, you were at the dentist this morning. Some emergency. Talk with a lisp.' Fran puts a coffee on Ana's desk as she mutters quickly, 'He's in a stonker of a mood. Makes his eyes flash. He hasn't actually shouted, just brooded. Intensively. If you want to swap places, just say the word.'

Ana looks up quickly, distracted. She's exhausted. By the time she'd fallen asleep last night she had been plagued with dreams of footsteps, a cap, bodies buried deep. She can hear her name being called from across the room. 'Thanks,' she says quietly. 'I owe you. Any word from Jack812?'

Fran crosses her eyes, which Ana assumes means a love-struck pose but also makes her look drunk. She grins and grabs her files. The chaos at home feels a world away. She'd caught up on the train on the way in, has a handle on the client.

Leith calls her, talks as he walks. 'Ana. There's a car downstairs. We're visiting the trial today. The offer has been made and it looks promising. We're just going along to observe the trial in action. The only real question is...'

In the car, Ana scribbles as he talks. She doesn't know Leith well. He sometimes asks about sailing, about when she is going out, demonstrates a passing interest. Not that she does it any more.

There is something familiar about him, that quality that some people possess. His hair is cropped close and is bright blond; he's tall, and he doesn't look at her as he speaks, but checks his phone.

Until the last minute, when he turns and catches her gaze intently. 'You were at the dentist today?' He hesitates over the word, implying he understands it might not be the dentist, that something else is going on.

She almost laughs, imagines telling him she'd been awake half the night because a body has been found. That she'd missed her train by minutes because of a police visit. Thinks of telling him someone knows her secrets, that she's poised on a knife edge, because if it is Leo, then someone is back for more. And she's terrified.

'Sorry. Last-minute thing.'

'No problem. Next time, if you'll be late, just try to call me first. You've got my number. We arranged this meeting last minute too and it would have been useful to know. If there's anything going on, you can tell me.'

She nods and opens her mouth to reply but he's already turned back to his phone, and the car pulls out of north London, heading up the M1, racing white vans that sit in the central lane, tourist buses making their way out of the city.

They pull up at a building that looks modern and sleek. It has spotlights. *Like a prison*, Ana thinks. *Like an expensive white prison.*

'Hello!' A man walks towards them, hand outstretched, and Ana is sure she recognises him but she has no idea from where.

'Leith Kirwan, and this is Ana Seabrook.' Leith shakes his hand, and when Ana does so she looks at him to see if there's any spark of recognition, but nothing.

'I'm Jack Thurbridge. Come this way and I'll show you round the trial set-up. We're just about to start, so it will be interesting for you to see what goes on. Or not, depending!' He laughs and then moves swiftly into the building, as modern and bright as the exterior.

Everything smells clinical. Clean.

He gestures to a large room with beds and chairs, which has a huge window running along the centre, looking into the corridor. A group of people sit chatting, and then another large window to the right looks into what seems like a sleek kitchen. None of it feels particularly medical.

'So this is where we run the trials and monitor the results. We always have an emergency medical team on standby. Trials can take a while. There are four main phases to any medical drugs trial. We're in phase two at the moment. It's still in its infancy. The first phase tests on only a few healthy people. Phase two is where we test the drug on people we're hoping it will be able to help. We're currently conducting tests in six centres, in six countries. The next phase is the big one.'

'Where do you recruit the volunteers?' Ana asks.

'Well, in this instance, we've advertised. It's all approved by an ethics committee. As Neprexine is a weight-loss stimulant, it's been easy to recruit.'

'And you've had good results so far?' Leith asks.

Jack nods. 'Yes, excellent. We're aiming to tap in to the cosmetic market after we've received approval to market the drug on medical grounds. Could be huge. It's been very encouraging. I haven't been told why you're here, but I can guess.'

Neither Leith nor Ana speaks. Merging companies frequently involves a staff shake-up and telling the staff isn't their remit.

Jack smiles. 'Don't worry, I'm a chemist, I'm not into the business side of things.'

Leith's phone rings. 'Sorry, can I take this?'

'Yes, but not here. The reception area? I'll get some coffee arranged while you're busy. The trial will start in about fifteen minutes.'

Ana looks at him. He's attractive, dark hair, and she watches him turn and call to another member of staff. It's the profile that jolts her memory. And she blurts out, before she can stop herself—.

'Jack812.'

He spins to look back at her. 'Sorry?'

Ana can feel her whole face heat up. The burn runs all the way to her toes. 'I'm sorry. I thought I recognised you... I...'

'Oh, Jack812! That's what you said!' He laughs again, eyes crinkling at the corner. He runs his hand through his hair. 'Bloody hell, that's embarrassing. We haven't dated, have we?'

'No! No... I mean. Not that... I'm not on the site, my friend...'

He places his hand on her arm and smiles. 'Seriously, don't explain. It's a murky place, the world of Internet dating. If I've been rejected by one of your friends then don't tell me! I'm quite new to it all.'

Her toes are still curling in embarrassment when she hears Leith return. She's aware that she's still bright red, still stammering, and Jack's hand is still on her arm. She sees Leith catch it all and raise his eyebrows in surprise, stopping for a second before saying, 'Ana? Everything OK?'

'Yes,' she says, mortified. 'Yes, I was just wondering where the loo was.'

'Down there on your left. Meet us back in the test

room,' Jack says, smiling, recovering quickly. 'Biscuits and coffee waiting for you there.'

Furiously, she pads powder over her face, her reflection still pink and patchy. At least she hadn't mentioned Fran. She can say she just noticed his face when she was scrolling through, but she doesn't think he will ask. He had found it funny, wasn't too embarrassed. She is so on edge at the moment. She checks her phone; a text from Mum:

> *Police have called. They want to come and see you 5pm. I've said you'll go to the station – you won't want them in the pub? Can you make it? Maisie getting in 3pm St Pancras xx*

Five o'clock would be fine. She has told Leith she has a follow-up at the dentist at 3 p.m., so she is already due to leave early. She needs to keep the two worlds separate.

If they're asking for her to go in, then maybe they've found something.

If it is Leo, finally, then there might be some kind of peace.

The steel of the sink is cold and she holds it, closing her eyes, balancing on the shifting ground.

Reflection arranged: professional, organised – she leans her head against the cool of the mirror before heading back out.

Has Ben heard? There's been no word from him.

Grief for someone alive is the hardest part. Sometimes it grips her when she's least expecting it. It lands now like a kick in the stomach. Her hands tremble.

Often, she wants to rail and cry. She has railed, has cried. It takes her nowhere.

But he must have heard by now. He must call.

Shaking her head out and standing up tall, she smiles into the mirror, confident. A touch of lipstick.

The volunteers are all overweight, either a little or a lot.

'Hope I get the real thing!' one of them says, a short man with curly hair. He must be about forty-five years old. 'I've been trying to cut back on the curries, but I think if I could just shift a bit then I'd have the confidence to go for a run, or go to the gym. I just need a bit of help getting going.' He smiles, rueful.

Jack hands out small paper cups with water and even smaller paper cups containing medication. 'Here we are. Now, as you were briefed earlier, you shouldn't feel any effects. We will monitor your heart rate and blood pressure this morning. Then we will invite you back in at regular intervals as outlined in the contract. Good luck, everybody!'

'Can we do a selfie?' the man says. 'A "before" shot of us all?'

The group laugh, and Jack nods.

'Of course!' he says. 'Let me take it.'

'No, I'll do it,' Ana says. 'You need to be in shot. I'll email it over to you.'

They bunch up. A group in gowns and Jack at the centre in his white coat, standing next to a slightly uncomfortable Leith.

'Say celery!' Ana calls.

Click. And as she presses, she thinks of another photo.

On the way out, Jack gives her a wink as he shakes her hand. Leith has already begun walking to the car, and Jack leans and whispers, 'Nice to meet you. Thanks for not bringing it up here. I'd get a right ribbing if they knew I was turning to the Internet.'

She smiles. 'Good luck, Jack812.'

14

MAARTEN

First, it's a movement in her fingers. Did it happen?

'Liv? Liv?'

Then a shake of the head. More sure, he shouts, 'Liv!' and runs from the room to the corridor, looking for the nurse to tell. 'She's waking up! She's waking up!'

Then he's back in the room and he holds her hand as her eyelids lift, and she coughs. She coughs harshly, and he grabs a glass of water and holds it to her lips.

The relief a wave, washing him through completely.

She stirs beneath his fingers, and he's overcome. He wants to speak to her, and he can't think of anything sensible to say. So he tells her their love story.

'I saw you first, riding your bike in Rotterdam. You wore a huge green jumper and your hair was tied up. I looked back, couldn't take my eyes off you... You headed into the café ahead of me. You met a friend and sat at a wooden table, with an old wine bottle as a candle holder, and the light flickered on your face. You

77

drank beer. And I'd never have dared speak to you…
but Klaus was there to meet me, and he'd heard your
English voices chatting, and he'd asked you where you
were from.'

He leans closer, whispers so his words land lighter
than breath in her ear. 'My life began then, *schatje*. I
didn't really live until that moment.'

She's still groggy. Still shifting slightly, returning from
the dark.

'And so much later, I held your hand like this when
you gave birth to Nic, and then Sanne. *Liefje*, my best
day is when you're home when I get home, or knowing
you'll crawl into bed with me if you're out late.
Knowing you're there. *Liefje*, I rely on you. You, you
are my home. Without you…'

His eyes are wet and he leans in to kiss her. He is out
of words. They pour from his eyes.

'Maart.' Her lips part and a wheeze rasps out; to him,
a melody.

He speaks quickly. 'There was an accident. The girls
are fine, your mum's with them. You're fine, but you've
been sleeping since. You're OK. The girls are OK.'

Thank God. Thank God for Liv. '*Liefje, liefje, liefje.*'

15

ANA

'Maisie!' Ana flings her arms open, pulling in her sister, all angles and blonde hair spiked, still carrying a huge rucksack. She can feel tears on her cheeks and she's not sure to whom they belong.

St Pancras is bustling. Someone is playing the piano nearby and the jumble of notes force their way through the Eurostar crowds, the passing commuters, and fill the high ceilings. A pigeon swoops low; people embrace, leaving, arriving, finding each other.

Bodies are dressed up, dressed down; all bearing the hallmarks of the heat. Suitcases wheeled, bags carried. Ana ducks from the sharp corner of a sign held up with someone's name. Tongues gabble in French, Dutch, Italian... freedom, possibility.

Europe lives here.

'How long are you here? I had no idea you'd be able to come so quickly!'

Maisie pulls back. 'I've got two weeks!' She waggles

her hands in the air. Jazz hands. 'I'm knee-deep in the thesis but I've done my research. As long as I can work somewhere each day it doesn't matter where I do it. Mum told me.' She smiles. 'Mum told me that Fabian is coming back to the village. I was writing, but Amsterdam is full of tourists at the moment and I need the calm of home. Everyone from my course has fled, so I jumped on a train. Here I am. Your personal protection service.'

'God, it's good to see you.'

'Look, let's go upstairs and have a drink at the Champagne Bar. I may be a skint PhD student but you're loaded, and living with mum. Bet you're not spending any on yourself. Except this make-up. This gets more and more sophisticated.' Maisie leans forward and clicks her fingers by Ana's cheekbone. 'Très chic!'

Picking up her bag, Maisie slings it over her shoulder, tanned and bearing a small tattoo. She wears a vest top and baggy pyjama-style trousers, printed with red stars on a black background. Ana smiles at the familiarity of her sister – thrifty, stylish, boho.

Ana laughs and they head towards the glass lift. It's busy in the station and they weave through the bar upstairs and find a booth. The 'Press Here for Champagne' button sits at the end of the booth and Maisie presses, asking, 'So, have you seen him?'

Ben is her first thought, and Ana's shaking her head before realising that Maisie means Fabian. 'No. Jess, the new cleaner, told us yesterday he's coming back next week sometime. The Irvines are holding their anniversary party at the pub. I've got a new deal, so I've been working late. Last night...' She shakes her head. She lifts her glass and takes a sip instead. 'Anyway, I can't have more than a glass of this.'

'He'll stick his dirty head round the bar. It's just a matter of time.' Maisie drinks the pink champagne quickly, reaching for the olives that had arrived with it and the tiny crisps, thick like pitta bread, salted and rich.

'I'm over him, Mais. Honestly, since Ben, the prison – I just don't think about him. He was...' She searches for the word but it doesn't come.

'He was a manipulating, mind-fucking arsehole, is what he was, Ana. A loser of the highest order, and because you left him, it will always be unfinished business to him. If he shows his face, you give him nothing. Any hint of anything and we're down to the police.'

'Did mum tell you about Ayot? The temple? The body...' Ana shudders. She checks her watch, due to be in the station soon. She hopes they won't mind wine on her breath.

'Yeah. You think it's Leo?' Maisie settles back against the thick leather of the booth. A pigeon swoops past. Two businessmen walk to the booth ahead of them, and one of them glances at Maisie as she lifts the glass again, refilled. He looks for slightly too long, slows his step a fraction. Unaware, she leans forward, holds Ana's hand. He moves on, ignored.

'Have you phoned Harper?' she asks.

Ana shakes her head. 'I wanted to. But…'

'Do it now. Mum said you're going to the local police this afternoon?' Her hand is cool on Ana's; the condensation from the drink trickles to a drop, slides down the glass and lands on Ana's arm. Her skin has risen in goose bumps.

'But aren't I jumping the gun? Won't she be busy? I don't want to—"

'Phone her, Ana. Phone her.'

The train rattles its way back. This time two faces reflect back. Same colouring, but Maisie's hair is short. Her ear is pierced a couple of times and, in this heat, she manages to maintain the appearance of cool. She's only a couple of years younger. Ana's hair is pulled up and back, her clothes more fitted, her face pinker. She looks like the grown-up, not the sister. Too old, she thinks. Too drained.

The nylon seats of the train are spiky under her legs. Half-drunk bottles of water roll around the floor, dumped by other passengers. Children lie on the seats, zombified with heat and iPads.

'Sure I can't drop you?' Ana asks as Maisie queues for a taxi.

'No, you'll be late. Go and do your interview. They must think it's Leo if they're dragging you in. Go and help them. We all want Leo to have some justice.'

The station is a big square building, just down from the centre of town. In a city so tiny, with cobbled streets and such a stunning cathedral, Ana looks at the police station and wonders how they managed to build something so grey and boxy. She walks up the steps and gives her name. She texts her mum to let her know that Maisie is on her way. Then she checks her emails.

It's cool inside, and she is shown into a room with a window. Sinking into the plastic seat, she says, 'Just water, please,' as the officer asks, then exits. There is a large mirror on one side of the room and she thinks of the two-way mirrors she's seen in focus groups. There's another camera in the corner. The inside of the station is far more technically advanced than its exterior would suggest.

'Hello, we met earlier. I'm DI Verma, and this is DS Atkinson.' The female officer from that morning enters the room, followed by a blond male with the first signs of sunburn peel under his eyes, and Ana rises, shaking both their hands.

'Ana, please,' Ana says as they begin with 'Ms Seabrook', and DI Verma continues.

'We don't want to raise your hopes. However, one of the possibilities we're considering is that the body discovered yesterday is that of Leo Fenton. I know there has been some speculation in the press – it was such a big local story at the time. We just wanted to find out if you've heard anything.'

She thinks of the photo she was sent, and she feels light-headed at the thought they know. Could they know?

Their words are surely only a fraction of the truth – more of a lie, Ana thinks. They must have more than location. There must have been something about the buried body that suggested Leo, but it's not her job to question them. She wants to mention the photo. This is the time to say it, but it sticks in her throat, and her mouth is dry.

'Well, I haven't—' Her phone beeps with a message coming in. 'Sorry,' she says, picking it up to turn the sound off. She glances at the screen, expecting to see one in from her mum. But instead, the screen is lit with LEO.

A message from Leo?

Holding the phone, she is aware that she is sitting silently, staring at the screen. The two officers wait patiently. DI Verma smiles, but her eyes slide towards Ana's screen and she turns it quickly face down. She practically slams it on the table, and it's a testament to their training that neither of the officers react. She feels her face heat up. The cool of the room is suddenly clammy and hot, and sweat trickles down her back.

'I—' she begins. But her mouth, if dry before, is like chalk.

'Here, please, have a drink.' The DS pours her a glass of water from the jug that has been wheeled in.

She holds the glass like a lifeline. She swallows slowly, giving herself a moment. She mustn't lose her cool in here. A swallow and then she's ready. She forces herself to smile. Her heartbeat has speeded up. It's racing so loudly she is sure they must be able to hear it.

'Sorry, it's my mum. My sister has just come home for a visit. I've forgotten to order the shopping.' It's a paltry excuse at best. She's babbling and her hands are clammy. 'You were asking if there's been anything?'

The DI nods, smiling. 'Yes, if someone has buried the body and it does turn out to be Leo, we'd be interested to know if you've noticed anything unusual recently. If there is anyone you've seen around who might appear to be suspicious? Any calls from anyone you haven't heard from for a while?'

The DI's face remains unchanged as she asks the last question. Did she see the screen? Do they know about the photo? Ana is desperate to find out. Should she say anything? The sensible thing to do would be to hand the phone over immediately. If she doesn't do it now, then it will seem much worse later.

But she knows she can't show them. She needs to read it first. Her mind flashes to the feeling of being followed. The man at the graveyard. The figure in the car park. Both wearing a cap. So familiar. Her job has taught her when to hold back and when to reveal. She remains still, but her mind is racing.

Could Leo really still be alive?

Aware that she's been sitting, staring, for a minute, she tries apologising. 'I'm sorry, it's been a long day at work, and I've only just picked up my sister from the station. I'm not really with it. I haven't seen anyone acting suspiciously recently.' She feels the lie lodge in her throat. It's bulging with things unsaid. She wills them to accept the statement, not to probe her further.

The light becomes sharper through the window; the sun must have swung further round, and it glares in her face. She squints, and she sees the two officers exchange a look.

'We understand that this must all be somewhat of a shock for you,' the DI says, rising. 'Thank you so much for coming in. Maybe we could speak to you again soon, and if you hear of anything, anything at all...' – Ana sees the DS glance at her phone again – '...then please give us a call. You have my card.'

As she shakes their hands, Ana wonders if they feel hers tremble. The posters on the wall blur in and out of vision; the colours in the room lift and vibrate. Her fingernails bite into her palms.

***

On the drive out to Ayot, the heat from the road looks like water up ahead on the horizon and the trees offer out wilting yellow leaves, exhausted from the sun. The country lanes are quiet. She passes a park: children play football, buggies scatter on the grass, basted in the heat.

Cars are parked on the verge and road in the village – it's hard to get through. There's a cricket match, so she parks at the edge of the village and walks from one end through the centre to their pub. She's still shivering, even in this heat. She passes the other pub in the village, the one with the aviary; it's bursting with cars. They spill out, stacked in the Friday sun.

Walking past it, she catches sight of a figure in a cap, and she thinks of the car park. The same sense of recognition.

Can it really be him?

She thinks of the photo, of the text message.

The sun is too hot now for black panic; it's daytime and the fear she feels is not the same as the night terrors. But it's still real.

Her phone is in her hand, like a hot stone. Her hand is ice cold.

'Leo...'

She steps towards the figure for a better look, but he heads out before her, turning off quickly. She doesn't see his face.

It's as she approaches The Frog that she catches sight of him again. He's sitting on one of the wooden benches near the field where the cricketers play.

The face is hidden. The cap is tilted forward. But it's the same cap she saw five minutes ago. And there's something about him.

Is Fabian back early? That jacket... She takes a step closer, and as she does so, the memories return, and she stands stock still, thinking of Fabian Irvine. Of the terror.

She'd caught him sitting outside her home before. He would sit on a wall, kicking his heels, reading a paper, drinking a coffee. He would sit in the bar near where she'd worked – would have arranged to meet friends there. And she'd end up leaving. Often, he'd come over and say hello. Often, he'd just catch her eye. If he was drunk, then he'd grab her hand and declare his love. Say that he was still waiting for her. Or say that she wasn't looking so great, that she'd put on weight.

She doesn't look at him. Speeds up her walk home. Pausing once through the main pub door. Allows the cool of the inside a second to let her catch her breath. Her palms clammy; her heart has started racing.

Leo.

Fabian.

Ghosts roaring back to life, swooping in; and she has nowhere to hide.

***

It is clear, once she enters the bar, that Maisie had entered to a hero's welcome: slotting quickly behind the bar, chatting to regulars, letting her mum have a seat. For once, Ana is back early and sits on a high stool; gin and tonic, a bowl of nuts. She gives herself permission to drink tonight. She's not in charge and there's nowhere to go.

The gin and tonic slips away quickly and Maisie passes her another, asking quietly, 'Is it him? Do they think it's him?'

'They don't know, not yet,' Ana says. She drains the drink. It sloshes in the empty pit of her stomach and her blood quickly warms. She thinks of showing Maisie her phone.

The photo. The text message.

She had read it once she was out of the station. She had meant to wait until she was out of view of the police windows, but she couldn't help herself. She had leaned back against the walls of the station for support and opened her messages.

Have you missed me?

It can't be Leo. There's no way he would send that, even if he were alive. And he's not alive. Is he?

But the photo she had received at work must have come from his phone. She remembers it being taken.

New York. She'd been in New York. The W bar, out for drinks after a work conference. She'd made an excuse and left the main group. They'd all gone on to the TAO restaurant and she'd said she was going back to the hotel.

Looking up, she sees Maisie laughing. The heat and the gins soften the edges of the moment. Maisie is in the middle of an anecdote involving a bike, a beer and the canal bridge. Ana blinks and holds it, a moment when everything feels normal. Like it was two years ago. Before.

Her limbs sink into the bar stool, and she loses the bright spots of stress behind her eyes that dot her vision like Warhol pixels. Jam brushes against her feet, comforting. Familiar.

'Ana, how were the police?' her mum asks, when it's clear Maisie can run things easily tonight. She sits by her, holds her hand.

'Fine,' Ana says. 'All fine.'

But something is very wrong, and she knows it.

16

ANA

It must be well past midnight. She checks her clock: 2.04.

The sheet is off, lying in a tangle on the floor. Her vest is damp. Her shorts are twisted round her legs. The dreams make her writhe in her sleep.

But it isn't a dream that has woken her.

She's tense. The beating of her heart is fast, her limbs tight. She forces herself to take a deep breath and to listen.

There. A noise.

Mum?

She runs to the landing, but her mother's door is resting closed, and she pushes it gently, peering. Fay Seabrook is fast asleep. There are gentle snores.

Maisie's door is closed.

The noise – this time it crashes. Something crashes downstairs.

Thinking of the footsteps in the car park, of the photo, the text, anger at her own silence grips her.

Who is she to expose her family to danger because of shame?

Why hadn't she called the police? The figure following her in the car park – someone is snipping at her sanity; calling up her demons.

Clutching her phone, she pounds down the stairs, which lead directly into the hall. The entrance to the house sits behind the bar and to the left; the house climbs upwards and over the pub and main entrance.

As she runs into the lounge, something is missing. She stands still, her breathing heavy in the room.

What is it? The feeling of something lacking.

There're no footsteps, she thinks. No padding of Jam's feet. No snuffle at her ankles. Even getting a glass of water in the night will raise Jam to her side. And that's if she hasn't snuck up to curl on Ana's feet already.

Walking into the bar, her foot stabs with something sharp, and she steps back, peering forward and padding the wall with the heel of her hand for the light switch.

'Shit,' she mutters, her fingers finding the light; the sudden glare of the bulb makes the red of the blood on her foot sharper. There is glass, broken and scattered. She leans to pull a shard free, and winces as it stings. She reaches for the blue roll of tissue that sits on the bar top. They must have left a glass out, and Jam has knocked it over, scared herself.

'Jam,' she whispers. 'Here, girl. Come on.'

She clicks her fingers, her eyes still blinking in the yellow glare. But there is nothing.

'Christ, Ana, what are you doing up? I heard a noise,' Maisie says, her voice coming from behind Ana.

'Don't move! There's broken glass. Can you go and get some shoes for me? I've left them by the house door.'

'Hang on.' Maisie vanishes and reappears, handing Ana a pair of thick-soled flip-flops, and she slips into them.

'Why are we up? Tell me why we're bothering with this in the middle of the night?' Maisie is tousled in sleep, dressed in a crumpled sleeveless band T-shirt. Her earrings catch the gleam of the bulb, flashing at the top of her right ear.

'I can't see Jam anywhere. She's knocked a glass. It looks like she's hiding. I want to check she's OK. She never usually comes in here at night. She wasn't in my room when I woke up.'

Maisie walks through the bar, Ana following her slowly, her foot stinging.

Jam is nowhere. Her bed is empty.

'Has she got outside?' Maisie asks, sounding sleep-drugged, but more alert. She steps forward quickly, breaking into a run. She knocks a chair as she does, which falls behind her, banging to the ground, but she doesn't break her stride.

'Ana, the door!'

The panic in Ana, which had started to recede with Maisie's presence, resurges. She tips forward, catching the edge of the bar and pushing herself into a run, following Maisie.

The back door to the pub garden, leading to both gardens, is open. And Ana knows she locked it. Someone's been here. But there was no sign of anyone in the house…

In the garden they both call, quietly at first, and then loudly, as their voices disappear into the dark, unanswered. Ana wants to get her phone from the house and call the police, but not until she's found Jam.

'Jam!'

'Jam!'

Ana runs to the end of the garden, the small strip that leads down from the back of the house, the private strip of land that is not part of the pub garden, and Maisie darts out among the tables, the toadstool seats and the children's slide.

Someone has opened the back door. Someone has let Jam out.

'Jam!' Ana calls, walking slowly to the end of the garden, near the new compost heap, built recently to try to make use of all the food scraps from the pub. Maisie had been pushing for it for a year, and their mum has finally got it going now Jess is here to lift some of the pub duties.

It's by the compost heap that she can see Jam.

And it's the shape in which she lies that grinds Ana's footsteps to a halt. The way her head is tipped back, as though she's been caught in deep laughter.

Moving again, tears already falling down her cheeks, Ana whispers her name, and it lands on the soil softly.

'My sweet girl,' Ana coos, as though calming her. She reaches out and strokes her coat, but she can see that Jam won't feel her again. Her eyes are open, unblinking in the pale light of the moon. They are glassy, and around her mouth vomit spills. Ana reaches out her hand and sweeps her eyelids closed.

'Jam,' she whispers again, and she buries her head into her coat, and cries.

17

MAARTEN

The station is loud with shouting. Maarten's head reels.

He's stayed the night with Liv and now she is sleeping. He's been home to see the girls, seen them into school. With Liv awake, they are keen to see their friends, Sanne to get her cast signed. Liv's mum has offered to stay for another week.

The danger has passed.

It's almost 9.30 a.m. and the shouting is loud. He's been up for hours and his head reels.

'It's just not appropriate!' He can make out Sunny's voice.

What on earth?

Passing Adrika, who has her head down and is striding towards the loos, he finds everyone standing around, watching the unfolding argument taking place on the open-plan floor. Sunny is puce, facing a woman who speaks firmly and has hair that flames red and catches all the light in the room. Luckily, he can't see the new Super anywhere. Tiredness makes him woozy.

'I was doing my job. Please don't shout at me,' says the tall woman, whom he hasn't seen before.

Sunny shouts back, 'I'm not shouting! And it wasn't your job. You should have called us!'

'*What* is going on?' Maarten drops his bag on a desk nearby.

They don't pull their eyes away from each other for a moment, locked in mutual rage. Sparks still fly. The air crackles.

The rest of the team begin muttering and moving away, heads bowed. But Sunny and this woman are still in a face-off.

'My office.' Maarten opens his door.

They come in, Sunny like a child caught in a fight: hands clasped, head bowed. But the woman looks at him coolly. She's tall, and her hair is twisted up into a grip. She's about Adrika's age and she wears glasses with thin black rims. There is something about her – the way she wears her clothes? Things hang sharply from her, curl round her. Younger than him, but she looks as though she runs Google. Maarten briefly wonders if she is the new Chief Super he has heard about.

He rises and holds out his hand. 'I'm DCI Jansen. And you are?'

'DI Carroll. From Holt Police. Call me Harper, please. I ran the initial investigation into the death of

Leo Fenton and your office called me to ask if I would share the file with them, as they have a potential ID on a body found. And I kindly offered' – a glance to Sunny – 'to come and go over the case.'

'Er, hang on. You've missed out a big chunk here. You haven't mentioned that you called the Control Centre direct and put in a request for them to organise a crime scene without having the courtesy to call us first.'

'What?' Maarten looks at the DI. 'You've requested SOCO? On what?'

'Not exactly,' she says. 'I was called this morning, very early, by Ana Seabrook.'

'And she is?' Maarten says, glancing at his notes. The name is familiar but the details of the case haven't sunk in, and he hasn't had a coffee yet.

'She's the partner of Ben Fenton, sir. The brother of Leo Fenton, a possible ID on our body.'

'Right. And how do SOCO come into this?' Maarten still feels like he's missing parts to this argument, like he's started at the end of the day, but it hasn't got going yet. 'Look, sit down, both of you. And stop this. I feel like I'm sorting out a fight at home over a biscuit. Sit down and calm down.'

They both sink into chairs, with Sunny muttering a 'Sorry'. The DI looks composed, waiting to speak. She's taller than Sunny. He sits hunched but she is upright, unabashed.

Maarten is reminded of the opening of an old black-and-white film, of the stars duelling at the start and ending up married. He bites his lip to stop himself laughing. They are a very unlikely couple.

This lack of sleep must be making him giddy.

Sunny's expression changes quickly, like he remembers he's left the iron on. 'Sir, I'm sorry. I heard she's woken up. We're all so pleased.'

Harper, seeing Sunny's face, remains quiet, head cocked to one side, watching Maarten.

'Thank you. Look, I'm rushed today. I need to get back to the hospital later. I don't want to have to deal with egos adrift. Quickly, DI Carroll, Harper, continue.'

She speaks smoothly, as though there has been no interruption. 'Ana Seabrook was distressed. She said that someone has killed her dog. And she believes it's related to the case. I thought, given that Leo Fenton is a possible ID, that it would be best to treat the dog as a crime scene. So I called your Control Centre and set off. I'd arranged to come down today anyway.'

'But you must have known you can't authorise a crime scene?' Maarten asks, part bemused and part impressed by the expectation.

'No, not me. But I followed protocol. They'd send a PC out regardless first to assess the scene, and they'd check in with you. I'm not delusional, I didn't demand the full-scale investigation, I just wanted to set the ball rolling. It was 5 a.m., your officers wouldn't have been here then. There was no one to consult and we all know that time is of the essence.'

Maarten nods slowly, conceding that this makes sense. 'And have we heard what the initial on-site inspection has turned up?' He addresses the question to Sunny.

'I called Niamh but she hadn't heard. She said she'll let Taj know if there's evidence that it's related to the body in any way – it'll be his crime scene anyway, if it's connected to the case.'

Maarten nods. There is nothing the DI has done that was out of order, except make a courtesy call. Sunny's nose is clearly out of joint, but then looking again at DI Harper Carroll, he would guess not much about her manner is designed to ingratiate. And this is something he understands well. The English value politeness above many things, occasionally above efficiency and practicality.

He feels a stab of sympathy for DI Harper. She had behaved well. But she had forgotten to apologise for it.

'Right. Well, we need to wait for Taj. I can see you're already convinced, Harper, so why don't you wait around. Sunny, you can go and bring Adrika in and I want a team catch-up. And no offence, Harper, but my team first. If you'd like to head over there,' he gestures, 'I'll get someone to make you a coffee and find you somewhere to sit. Thank you so much for driving down. Your input today is going to be of enormous value.'

She nods and rises, and Sunny shows her out, going to find Adrika.

Swivelling in his chair, Maarten turns on the computer. There are three meetings he is supposed to be in today, including the always depressing Resources, but he cancels them all. The Super had been kind on the phone.

Adrika and Sunny re-enter and Adrika turns on the interactive whiteboard, filled with notes.

'Adrika?'

'We have a body, but no identity as yet. A possible suspect of Leo Fenton, based on a potential soil composition match of that found with the body and the area of Leo Fenton's death, and also the fact that his body was never found. He was born in St Albans, and the partner of his brother lives here, in Ayot. We're waiting on Forensics for anything further. Leo Fenton was declared dead a little over eighteen months ago. Two years ago, he was camping overnight with his brother, Ben Fenton. When Ben woke in the morning, Leo wasn't there. Ben was covered with Leo's blood, as was the tent. There was no one else around; no subsequent proof of life of Leo Fenton. According to Ben, a cyclist who passed their camp could testify that he and his brother had a civilised evening, but no other witnesses report seeing a cyclist on the coastal path at that hour. Ben Fenton was held on remand and went to trial, now convicted for his murder. They were camping near the sea, on secluded yet public land, near a small cliff that led down to the beach. The jury found him guilty of killing Leo and throwing him over the cliff to get rid of the body. The body was never recovered. Traces of blood were found at the edge of the cliff, as well as a trail of blood in that direction. Items of his were found on the seabed. It was an unusual case, but there was an inheritance sum at stake, and the lack of alternative DNA at the campsite presented Ben Fenton as the only suspect. His statement about the cyclist was dismissed as fiction in court. Apparently the lawyer was very convincing – pulled up a lead case from 1955, that of Michal Onufrejczyk, where no body was found, only substantial amounts of blood at the scene. Fenton has maintained his innocence. Lead detective in the case was...' At this point she pauses and Maarten looks up. '...DI Harper Carroll.'

'And DI Carroll has briefed you both on the details?'

'Yes, sir. However, the murder weapon was never found. And this morning, she phoned in a further suspected crime scene.'

'She didn't mention anything that would suggest foul play?' Maarten says.

'Well, she's only going on the call she received from Ana Seabrook, who was mainly distressed about the death of her dog.'

'So the dog was stabbed?' Maarten asks.

Adrika shakes her head. 'I don't think so, but I'm not sure. We'll know more soon.'

'If we can find some correlation between the body and a possible other crime scene in Ayot, then this will make it much easier to progress. We can search for the identity of a John Doe for a very long time.' Maarten taps his pen again. 'What I don't understand,' he says, 'is why Seabrook called Carroll. Why would she even think she'd be involved in this case?'

Sunny lifts his arm in agreement, making a slice with his forearm. 'Exactly my point! Carroll should have directed her to us.'

Maarten shakes his head. 'No, that's not what I'm saying. It doesn't really matter who does what, as long as it gets done. Carroll hasn't broken protocol. My question is why Seabrook would call her and not us, at 5 a.m. – were they friends?'

'It seems…' Adrika is doing a bad job of keeping her voice steady, Maarten observes. 'It seems that DI Carroll and Ana Seabrook developed a friendship during the case, and Seabrook still had DI Carroll's number. They seem to have become close.'

Maarten taps the pen on the desk as he looks at the notes he's made. 'So, we have a body, which we suspect is a murder victim of two years ago, and now we suspect we have further activity on the case, involving a dead dog?'

He gazes out of the window. The air conditioning in the police station makes this the only place in St Albans at the moment where he feels cool. No one is allowed to open the windows, which he still finds bizarre in the summer. *Don't let the heat in.* It feels a bit like the war.

'Any witnesses? Fingerprints? Anything from the graveyard that will shed any light on the case?'

'Not so far. We have eyewitness accounts of a van, and there is CCTV, but the number plates had been caked in mud. We assume deliberately. There was no useable image of the driver of the van in any of the footage.'

'And was Ana Seabrook ever a suspect in the case?'

'I don't know, but I can check.' Adrika makes a note.

'She was a bit jumpy when she came in to speak to us yesterday,' Sunny says.

'Really?' Maarten glances at his notes, adding a line. 'Jumpy how?'

'She had a text message halfway through. She glanced at it – I'm not sure she even read it, but she went white as a sheet. Like she'd seen a ghost. She didn't really recover herself in there.'

'Did you ask her?' Maarten asks.

Adrika shrugs. 'I wanted to. I gave her the opportunity to tell us if it was important, but she wasn't going to offer anything up. And we don't have anything concrete to go on. I can't ask to see her phone.'

'No,' Maarten agrees, nodding slowly. 'And yet here she is again.'

'You think she's involved? That maybe she was an accomplice to the actual murder?' Sunny asks.

'I think we need to consider it. And the body. But

we need to think about why, and why now, two years later. If someone commits murder, and let's say that Ben Fenton is innocent, then why hang on to the body and drop it into the lap of the police two years later? What is there to gain from it all? The answer is like the body – buried deep. We're meant to dig for clues. I'm certain of it. I bet if Seabrook's involved there will be other evidence. If we do end up going round today, then keep your eyes open.'

Sunny dips his head, stares at his feet. 'Sorry about earlier.'

Maarten shrugs it off. 'Don't even think about it.' He stands, stretching, and his phone rings.

'Taj,' he says as he answers. He nods. 'See you in about half an hour.'

'We're on,' he says. 'Let Carroll know.'

Checking his watch, he thinks of the things he needs to do before he collects the kids from school. He's asked Jane to get some clothes together for Liv. The doctor had said she's likely to stay in for at least a week to be monitored. Shock can be a dangerous thing.

Glancing through the glass of the office, he sees Harper Carroll by the window. A cluster has gathered around her. Things are picking up pace.

It is lucky, Maarten thinks, that the gardens are separate. The public garden is accessed via the main door and the car park. They have swept most of that and it's been determined that the dog made its way out of the back pub door and only went into the private garden for the house, so it's easier to keep it separate. There has been some tampering with the lock on the back door.

The scene is sun-soaked. Faces are slowly turning red. Half-empty bottles of water are strewn on a far table. The suits and plastic of the crime scene make the whole thing feel hotter.

Despite the heat, Ana Seabrook sits in the kitchen of the pub, shivering. SOCO are almost finished inside the pub, but the family are still kept out of the way.

'It's definitely a knife,' Adrika says, walking up to him. 'It looks as though the dog uncovered a knife and a pile of pills.'

'Any update on the pills themselves?' he asks.

'They'll need to be tested, but they're stamped with one of the brands of zolpidem, a sleeping pill.'

'Really?' Harper Carroll comes up behind them. She has been busy talking to the Seabrook sisters in the kitchen, and she comes out cool, sliding sunglasses up the bridge of her nose. 'Well, that's interesting.'

'Go on,' Maarten says.

'When we did the original investigation into Leo's murder, Ben Fenton claimed he'd been asleep. Slept through the whole thing.'

'Quite a claim, and very convenient,' Maarten says.

'Yes, exactly. We did a blood test, toxicology, and the urine test was positive for zolpidem. It disappears quickly from blood but stays in urine longer, and hair for about five weeks. Combined with the alcohol in his system, it's feasible he would have slept through it. The problem we had was, without the body, we had no clear idea of when the death took place. There is no knowing if the pills were consumed before the attack, or afterwards as an alibi.'

'Did he have the drugs on him?' Maarten asks.

Harper shakes her head. 'We found a bottle tossed in a hedge nearby. They contained only Ben Fenton's fingerprints, but only half a print, so nothing conclusive. But it worked against him in court.'

Maarten looks over at the end of the garden, where the pills are bagged and the knife is being extracted slowly.

'So he maintains that someone drugged him, and yet he could easily have killed Leo, then popped the pills and lain back down.'

'Yes. There were no other witnesses. Ben reported a cyclist had passed them and stopped for a drink, but we have no corroborating evidence, and despite requests for anyone to come forward, there was nothing. The evidence suggests only Ben Fenton was there. It seemed open and shut. But I always felt we were missing something.'

The flies are back. He can hear the sound of crying and he sees Ana Seabrook stepping outside. She's with

RACHAEL BLOK

Sunny, going over the lock on the door. She glances down to the end of the garden.

'And now there are the same pills here?' he asks. 'Think she's had them the whole time, and they've been buried?'

'That's what it seems like, sir,' Adrika says. 'Or is meant to seem like. And the possible murder weapon. The mother was telling me that the compost heap is newly built. The ground has been more recently turned over at the bottom of the garden, so something buried deep a few years ago may have shifted closer to the surface, and the hole has been dug freshly – looks like by the dog. The bag the pills were kept in was open and they'd spilled into the earth. It wouldn't take much for her to overdose.'

'Did Ana Seabrook build the compost heap?' Maarten asks.

Sunny has joined them, and he shrugs. 'I'll check, but I think it was the mother. If Ana Seabrook was an accomplice two years ago and buried some of the evidence here, then she won't want it digging up. Seems her dog came a cropper of her own tricks.'

'But why bury the body now?' Adrika asks.

Maarten thinks the answer in his head, but Sunny is one step ahead of him, and seems already convinced. 'To get him out. If they can make it look like it was someone else, then Ben Fenton walks free, doesn't he. They do the crime, he's done some time. Then they get the rewards. Go on, DI Carroll, tell him about the money.'

Throughout, Harper has stood silent, looking at the bottom of the garden, though Maarten is convinced she's listened very carefully.

'You're correct. I really don't think this is Ana, but there was a pot of money. Leo Fenton was involved in a company sale. He worked for a firm in New York and was involved with bringing a new drug to market. The company was bought out and he took a substantial share in the profit pool. Over a million dollars.'

'And on his death, where did it go?' Maarten asks.

Harper has exchanged her earlier glasses for sunglasses, which are rimmed with silver and flash the sun from the red of her hair as she turns towards him. He finds himself blinking, reaching for his own sunglasses, sitting in his back pocket.

'Ben Fenton,' she says. 'He was due to inherit the lot.'

'Well, that,' Maarten says, 'is interesting.'

'Want me to bring her in?' Sunny asks.

He shakes his head. 'No, give her a couple of days. Let's see what the knife comes back with. And let's see if anything else turns up. This case seems to be writing itself. A few days might help build it. If we go in, we can go in hard.'

18

Friday 15th June

ANA

Nail varnish, perfume, power-laced air: the scent is heady. Flesh is bare on arms, legs; dressed in white coats, the counter assistants smile, offering out the smell of summer, of sunflowers, of numbers 5 and 19.

Ana has half an hour, as the meeting she's been in has finished early. The air con in the meeting room had broken. She had been expecting another hour of deliberate pig-headedness, of each side holding firm until the other broke first. But this heat had meant no one had wanted to linger. The lead on the opposing side had carried a chunk of flesh around his middle and the buttons on his shirt had pulled when he'd sat down. His face had gradually gone from pink to red to puce. He had mopped at his brow with a handkerchief.

Ana had almost felt dishonest when she had pushed their agenda: an additional 2 per cent in the final deal, an extra seat on the board. He had nodded, practically asleep, dozing and jerking awake. He had been sitting with his back to the glass in the meeting room. She hadn't worn tights and she'd slipped off her shoes for the private cool of beneath the table.

Occasionally, the relentless sun was a blessing. People ran to the park, to the nearest water. Less time for posturing. More time for life.

More time to look for answers to her melting face, applied quickly when she'd left Ayot. The police hadn't left until the early afternoon, and by then she'd been all cried out, with the tracks of tears scorched into her skin. There had been one meeting she couldn't cancel, and it had actually been a relief to board the train and to turn her thoughts to something else.

She has over an hour before catching the train home, and John Lewis had beckoned as she'd walked towards the Tube on Oxford Street. She deserves half an hour off from everything. She can feel herself cracking beneath it all.

'So, this is hyaluronic. It pulls all the water up to the surface of the skin. Look, it's quite dramatic.' The counter assistant stands back, holding up a mirror for Ana to look back at herself.

Is one eye slightly less baggy, lighter than the other?

'Are you drinking enough water?' the assistant asks, her curled red hair flipping to the side as she bends to blend, to pat.

'Trying,' Ana says, thinking of the relief of knocking back a pint after yesterday's morning run, watching Jam lap almost a whole bowl of water, her paws damp with dew, brown with the rust of baked earth. She shakes her head, feels the tears stirring.

'And sleep, you need to get some sleep. The edges of your eyes are dry. Here, let's try this.'

Sitting in the chair, Ana feels the sleep, so absent last night, finally settle in her shoulders, her eyes, lids drooping.

'You close your eyes for a few minutes, and I'll just do the rest of your face.' The voice is kind, the stroking along her cheek, the highlighter on her brow bone, soft.

She's drifting into sleep when the image of Jam flits across a daydream, and her eyes fly open to the brightness of the counter. The mirror dazzles with light, but squinting, she sees the edge of a cap. And she might be going mad, but it's the same cap, she's sure of it. She feels sick. She's not afraid exactly, it's more like there are rocks in her stomach. There's anger there now, she's becoming hardened. Now that Jam has died, on top of everything else.

But who? That sense of familiarity, like a haze.

'Fabian?' she calls loudly, and the assistant looks at her in surprise.

'Fabian Irvine?' This time she shouts. She can see the cap reflected in the mirror she's facing, and the assistant pauses with the eye pencil, the point close to her eye.

There is no reaction. The cap is still there, bent over a stand.

'Sorry,' she mutters to the assistant, and she stands and turns, moving quickly. Almost as soon as she moves, the figure is lost in the crowd. It's Friday evening and the store is busy. She can't see him, but by the door she pauses, catching the back of the cap exiting to the street.

'Fabian Irvine!' she shouts, but he is gone. A crowd of shoppers stare at her, muttering, and she realises only half her face is done and she has left her bag at the counter.

Walking back, the sense of familiarity crushes her. It's not the profile that seems similar, it's the cap. It would be like Fabian to wait for her, and the actions are the same – she feels hounded, and he hounded her. But it's the cap that is so familiar. And it's familiar because it looks like Leo's. It's like Leo's cap.

'Sorry, I thought—' she says to the assistant, standing stock still by the stool. 'I thought I saw someone I knew. Who I haven't seen… for a while.'

The assistant is kind; she helps Ana back onto the stool, raising her brush quickly and continuing as though Ana hadn't left so unceremoniously.

'You're tired,' she says gently. 'Here, let me finish, or one side of your face will be different for the rest of the day.'

Ana's mind works rapidly as the brush strokes finish their work. When it's time to leave, she leans forward, but her legs refuse to let her stand. She says, 'I'd like to buy the eye cream, and the mascara, the one with the serum in it.'

'Here,' the assistant says, 'have these free samples. This exfoliator is amazing.' She smiles warmly at Ana. 'And try this lipstick. We only got it in last week.'

'Thanks,' Ana says. 'You've done a brilliant job.' She takes her small bag, finished with ribbon.

A tear starts at the edge of her eye, and that in itself almost makes her cry, as all that make-up, so carefully applied, will wash away. She blinks it gone.

And it is heavy on her, like the heat that crushes – that Leo's killer might be targeting her, that it could be Fabian. For certain, someone is following her. Someone is creeping round her.

How long had he tracked her to find her in John Lewis?

Will she see him on the Tube? On the train?

Even if he's not there. She will start to imagine him. What does he want?

When Fabian had tracked her, after she'd left him, she had started to second-guess his presence, to feel her skin prickle and itch, even if no one was there. It was like a rash.

Does his return from the US have anything to do with the body? Or is it Leo? Had he faked his death?

She wilts on the Tube platform. The announcement that you should 'carry water' on your journey, to 'alert a member of staff if you feel unwell', is loud. The danger of these temperatures, making the old and frail faint.

Pushing everyone to their limits.

19

Friday 15th June

BEN

They're in the library. Ben hands a book to Tabs. 'This one's good. I read it last week.'

Tabs takes it and smiles. His right eye is black with bruise, the edges mottling to blue, and another, higher up, has become yellow.

'Why do you take it?' Ben asks.

'Got no choice, mate. You know what they do in here to sex offenders. I just need to wait it out. Hope I get out the other side.'

Ben picks up another book. It's quiet. The library is popular with the inmates, they're usually well-behaved in here. True crime is the most popular genre, but the librarian prides herself on encouraging wider reading, building a love for books. She organises creative writing classes, drama groups. The prisoners behave: they don't want to lose the privilege. And it's staffed by a civilian – it's the uniform that they hate.

But today is hot. And the library is like an oven. It's almost empty.

'You were a teacher, weren't you?'

'Yeah. Won't teach again, though.' He shrugs.

Ben looks at the book he's holding and thinks of Tabs in a classroom. He never asks about the charge. 'Your sentence isn't long?'

'No. They couldn't really prove anything. They found photos on my phone; there were some allegations from a couple of young girls about a few things. You know what I'm in here for, mate. That was enough. It's a short enough sentence. Almost done. Been in here three years.'

Placing the thick book down, Ben picks up another. The dust on the top flies upwards, and it catches the back of his throat.

'You didn't do it?' he asks.

Tabs smiles. 'Oh mate, we're all innocent in here. You didn't do it either?'

Ben shakes his head quickly; he suddenly wants to cry. He is in here, friends with a sex offender. A convicted sex offender, so indifferent about his crime. His only friend. How did all this happen?

'Any news?' Tabs asks. His tone is gentle.

'Not really.' Ben has written to his solicitor, and the only letter he's received back had promised to look into things. 'I've heard nothing on getting out. I guess they need to investigate first, but if it is Leo's body, then I couldn't have moved it, because I've been in here.'

Nodding, Tabs tilts his head left, looking down at a book. 'I hope so, for your sake. Be good for you to get back home. I like St Albans – I used to teach there for a year or so. Finlay Comprehensive.'

'Oh yeah, I remember now you mentioning it before. That's my old school!'

'You said you don't remember me, though? Fair enough, we hit it at different times. I was only there for a bit. You must have been doing your A levels, or have left.'

'Nah, I had a think after we talked about it last time. Sorry, mate. Maybe because me and Leo and Ana used to bunk off a fair bit. I've never been the most academic. Ana pulled it back later on but she had a rough time with her dad. She didn't focus too much for a year or so.' Ben grins. 'How long did you stay?'

'About a year? So you been with Ana since school then?'

The mention of Ana makes Ben's eyes soften. 'No – we were just mates back then. Well, she was friends with my brother, really. But that year – do you remember? – that was the summer… well, there was that thing with the girl. I think the school changed a lot after that. Tightened up a lot on watching kids. Bunking off wasn't easy anymore for those two. The three of us stopped hanging out, and I'd left anyway.' Ben's mind is dusty in here, like the books. But these memories are clear, sharp-edged.

'Yeah.' Tabs scratches his stubble. 'Hanged herself, didn't she? Poor thing. Sad what the pressure of school can do.'

Ben takes a breath.

'You remember me?'

'Sorry, mate. The only one I remember from your year was that bragging lad. Can't remember his name, but thought he was something. Gone on to be a producer I think, now. We got into a bit of a to-do and I ended up dragging his arse to the Head. Little shit, he was.'

'You mean Irvine,' Ben says, with a quick shake of his head. If he had Fabian Irvine on his own, he's not sure he could control himself. When Ana had told him what he'd done...

'Yeah, think that was his name. He was trouble. But he was clever. He's the kind that should be in here, but will be slippery.' Tabs stretches then reaches for another book.

It's good to have some quiet. Ben has to be careful talking to Tabs too much. There's a code of agreement that he should take a beating whenever possible. Ben doesn't want to earn the same treatment.

'I don't remember your girlfriend, but I think I taught her sister. She would have been in lower school? You said she's called Maisie?'

Ben nods, smiling at the thought of Maisie.

'Small world. Police been on to you yet? Any mention?'

Ben shakes his head. His solicitor had given him some information. 'Apparently if it does turn out to be Leo, then I have to wait for a formal ID before they can do anything. There's nothing to suggest it is him. But I can't shake it. I can't get rid of the feeling that something is happening. I keep thinking about who it could be. Who might have been so angry with Leo, with me or Ana… I've just got to wait.'

'Well, we're good at that.' Tabs winks.

Friday evening and they have the dogs out, searching for drugs – sometimes only the size of an earbud, but the dogs can root it out. They can clear a corridor of rooms in five minutes, noses out, tails wagging. When they find something, they bounce on the spot, like they've found a Christmas present, a treat.

The barking fills the wing and there are shouts from prisoners. He can hear Kiz on the top bunk, busy with something.

Searches make the men uneasy. It's not just the drugs. They keep their SIM cards tightly hidden. Internally sometimes. Phones too. The phones themselves are shorter than a stick of chewing gum. Easy to hide. They get smuggled in. When the searches begin, it can be all encompassing. The men are uncomfortable, irritable. Pain and money are involved in all these transactions. A piece of flesh. A piece of your soul.

Ben knows that Kiz is up to something and he is best left to it. The wrong thing to do would be to accidentally see something Kiz wishes that he hadn't. He lies flat on the bed, thinking of other Fridays. Of nights outside the prison. Nights outside this hell.

'Benny, they nearly here?' Kiz whispers down.

'Yes, mate. A few cells along.'

Kiz drops down from the bunk and leans hard on the glass in the window. Their wing is old. The glass clicks out if you lean on it, and it rests against the bars that line the outside. He drops a handful of something out and jumps back up on the bunk.

The door opens and the dogs run in, barking. There's shouting from Kiz, about allergies to animals.

Ben allows it all to wash over him. He can see Tabs walking past, escorted out. Fresh blood pours down his face.

There are shouts from further down the wing.

'Aye, aye, seems like Macca's been caught. Someone'll pay for that,' Kiz says, peering to see as much as he can from the door screen. 'Someone's getting him fresh supplies in. Wish I knew who. I reckon it's one of the guards. Maybe Mr Shaw, whatcha think?'

Ben shrugs. He knows it is the young one, with the black hair. But it doesn't do to know things.

'Macca's being pulled out.' They're on their own again, and Kiz is glued to the barred window in the door. 'Reckon he'll get The Seg, and they'll nick him for this if they can prove it's his. Someone will pay; he'll want to lash out,' Kiz says again.

And Ben worries about the blood on Tabs's face. Whether someone is already paying.

He needs to summon Ana. Thinking of what he told Tabs earlier, of their bunking off, he drifts back. They'd bike down to the park, sit by the lake and smoke roll-ups. In school, summer couldn't be too long and the sun always shone. He thinks of the tang of the first roll-up hitting the back of his throat, of cheap white cider in glass bottles that used to bash his front teeth after a few, the fake ID he'd used. Ana had given him sideways glances, and he'd known she'd had a crush on him. But she'd been a kid. His little brother's sidekick. It had been when he'd met her again at Leo's birthday. She had been in her first job and she'd gone from a kid to a woman he shrank before. She'd walked in, all her childish awkwardness morphed to grace, and that had been it.

When Leo had visited from New York, they'd still fitted together; Leo dropped in like water, absorbed seamlessly, no fractures.

But when he'd died, they'd frozen like ice, and shattered. There's a shard in him now, lodged in his core. Leo dying had driven it in and it hurts him to even think of it. Of the blood... what had happened.

To go back to those long summers, to sit with Leo, to be with his brother again...

He wills Ana. She arrives like a breeze.

20

Ana

'I thought you might want a lift?'

Ana walks out of the station, the humidity close, sultry and sticky. Her mum is sitting on the low wall that runs down the edge of the station. Anna had left the car at home for Maisie today. She feels her hair starting to curl, her feet hot in her work shoes. Her smile seeing her mum is wide, and she shakes her head, pulling her hair out of its hold; the week has ended.

She has checked over her shoulder all the way back. When she closes her eyes, Jam lies flat, mouth laughingly wide.

'Yes, please. Want to get nails done first?' She kisses her mum on her cheek, links her arm. She doesn't want to go straight back to Ayot. She thinks of bodies, knives: creeping. Something is coming and she doesn't know from where.

Her mum laughs. Ana has talked her mum into getting her nails done twice before. Each time a success, but she comes from a generation where nail bars were unheard of.

'You know I can just paint them myself?' says her mum.

'You can, but they never quite shine in the same way. And now you're not doing the cleaning, you can't say there's no point, that they'll chip off in two days.'

The chatter in the salon is quick. They slip into the chairs, and Ana relaxes as the lady massages her hands, wipes with cotton wool. The dark red slides away. She chooses an orange for the weekend. Burnt, like the ground.

'How was it? The meeting?' her mum asks, then follows up in a rush with, 'I'm so sorry about Jam.'

Tipping her head quickly one way and then the other, Ana says, 'So-so. And I know. We'll all miss her. And you know they found... Well, you know they think she might have died because of some pills that were buried?' She doesn't talk about the knife. They hadn't really talked that through. Hadn't even touched the sides. She tries to keep things easy for her mum. Gentle.

Her mum had left quickly after the police had said she was free to go. Watching them walk round her garden had been too much. She'd gone to meet a friend in St Albans for lunch. She hadn't heard all the details.

'Oh?'

'They were the same pills they found in Ben's system, after Leo was killed. I think there'll be some repercussions, but I don't know what. We should be ready for a bit of upheaval. I'm sorry, Mum.'

'Ana.' She breathes it out, shocked. 'Surely no one would bury something like that in our garden! Who would do such a thing?'

'I'm guessing it was whoever buried that body, Mum. Someone has started it all back up again. I just hope it means that Ben is free. I hope it means Ben is almost out.'

The paint goes on in long, slick strokes. The chatter all around them is of Friday night, of the weather: 'too hot for me', 'when will this break?', 'state of our garden'. It's a gentle hum, but Ana's mum is quiet next to her. She wishes she could take it all away, just leave here with shiny nails, with a relaxed weekend ahead of her. Instead of bodies, bloodied burials, and a grief so deep and wide that there's no climbing out.

'You know, when your father died, I lost the plot a bit.'

Ana glances sideways; her mum is studying the colour on her nails, wet and bright.

'You probably remember, or maybe I hid it, I don't know. But I drank a lot of gin. I used to have a glass when I woke up sometimes. I knew I was heading in a direction I didn't want to go, but I missed him, Ana. I missed him with my heart, with my teeth and hair and nails. Every inch of me. Every inch of me hurt with missing him. The idea that I'd never see him again. That his side of the bed would be empty... I tried sleeping on his side for a while, and it helped. I slept in his clothes. I chatted to him when I cleaned, when I was in the car.'

Tea is brought over. 'Feet now?' the woman asks, and Ana nods. They place their feet in bowls and sit with their fingers outstretched, splayed for the drying. They drink iced tea, holding the glasses with their fingertips.

'I know what it's like, to miss someone. I've been so proud of you. I know it's been hard. You coming home. But you did the right thing. That huge flat you shared in London, you would have rattled around. Rattled off the rails... who knows.'

Ana thinks of it. Of how she had tried to carry on. But she had been so alone. And she tried a flat-share with a friend, but they would open wine, head out to cocktail bars. She just couldn't. Ben being sliced away had left a wound; sometimes she's so angry with him for not seeing her, her future looks hazy and unreal, like the mirage of the heat on the roads. She has no idea what the future holds.

Going home had felt like the only option. The easy commute, the bed still waiting. Ayot knew about the trial, but it had happened in Norfolk, it hadn't really soiled their doorstep or asked them to take sides. Ben and Leo had grown up in St Albans, so the village had Ana's back.

'The moment I knew I had to stop was one Christmas. I had drunk so much gin by ten that morning, I couldn't read the numbers on the oven to put the turkey in. Do you remember? I told you both I had the flu. You made scrambled eggs. I went to bed, and I cried. Sobbed so hard. I could hear you both downstairs, watching the TV for the whole day.' She shakes her head. 'That was it. I stopped. I kept a firm hand on it. Until I could cope. Until I could face the day on my own. As raw as I might feel.'

Ana does remember that Christmas. She and Maisie had sat under the blanket on the sofa and huddled together, watching movie after movie. Ana had drunk, too. Not Maisie, she hadn't let Maisie. But she had seen her mum drink. She had known where the bottles were stashed; she missed her dad as well. She had got into the habit after that of finding her mother's drink and downing some before nights out with friends. She'd carried on for months, drinking before she went out, looking for excuses to drink, to pretend she was having a good time. The night she'd turned sixteen she'd been out of it. The knowledge that her dad wasn't there to see was a hole inside her. That was the night she had kissed Andy Miller. Slept with Andy Miller. When Andy Miller had had sex with her. She still couldn't straighten it in her mind, work out the correct syntax.

She didn't need to tell her mum that. The next day her birthday present had arrived. A tiny puppy they had decided to call Jam, and Ana had stopped stealing drinks from her mum's supply. In fact, she thinks, her mum's supply had slowly disappeared. They had all worked their way through, round, up and down, zigzagging and reversing at times, but all worked their way through the loss.

'All done. You have flip-flops?'

As they walk out, the air is still sticky, the sun bright, and the streets of St Albans are filled with an early evening buzz. Tables line the huge broad street outside of cafés; the big museum in the centre is new, bright and white, almost finished. The cobbles that lead down to the cathedral gleam in the balm of the pinking sky.

'Come on, love. Let's head home.'

Ana slips her arm through her mum's.

21

LEO

'Another beer?' Leo heads to the bar. The release from earlier has vanished. His head has begun caving in, locked in a turning vice.

The White Horse isn't too busy. It sits on the tiny high street that runs down to Blakeney Harbour. A family sit round a bar table playing a game of cards, and there's a couple nearby having dinner.

They've covered the rings – what Ana's mum will say, where to go on honeymoon – albeit briefly, not too much depth. They've covered the deal in New York and Leo's new-found wealth. They've talked about Fleeta leaving. They've planned their next trip. They've moved on to the disastrous end of season for Arsenal.

But it's June, and they're no closer to talking about *it*.

The thing is, Leo thinks, men are just supposed to *get over* things. Carry on. If he were a woman, he could rock up to a friend's house with a bottle of wine and have a good cry. Would that help?

It's been years. Years and years, and therefore he should have moved on. But he can feel it crashing in. Every June.

Ordering two more pints, he gets himself a shot and knocks it back before heading to the table. They're sitting down the few steps at the bottom end of the bar. He knows the barmaid by sight, and he cracks a joke before carrying the beers back down. Something banal about the weather. He barely even registers what he says as he laughs to follow it through. If he were looking at himself, he would see nothing wrong. He could throw up right now.

As he takes the first step down, he looks at Ben, on his phone, probably texting Ana. His brother is all he has left in the world. And yet anger floods his veins like fire. Why does he get off so lightly?

When it comes down to it, he blames Ben. He had told Ben immediately. His big brother had finished his A levels and almost been out of school – surely he would know what to do? And it had been on his brother's advice that he'd fled. Those terrible three days – no sleep, cursing himself. He had locked himself in a room and turned off his phone. But he had come out to do the right thing. He had looked himself in the mirror and known who he was. What he had to do.

It had been too late.

Each step down to Ben cranks up the tearing in his head. The pressure is too much. Every June. Every single year.

It doesn't get easier. He had talked to a therapist once. Fleeta had made him. He hadn't told her what it was about, but she had guessed there must be something. She had seen his mood change with the season. He had managed three sessions and had even said aloud that it hadn't been his fault. He had said he needed to forgive himself. But he can't. It's just not that easy. He's swallowed by guilt the size of Jonah's whale, and it won't let him go.

The grief of it. The loss.

Ben looks up and smiles. 'Here, let me take those. Look at this! I took a film with the GoPro and this bit is sick!' He holds out the screen and as Leo looks down at the blue of the waves, the speed of the boat, he knows that he is about to tip it all over. He can't bear Ben smiling on this day of all days. He's going to burn it all down.

22

Friday 15th June

MAARTEN

'DI Carroll has asked if she can sit in on this last meeting and I've agreed. She's heading back to Norfolk later today.' Maarten glances at the three of them. Adrika and Sunny sit quietly, notepads out. Harper smiles up at him, leaning forward, and she swings her phone up, glances at it, pursing her mouth. *She's checking her lipstick*, Maarten thinks. *She looks like she's checking her teeth, her lipstick.* Then she turns it face down on the edge of his desk.

He's anxious to get back to Liv. The girls are at a friend's house. The families at the school have been brilliant. Even just collecting the girls: the fast turnaround of tea from school to hospital had been baked beans, toast with cream cheese; but there had been green mould on the top of one of the cheeses where the lid hadn't gone back on properly. He'd insisted he didn't want Jane overworked, but had quietly stepped back, grateful that she had found the rhythm of the girls' lives quickly.

The kindness of people has moved him. Liv had always been the one who'd known most of their names, but they've introduced themselves: 'I'm Gill, Alfie's mum', 'I'm Josh, Phoebe's dad'...

'I think we have to look at the possibility that Ben Fenton is innocent, or at least if he is guilty, there is someone else involved, someone else we're hunting for: an accomplice, possibly. If so, then who does that leave us with?' Maarten settles back, tired eyes heavy. He picks up his coffee to take off the edge.

Adrika stands and picks up the pen for the large whiteboard. 'Well, I think we have to put Ana Seabrook up there. The presence of the zolpidem and the potential murder weapon buried in her garden is either persuasive evidence or a glaring red herring. And I have the feeling she's hiding something. I think we need to take her phone in and search the house. The presence of the weapon should make that easy. No other fingerprints are on the knife, but Forensics are working on blood traces. We only have her word that they must be newly buried; that's what opposing counsel would say. She's certainly on our list.'

'Anyone else?'

'Well, we looked at this at the time. If you've had a chance to read the file, then—'

Harper takes the pen from Adrika, tugging gently as

she does so. It's the first time he has seen them look at each other directly, and Adrika flushes a pale rose underneath the brown of her skin. She doesn't let go of the pen immediately. Maarten exchanges a look with Sunny, who shrugs his shoulders.

'The other suspects at the time were limited. One of the leads we never managed to follow up was the cyclist who had run into them around sunset. Fenton reported that he'd come off his bike, not badly, but that Leo had brought him up to the tent for a beer. Fenton said he stayed for about half an hour, then went on his way.'

'Was he a suspect?' Maarten asks.

'He was a person of interest, not really a suspect. There was no other DNA found in the tent. Just Ben and Leo's. But it would have been useful to have spoken to the cyclist, to get a report on the mood of the two men. All we've really got is Fenton's word on things. The idea of there being a mysterious cyclist was dismissed quickly in court – too easy to say and impossible to prove.'

'There wasn't any acrimony between the two?' Sunny asks.

'There was a report of an argument in a pub. They'd been out for dinner in a pub in Blakeney, and one of them stormed off. We checked CCTV and it was Ben who left. Leo finished the drinks and then paid the bill, following an hour later. The pub is a quiet family place. They stood out. They're known by sight by some in Blakeney, and their behaviour was unusual. They argued about something that night.'

'And no idea what the row was about? Ana Seabrook didn't know?' Maarten asks.

Harper Carroll shakes her head. 'She was a mess in her interview but no, she said she hadn't a clue. Nothing reported from any of the others. And we interviewed widely.'

'And you never found the murder weapon?' This time Adrika asks the question, and Maarten sees her writing in her notebook as she does.

'No. No body, no murder weapon. But it was Leo Fenton's blood alright. He gave regularly as a donor and we were able to match it exactly. And so much of it. And traces found leading to the edge of the coastal path. They found an item of clothing beached up, still with traces of blood, and his watch was recovered from the seabed. His body was presumed lost at sea. He has never been heard of again.'

'They were quick to convict, with Fenton? There must have been some kind of motive made clear.'

Carroll crosses her legs, tilts her head to the right. 'Well, apart from the row, it was the sheer volume of blood – the fingerprints of Ben and Leo everywhere and nothing else. Plus, as discussed, there was an inheritance of roughly a million dollars, and Ben Fenton's finances were not strong, certainly not compared to Ana's. And that's a problem for some men – their partners out-earning them. Usually, as you know, they have to wait a certain period of time to declare a death without a body, but these were unusual circumstances. There was so much blood. He was dead and Ben was the only other person there. Apart from the cyclist, but as I said, we've never traced him.'

'That's strange, don't you think?'

'It depends. Ben Fenton said he thought he sounded South African. If he exists, then he possibly went home from his holiday and never checked an English paper. That coastal path is a popular place to cycle. It's so remote – come and see it. Why don't you visit?'

Maarten nods. He should. This case needs a few leads stretching somewhere.

'So, if it wasn't the cyclist, it had to be Ben? Or maybe Ana Seabrook?' Adrika says, so rhetorically that no one responds.

'Nothing else, no clues about anyone else being involved at all?' Maarten watches as Harper loops Ana Seabrook's name to Leo Fenton's, to Ben Fenton's, but she shakes her head at his question.

'No. We did look into Seabrook. Whether there was any pay-off for them, that maybe it had been planned between them. But there was no indication of anything. She was at home that night and ordered a takeaway, and we have a statement from the delivery person. In theory, she could have left in the middle of the night and driven to the scene. The drive is roughly three hours, but fast at night. Then she'd have to get herself to where they were camping. But there was no evidence of her there, and she has no motive. She's been friends with them both since school, she seemed devastated by Leo's death. It looked like a fight, possibly that got out of control. Just the two of them. By Ben's own admission, they'd been drinking. The knife they used for fishing was gone in the morning, and it was assumed that it had gone into the sea with Leo Fenton.'

'And the knife that was found yesterday?' Sunny asks.

'Yes, a fishing knife. We're still waiting to hear on the DNA. The dried blood on there is old. As you know, DNA breaks down in sunlight and water, or else is consumed by bacteria. It's unlikely we'll get a confirmation, but we could look to trace the knife. Luckily, it was bought new for the trip. We have the receipt for it in the file. We went through Ben Fenton's bin after the murder. He was the one who purchased it. If we can confirm that the type and make of the knife are the same, then I think it will be useful evidence. You can look it up?'

Maarten nods and sees Adrika making notes. Harper is writing it all up on the board as she speaks. She's efficient, he thinks. She's good at her job. Her work, her brain, is sharp. He doubts she missed anything two years ago. They're missing something now, though.

'So, who else do we have as suspects? Can we think of anyone else who would have hurt Leo Fenton?' Maarten leans back, studying the board. There must be another way to look at this.

'Well, let's forget Leo Fenton for the moment. If someone is burying sleeping pills and a fishing knife in Ana's garden, then there are three possibilities. One, someone wants to get rid of evidence. They bury it in Ana's newly laid compost. Unfortunately for them, her dog digs it up. Two, someone has planted the evidence there to put Ben Fenton in the clear.' Adrika taps her pen against her notebook. She has risen, and she picks up the pen, scribbling on the whiteboard.

'And the third?' Sunny asks.

'Well, the third is to scare Ana. If she isn't the murderer, and I don't think we can cross her off just yet, but if she isn't, then someone is targeting her. They are coming to her house in the dead of night. If I were her, I'd be pretty scared right now.' Adrika finishes noting this down and turns to the team. 'Maybe we should investigate motives to scare Ana Seabrook, and maybe there is some crossover with Fenton's killer? At the moment, let's not assume the two have to be mutually exclusive.'

Sunny whistles through his teeth. The sound makes the air sharp; Maarten thinks of a squeal of brakes, the jolt of an impact. The trace of a scream. He shakes himself back into the room.

Sunny is still speaking. '...on it. I'll head over there later and have a chat with her.'

Glancing out of the window, taking a breath, he sees the sun has shifted in the sky; two children with sun hats carry ice cream. One takes a lick, and the scoop flies off and lands on the ground. He can hear the cries in here.

'There's another possibility,' Maarten says. He looks back at his team, then to the board. 'The only other person who could have had easy access to the murder weapon, the watch and the blood of Leo Fenton, is Leo Fenton himself. Let's consider the possibility that he isn't dead at all. That in fact, the body we have found is someone else entirely. It's just a thought. But we need to look at it.'

'And the body?' Carroll asks.

'The identity of the body in the grave hasn't been determined yet. Let's just make sure that Leo Fenton had no obvious reason to disappear for two years. It wouldn't be the first time that it's happened. Open another Proof of Life.'

He rises and extends his hand. 'Thanks for all your input, Harper. It's been good to have a head start on this. If we get anywhere, we'll be sure to let you know.'

She hesitates, but nods. 'Good to meet you too, Maarten. And I'm pleased to hear your wife's on the mend. I'll head off. Friday is bad on the roads.'

Sunny has stood to shake her hand. Adrika stands too.

'Sunny, Adrika,' Harper says, and she moves to leave, hanging on for a second as though there's some kind of elastic that won't allow her to release. She looks round one more time, smiles. 'You'll keep me updated?' she says.

Maarten nods as she exits.

'Phew. She's good, but that was exhausting,' Sunny says. 'I haven't written so fast since GCSEs. And she's quite intense.'

'She's good. We're lucky to have had her input. The file will be invaluable,' Maarten says. 'Adrika?' He hands it to her.

Adrika shakes her head slightly, starting to collect the pens.

Maarten stretches, ready for the weekend.

Heading out towards Liv, the sun still hot on his back. The handle of the car is hot to touch. He notices the border that runs the edge of the station has paled to a yellow. The sun has aged the ground, the grass withers. The countryside of England now more of a dark lemon than a green, green grass of home.

23

ANA

Ana wakes – there's a noise. Fresh from the garden discovery, she lies tense.

The moon is heavy outside. It hangs in the cloudless sky like it's been stitched into the night and painted, sprayed luminous. It glows. She watches it, listening carefully.

A sound outside. It could be a cat.

Maisie and her mum are in the house. The knowledge of this arms her, makes her feel like she can check downstairs. Even if something is lurking, she has backup. She won't be able to sleep like this. She won't be able to calm the shadows of the dark.

When she was younger, she had been fearless. Andy Miller and Fabian had left her looking for monsters in the shade. Ben had lit up the dark corners, chased away demons. But monsters had turned out to be real after all. She had realised that when Leo was killed.

It's hot, sticky. She walks barefoot across the thin rug

that lies on her bedroom floor, and is careful not to step on the floorboard that creaks on the landing.

Downstairs is hotter still, with the windows all closed. She double-checks them; all locked. Checks the doors. Re-checks.

Something sounds outside, like a can falling. A cat in the recycling. She is terrified. She can't carry on like this: not sleeping, jumping at every sound.

No one can get in. Everything is locked. They are locked in and anyone else is locked out.

Sleeping beside Ben had been the last time she had felt utterly unafraid.

Like sequins, the stars blink as she gazes out of her bedroom window upstairs.

Can Ben see this sky? Can he breathe this air?

Wrapping her arms around herself, despite the heat, she thinks of the nights she spent with Ben. His arm falling on her in his sleep, his snuffles. His snores after too much beer.

She thinks of what she's never told him. Of that photo under her pillow, burning a hole with guilt. She'd worn make-up in court to paint over any glimmer of it.

Lying down, her sheet pushed off the bed, she stretches in her single space and feels its confines, its invisible wall. Ben had opened up a world in the night. A world of velvet, of pearls. Without him, it's just a bed.

Just a bed.

***

'Ana!' Maisie's shriek is loud and Ana bolts down the stairs. She runs so fast she almost falls, and tips forward. She has to grab the rail and leap the last few steps in order not to plunge and crash. The morning light is still grey in the lounge, the curtains pulled tight.

'Ana!' Maisie turns and her face is wet with tears. Streaked. Mascara lining black watermarks, and her sobs come up from her in belches. She stands in the bar, the stone floor cold beneath their feet.

'Maisie,' Ana says. She steps forward, ready to comfort. Her voice is soft and she doesn't know what's caused this distress. She'd seen their mum in the bathroom on the way down, which is always her first concern. 'Maisie, what is it?'

Crying, Maisie is shaking, and Ana realises it's more rage than sorrow.

'I've just seen Fabian Irvine outside. He just walked past the window with a newspaper, milk and a coffee. A fucking coffee! Fabian is back. Ana, I bet he was here yesterday. And I bet he killed Jam!' Maisie's heart-shaped face lifts, twisted with rage and tears. She uses the side of her thumb and brushes them up and back from her cheeks, shaking her head. 'It's got to be him. Such a crappy, spineless act. Killing a dog. To get back at you. I'm going round.'

'No!' Ana puts her hand out. Her mind is filled with

murder weapons in the night, photos she hasn't dared confront. And now Jam. Jam. 'Maisie, we don't know it's him. We don't know.'

'Of course it's him! And it's just the kind of lowlife act he's capable of. It's a belly-crawling act. It's guttural. It's snake-like. That's how he worked, Ana, he kept you locked in a cage for two years! Mean words, manipulation – he had you thinking you were nothing! And then you walked away from him. And this is how he deals with it. He takes away your dog. *Our* dog!' She walks backwards, shaking her head. 'I'm not letting him get away with this. He's got me to answer to! I wouldn't be surprised if he's behind all of this!' She opens the door and leaves it to fall slamming behind her. The gravel of the drive flies up in puffs of dust. Fabian's parents' house is on the edge of Ayot.

Ana looks back to Jam's empty basket. They haven't wanted to move it yet.

She runs upstairs to throw on some clothes, grabbing her phone, her keys. Maisie is too hot-headed. She will need Ana's calm.

Concentrating hard on not thinking about speaking to him, she prepares herself. Her skin still crawls with the time he'd let himself into her flat and she'd slept with him rather than argue. To get him out without riling him. Then she'd changed the locks. She rubs at her skin, then thinks of Maisie, and runs down the stairs.

24

Saturday 16th June

MAARTEN

'Do you think it was about giving rest to someone?' Adrika's voice is distant down the phone, on the Bluetooth speaker. He's driving in to see Liv. Nic and Sanne are in the back singing, and he struggles to hear.

He leans hard on the horn as someone goes to step out onto the road.

'You mean the body?' Maarten asks.

'Yes. Why bury a body you've murdered, two years after you've done it? You clearly want it found, so why go to the trouble of burying it? Why not just leave it where it's easy to get to? The effort it took – in the graveyard in the dark, risking being caught... What's the point?'

'Maybe,' Maarten says, indicating and turning off towards the hospital, 'maybe it wasn't about giving rest to the person who's been killed. Maybe it's about rest for someone else entirely.'

'Hmm,' Adrika says.

'And maybe it's the act of burial – there, in that place – that we're meant to notice. That spot has been carefully chosen. But why? Why not Norfolk? Or Leo's local cemetery? The only link we have is to Ana's parents' village, but Ben wasn't living there when Leo was killed. We're missing something, I'm sure of it. Hang on—'

He reverses the car into a space and smiles at the girls in the back. They are loaded with presents for Liv today; their excitement is through the roof.

'Look, I'm just heading in. You said you've had a call?'

'They've dispatched uniform, but as the call is from Ayot and the report of a disturbance involves the Seabrooks, Niamh thought we should know.'

'Will Sunny be there?'

'No, just me. Niamh called this morning.'

'Thanks. Let me know how you get on. Good luck.' He climbs out of the car and joins in the last line of the song, letting the words rip from him in a howl, to protest.

'Papa, stop singing, you're ruining it!'

He laughs. 'Come on. Let's see Mama.'

Liv is in a side room. The cannula's still inserted into her hand, but most of the other wires have gone.

'Mama! We made you cookies!' The girls fall into the room, and Liv raises her finger to her lips, gesturing to the bed nearby.

'Not too loud, girls. There's a lady sleeping. Ooh, can I see the cookies? I'm starving!'

'How are you?' Maarten kisses her, smoothing her brow with his hand. He sits at the edge of the bed as the girls empty their bags at the foot of it: biscuit tins, drawings, a cuddly toy. She is still pale. Her face clammy to his lips.

'Much better, I think. But they want me to take a course of antibiotics before I go home – said my temperature had gone up quite high last night. Doesn't look like I'll be out for at least a week. Maarten, how are you coping? I'm so worried about you all.' She falls back on the pillow. Speaking seems to have tired her, but her colour is stronger than before.

'We are coping just fine,' Maarten says, holding her hand. 'Your mum is running the house with military precision. It's so hot at the moment, we don't seem to need to do too much. The girls are only in shorts and T-shirts so there's not much washing, we're eating a lot of fruit and salad – not too much cooking. The girls have been on loads of play dates – everyone's been great.'

'How's work?'

'So-so.' Maarten shrugs. 'We're not getting too far with this case. No real leads at the moment, but I've got a feeling it's going to spring to life quite soon.' He thinks of Adrika on the way to Ayot. That village is hiding something. He'd been thinking about it during the night; the heat had been sticky and he hadn't slept. He'd circled round the case. And he is pretty certain location is their biggest clue. Location is everything. Whoever has buried that body in that graveyard is trying to make a statement about something.

Decoding the statement will take time.

'Are you OK in here?' he whispers, gesturing to the sleeping mound on the next bed. 'Do you want me to try to get you a private room?'

'No, she's OK. She's called Aggie; she's quite old. She's in here with dementia. She had an accident at home, and they're trying to work out where she should go next. The nurse was telling me. Apparently, she was a midwife years ago. She doesn't say too much, calls me Katie every now and again.' Liv smiles. 'It's nice to have the company, to be honest. I'm not required to speak too often and there's only so much daytime TV you can watch. Without going insane. Let's hope a week is all I'm here for.'

As if on cue, the bulk that is Aggie shifts in the bed. She moans. Then in a hushed, sing-song voice, she murmurs in her sleep: 'And no one knew. I told no one.' She throws the cover half off her, then turns back, muttering, 'That poor little thing went in the night. She loved it, didn't she. I didn't tell no one.'

'What's she talking about?' Maarten asks.

'Who knows. She just rambles on.' Liv smiles. 'She's very nice, though whenever she thinks I'm Katie she gets quite upset.'

'Mama, I made you this!' The girls jump up to the edge of the bed and Maarten slips into a chair, pouring Liv a drink. There's a jug of warm water and a beaker, which is cloudy from too many dishwasher cycles. The fresh juice he'd brought in yesterday has all gone and he curses himself for not bringing more.

'Did you bring me a coffee?' she whispers. 'The nurse frowns on it, but I'm missing it so much.'

Smiling, he brings up his paper bag with two reusable coffee cups filled. 'Stopped at a coffee shop on the way out of St Albans.'

His phone buzzes. There's a text from Adrika: *Ayot's gone mad. Will phone in a bit. I can deal with it.*

He can feel it. Something will stick its head up soon.

He smiles and the girls pull out drawings they've done, immediately fighting over who gets to explain the picture first.

Nothing stays buried for ever.

25

Saturday 16th June

ANA

'You killed our dog!'

Ana runs flat out. She almost gets to Maisie before she launches herself at Fabian, but not quite.

She'd made it to the edge of the street and had seen Maisie standing outside the Irvines' house, screaming up in the denim cut-offs she'd been wearing last night. They'd agreed on a lie-in on the Saturday morning so no one had risen until 9 a.m.

She doesn't flail: standing feet hip-width apart, head up, shoulders dropped and steady – Ana can see she's angry. She had been standing in the street screaming: 'Fabian Irvine! Come down here!'

Now, he has finally descended and Ana makes it to Maisie a second too late. But unlike the attack she'd been expecting, Maisie isn't hitting him. As Ana runs up close, she can see that Maisie's whole body stands an inch away from Fabian's. Only an inch. It's both confrontational and threatening, but it's controlled.

She shouts up at him and he turns away. Ana can tell he doesn't want to be seen to back down, but he's flustered. He glances left, right. He's looking for a port in the storm.

Feelings drown her. The wave of familiarity at the sight of his face, his chest, the outline of his shoulders. Familiar. Repellent. He's still as attractive, maybe more so. His clothes are expensive, casual, and as his hair falls forward she thinks of Ashton Kutcher. He's dark from the heat, and his legs, poking from beneath his khaki shorts, are muscular, thighs broader. He looks as if he's taken up some serious sport.

A tattoo peeps from beneath his heavy watch strap, shiny with loose links. It lies over his wrist in the shape of a bird. But Ana knows that underneath the wings lies the word *Ana*. He had it done after she had left him. He had greeted her one morning with it raised in a salute. Because if she was inked into his skin, surely she couldn't leave? A retrospective claim. Ownership by nomenclature.

But looking at him now, she's also surprised, taken aback. She would say he has no idea why Maisie is shouting at him, why he's the target. Two red patches are burning in his cheeks, like hot pennies.

'Why Jam? Not content with oppression? With quiet whisperings that she shouldn't go on that girls' night out? That weekend away with friends? That she was starting to put on weight! A year of using her diminishing confidence to bolster yours? You have to kill her dog? Our dog?'

'Maisie.' His hands lower and are held up, like a white flag. 'Maisie, I don't know what you're talking about. Is Jam dead? Why would anyone kill a dog? Maybe she's just—'

'You killed her! You did it. Someone has poisoned her, and I know it was you!'

Ana slides to a stop. Her trainers are slipping on her feet. She hadn't quite got them on properly before sprinting. She hadn't had time to put on a bra and her chest aches from running – she's suddenly aware she too has just pulled on last night's dress, and she has no underwear on, she hasn't brushed her hair and she feels part naked. Not the ideal outfit for this first meeting, after a year of feeling bruised and haunted.

'Maisie,' she says, touching her sister's elbow. It stands out at an angle, and it's shaking too. But it's not dropping.

'Ana.' His eyes glide to her and she refuses to look away. Like a child's staring competition, she won't blink. Her stomach rolls like she's at sea; she holds his look.

Finally, he shrugs. 'I didn't kill your dog, Ana. It's good to see you.' His tone is bored, but his eyes are hard, like flint.

Sirens sound behind them, and from behind the door, Fabian's mum appears and looks sheepish.

'Ana, it's you. I had no idea – I heard shouting and I was scared. After the body this week... but if I'd known.' Valerie Irvine pulls her dressing gown around herself tightly. She hasn't quite come out of the house, but the door is ajar. They all stand, slightly unhinged.

There's a pause as footsteps come running up behind them.

Maisie is quiet now. She is still standing up against Fabian, unrelenting, but she has said her piece.

'Hello? What's going on?'

'I'm sorry, Officer. I think there's been a misunderstanding,' Valerie begins. Ana admires her stepping up to it, wanting to calm the situation down. But then she's had years of dealing with his moods. If Valerie has seen Fabian at his worst, she must be a master at the role of pacifist, apologist. Ana has always liked Valerie, but also feels a bite of pity. What it must be like, to have to live with that ego. To love it unconditionally. Love and fear.

There are more steps behind, and Ana recognises one of the police officers who had been to her house. The short, dark one. Today she pushes through the gate with her head up, and the uniformed officer defers quickly to her by stepping aside, turning towards her to report the situation. She nods at him, but doesn't turn full round. Her eyes are looking at the four of them, and despite Maisie's stance, her gaze lands on Ana, and is appraising.

'Ms Seabrook. Would you like to tell me what this is all about?'

Ana steps forward and opens her palms, like she's holding wool that is being wound. 'Our dog, and we saw that...' She doesn't dare accuse Fabian. It might have everything to do with Fabian Irvine. Or it might not.

'There's something new, after yesterday?' She takes a step forward and nods to Valerie, to Fabian, to Maisie. 'I'm DI Verma.' She smiles warmly at Valerie, who Ana can see is frightened at the formality of this officer, so obviously a step up from the uniformed PC.

'Would you like to come inside?' Valerie says. Her eyes peep up the road. Ana knows she will not like dirty laundry aired in public. They live in a big house, and have a biggish reputation in this small village. Dirty laundry should be kept firmly behind closed doors.

There is a crowd now. And it is for them, Ana is convinced, that Fabian shakes his head, and exclaims, 'Whatever,' and steps back, disappearing into the house.

Maisie looks at her, raising her eyebrows, and Ana nods. She takes her hand. 'Come on,' she whispers.

DI Verma follows them in, and the door closes. They are locked in the room now. The air, already stifling, thickens still. Ana glances at the door, claustrophobia crushing her chest. She wants to cry for Jam. She will not run from him. For Jam she will stay and face him.

Now that she has seen Fabian, he doesn't seem to fit

the figure in the cap. The profile is wrong, somehow.

If so, it means there is someone else. That there's someone out there, lurking in the hot darkness after the sun goes down. Creeping around her house. Can it really be Leo? Back from the dead? Would he want her to feel so afraid?

The thick heat of the sun has raised something. It's killing the roots of the trees, the grass, the flowers. It slaughters life all around it. But something beneath it is thriving. Something rotten. Something coarse.

Evil lies festering.

Unearthed. Unknown.

26

Monday 18th June

Maarten

'How was the weekend?' Adrika asks, coming into Maarten's office for the morning briefing.

'Good!' He stretches back in his chair. 'Liv is really on the mend. In between hospital visits we managed a walk, took the girls swimming in the river. *Voortreffelijk!*'

Adrika laughs at his good mood.

Maarten knows he is usually not the most effusive, but Liv is doing so well and the girls are sleeping much better; he is sleeping much better. Even the heat has not soured his mood. It lies heavy over the country, hanging in the air with its power to flatten. He'd caught a discussion on the radio on his way in about global warming, field fires; even then his mood had held.

'Morning.' Sunny arrives with coffee for the team. His face, Maarten notices, has darkened to a tan, rather than a burn.

'Thanks,' Maarten says. 'Good weekend?'

Sunny nods and says, 'Yes, and I've got good news for you.' He and Adrika exchange a look.

'I was in the pub with some friends at the weekend. You know I went to a comp in St Albans, different one to Ana Seabrook and Leo and Ben Fenton, but there aren't more than a few years between us. One of my mates from the cricket team was at school with them, and he said that Leo and Ana were thick as thieves when they were young. Ben didn't get together with Ana until much later, but Ana and Leo always had a special bond. Said he wasn't surprised to hear there'd been trouble over the older brother getting together with her. I obviously didn't comment, but they're all talking about the case. It's made local news.'

'Now that,' Maarten says, 'could be nothing, or it could be very interesting.'

'Ana Seabrook didn't talk about their childhood at all. I guess it was fairly tangential to the case,' Adrika says. 'There's not much in the original file.'

'Something else we can talk to Fenton about. Good work, Sunny,' Maarten says, scribbling notes.

'No problem.' Sunny smiles.

'And on the subject of weekend work, we have a newly entered Fabian Irvine in the mix,' Adrika says. 'The Seabrooks, or more specifically Maisie Seabrook, the younger sister of Ana, has accused him of killing their dog.'

'Who?'

'Ana and he were in a relationship a few years ago. Abusive, as far as I can tell from what was being shouted in the street. The PC got there before me and heard quite a bit. Nothing physical, but emotional abuse, wearing her down, veiled threats et cetera. Anyway, he usually lives in New York, but was seen in Ayot on Saturday morning. We checked flights, and he actually landed in England over a week ago – before the body was buried – but he claims to have attended a music festival when he got here, and said he only got to Ayot late on Friday night. Maisie Seabrook believes killing the dog is within character.'

'What does Ana say?'

'Very little, to be honest. I get the impression she's holding something back, but it's nothing I can put my finger on. She's got a lot to cope with at the moment, I suppose. The dog's blood test suggests she died from the pills – I think we can presume poison, either accidental or intentional.'

'Well, if Irvine is involved, it will be more than killing the dog. Was he ever a suspect in the original killing?'

Adrika shakes her head. 'No, but Maisie Seabrook has accused him of jumping on the back of the news of the body and planting some pills and a knife as a way of harassing Ana Seabrook. She said he wants "to crush her".'

Maarten tips his head to the side, making notes. 'That's quite a claim.'

Adrika shrugs. 'Maisie shouted at Irvine, but nothing else. There's nowhere to go with it. I've sent some PCs out to take statements, CCTV, any witness reports et cetera. I'll leave it to them. It's not really part of our investigation at the moment so I'm leaving it to uniform. Nothing to connect it to the body other than an accusation. Nevertheless, we'd be fools to dismiss it entirely.'

Maarten drinks his coffee. His mind is filled with the act of killing a dog. Who would do that? And how do you do it in the night?

'Do we have anything new from SOCO?' he asks.

'Nothing other than the confirmation on the pills,' Adrika says, drinking from the coffee she'd brought in. 'But we'll know more later. Still waiting on the knife.'

Maarten taps his pen, underlining a couple of notes. 'Let's follow up with this Fabian Irvine. You're right to leave it to uniform, but keep me updated. How long has he been in Ayot?'

'He got back the afternoon before the body was buried,' Adrika says. 'What time did his flight land, Sunny?'

'Two p.m., and the rental car was picked up at 2.45 p.m.'

'And no word on our body yet?'

'Not yet,' Adrika says, shaking her head.

Maarten sketches out his list of suspects. It's too vague. There's something they're not seeing. 'I think we need to go backwards a bit. It feels like we're starting at the end of the puzzle, not the beginning. There's something else, I'm certain. Can you call and get an appointment to drive up and see Ben Fenton?'

Sunny notes it down. 'Of course. He's not too far from here. Try for later this afternoon, is that OK?'

Maarten nods. He draws a black circle around the name Fenton on his list. 'Fenton is doing his time for this murder. Whoever has buried this skeleton could be working with him. The burial implies Fenton's innocence, no? If Fenton was inside when the body was discovered, then it hasn't been him hiding it. Unless he's paid someone to do this. And the same for the murder weapon.'

'Someone wants the two acts linked, they must do,' Adrika says. 'Does that draw a link between Fenton and Seabrook?'

'It would seem to show both of them as innocent, or guilty. What about if they're in it together? If Fenton did kill his brother, and did time for it; and then the body comes along two years later, and he gets let out, then he gets away with it... What if Seabrook's been hiding the body the whole time?'

'That works,' Adrika says.

'Best double bluff there is, innit,' Sunny says. 'Clever as.'

Maarten gazes at his list: Fenton, Seabrook, Irvine, the mysterious cyclist.

'It's still too short. This has been planned for a while. No fingerprints, no evidence, somewhere to keep the body... someone is invested in this. And why the graveyard? Why *that* graveyard? Let's try to start from the beginning. Let's rework the case. Who's got Harper's file?'

'I have,' Adrika says.

'Great. Go over it again. From the start. Go over interviews. See if Irvine comes up in there. If it's not Seabrook behind this, then she's certainly on the receiving end of a lot of it at the moment.'

Something's buried. It needs digging out.

27

BEN

Still nothing of any use. He chucks the letter on the bed. Useless solicitor. No plans to visit him. Just writing expensive, complicated letters.

He's thought long and hard about who could have killed Leo. And he's never come up with anything. Played that night over and over.

He thinks of Leo's smile as he handed over the last beer. The sun had set behind him like the sky was on fire: the clouds violet, the light over the sea all the shades of yellow and orange. They had crossed the necks of the bottles, like they'd always done. The anger from earlier gone – the air still and warm. He had loved Leo; waves of love sun-warmed, sitting where they sat every year. The camping ground held their history. Even as boys, when the house behind them had been theirs, they would sneak down to this spot, drink beers stolen from the fridge; they'd tried their first cigarette there.

Ben wipes the tears away, pleased Kiz is out on duties. In the same way he has banished Ana, he daren't let himself dwell on Leo. The grief is a hole inside of him and also one that threatens to swallow him. Who could have done this?

Leo was all the goodness in the world.

It must have been some random attack – as unlikely as the court had seemed to find it. They had no enemies. Unless you counted... Well, that was ages ago. Surely that can't have had anything to do with it? They're all grown-ups now, concerned with being grown-ups. They owed no one money.

He squeezes out a blob of toothpaste and sticks the letter to the wall. He's got the other stuck up there, and he'd cut out the newspaper article the librarian had saved for him. His file notes.

Reading again, he circles the church.

Why there? Why did they bury the body there? Ana is from Ayot, but he and Leo grew up in St Albans. Why kill Leo in Norfolk and bring the body back here two years later?

He scribbles notes quickly, then there's a bang on the cell.

Lunch.

The food tastes fake. Fake food. Play food. He talks himself into eating it. One day at a time. One hour at a time. One minute at a time. Oblivion, for many of them, was the goal.

Kiz enters, jittery. 'Alright, mate? Just been for a bit of exercise, like.'

There's a gleam in his eye. He flicks on the TV and jumps up on the top bunk.

They don't normally share a cell. The one Kiz is usually in had been wrecked. Kiz had been in a fight that had got out of control. They were sorting it out. Ben has come to know Kiz's ways quickly. He is not a complicated animal.

From the gleam in his eye, Ben would guess Kiz is going to take spice. Where he's found the money Ben has no idea – he's subbed him from his canteen already this week.

But Kiz is as blatant as a kid stealing sweets; Ben knows his patterns, his routines, and he's been fidgety for a few days. He's been doing something to earn a supply. Since the dogs there's been a quick trade. They reckon they've got a few weeks.

The first sign is quiet. Kiz is never quiet. Usually when people are excited, they babble. But babble is Kiz's status quo. His quiet is louder than someone else's shout. Ben hears it all the way down from the top bunk.

'Turn it up, mate?' Kiz shouts down. Ben flicks the TV and lies against the wall on his bed.

It's none of Ben's business. He will call a guard if it looks like it's going bad. Sometimes they just fall flat. Sometimes they fit. Then they need medical assistance, which comes running.

But Ben doesn't want Kiz to die. And that's the end product of it going bad.

Kiz is putting down his plate. Ben listens, decodes the signs.

There, he's unwrapping the paper. There's a gasp of excitement, like a puff of smoke.

Kiz's vape lights. Spice can be smoked, but not in here, not without detection. Vaped is much easier.

Ben counts out a full three minutes. That was how long it took last time for it to kick in. He stands and glances at the top bunk, making as if to turn off the TV. It's second nature not to engage Kiz. If Kiz is quiet, you leave him be. Unless, of course, you think he's dying.

There's no sign of anything. Ben leans in and whispers, 'Kiz, you still with me, mate?'

Kiz's gaze back is zombie-like. His colour is still there and he's still breathing. He's closed for business.

Ben flicks over the TV. He gets to watch what he wants. He tries the news. There's been nothing since that first news report and he's been scouring every chance he gets. He flicks around and finds a local channel, but nothing. It's taking too long. Why is it taking them so long? His solicitor had said to wait a few days.

Flopping back on the bed, he lies and watches the world unfold before his eyes. A lot of it is about the weather. Would there be a hosepipe ban? Advice on sun cream. Not going out between 1 and 3. It finishes with a montage of photos of the country surviving in the heat. Sunbathers stripped down in Hyde Park, and on any scrap of grass in London. Old building foundations rising out of the scorched ground, visible for the first time in centuries.

And out had risen Leo's body. Leo's poor bloodied, battered body. The image of it has plagued Ben's dreams for the last two years. He thinks of the smell. It had been the smell of blood. Here's the smell of blood still.

And now unearthed. Arisen.

How long will it be? How long until they unlock the door and let him out? Surely it must be clear to them all he couldn't have done this? Surely he will be allowed home soon?

To Ana. Ana. Ana.

He just wants to hold her hand, sit and watch TV as she lies against him and falls asleep before the end of the film, so he has to go through the final fifteen minutes again. Even pull her hair from the plug in the shower, listen to her moan at him because he's left his wet towel on the bed again...

Rising, Ben leans in to Kiz. This time, his breath has slowed, and his colour is not strong. The tint of blood in the cheeks disappears as Ben leans even closer. He whispers, 'Sorry, mate. Time to bring you back.'

'Quick! In here! Overdose!' he shouts through the door, and he hears an alarm sound. Four of them come running. He stands flat against the wall as they do their work, bringing him round. He's seen them do it before.

'Oi, Benny. Someone coming in to see you later.' It's Mr Burke.

'Me?' Ben says. 'Who's coming?'

'Coppers, I think. They didn't say what about. I'll come and get you when they're here.'

Ben lets out a breath. Coppers...

He looks through the slits of windows that sit in the walls of his pad. The bars. There's a trace of the yellow grass he'd seen in the sun-blasted montage.

The sun is bright.

28

MAARTEN

It looks, Maarten thinks, *almost corporate.*

He's been to a few prisons and they all have their own character. Some more threatening than others. With this one, the clear sign at the front names the prison as if announcing a large factory or a research centre. The doors are freshly painted. It doesn't stick out. The fences are out at the back, on the fringe of the town. It's a short walk up a path, with flower borders either side, set just off a street that climbs the hill from the main road.

About half an hour's drive from St Albans; the traffic had been clear. School holidays are only a few weeks away. At the weekends the country sits in paddling pools, splash parks, drives to the beach. On Mondays they haul themselves to work, apply after-sun, wilt at their desks.

Maarten is already wilting inside. This prison has heating, but no air conditioning. It's Britain, he gets it. But it's 28 degrees Celsius outside. Feels hotter in here. He has already taken off his jacket, but still, he's in a shirt, with long trousers, and shoes with laces and socks. It's like torture.

They'd had a brief tour. He finds it helpful to know the environment when he's interviewing. Helps him make sense of the person, their circumstances. Doors on each floor. Doors in, doors out. Doors everywhere. Prison officers carry bunches of keys that jangle like currency.

Fenton is brought into a room. He sits with no handcuffs and an officer stands to the side.

'Want any drinks bringing in?' the guard asks.

'Just water for me, please,' Maarten says. 'Adrika?'

'Water's fine.'

Maarten can feel Fenton taking him in. He'd read the file: a comprehensive in St Albans, Southampton University; done some travelling; worked on boats, doing up old ones and selling them on, a place on the edge of London. He'd also run sailing courses every now and again for schools in Hertfordshire. He had lived in a rented flat with Ana Seabrook in London. His brother had worked abroad for a pharmaceutical firm but sailed competitively in his spare time. He had made quite a name for himself. Their parents had owned a holiday cottage near Blakeney, family holidays had all been up there. He and his brother would often go for the weekend, cycle the coastal path, sail and camp, now the cottage had long been sold.

He'd asked Adrika to drop in the questions about the relationship between Leo Fenton and Ana Seabrook. You just never knew what would prove interesting in the long run and it was always useful to watch reactions.

They begin with the usual introductions, the gentle preamble of confirmation of the basic details.

'Could you tell us a little about the cyclist?' Maarten asks.

'The one we had a drink with?' Ben asks. 'I don't think there's anything new I can add. It was all pretty normal. So normal that until the situation became anything else, I'd not really taken any notice of it. He was cycling along the coastal path. We were camping out there, further up the bank. We pitched a tent where we always do, on a stretch of land just down from where our parents' cottage is – was, anyway. They sold it just as we started secondary school, before the property hikes up there. They were tired of the upkeep. They're dead now – their boat capsized on a sailing holiday up in the Scottish lakes.' He pauses, scratches his arm, shrugs. 'We're a sailing family. Leo and I still go back up and camp outside the old place. It isn't a campsite as such. Leo saw someone. A bloke fell off his bike.' Ben frowns, shakes his head, turns his palms out flat and then in again. 'I'm sure he was called Matt. I'm pretty sure he was from South Africa. But maybe that's not quite right. Leo chatted to him. He came up and had a few beers with us.'

'What did you talk about?' Adrika leans forward to ask, lifting her glass of water. Maarten notes that she's sweating slightly. Looking a little pink around the gills. His head begins to ache with the weight of the air in the room.

'Honestly, I wish I could remember. But it was all so normal, just banter. He was doing part of the coastal ride. We'd been sailing that afternoon. We were just hanging out. We did it a lot and have been doing it since childhood. It's like our second home. Leo's job in New York had gone well, and he was starting something new, taking a few weeks' break. New York was where he was working when…' He shakes his head. 'Anyway, we chatted about nothing. Bikes, boats. I remember the bloke said he had a sister when he found out we were brothers. I can't remember her name, but I do remember him saying she'd died when she was young. Then at some point he was on his way. He seemed a decent enough bloke.'

'He was the last person either of you saw?' Maarten asks.

Ben nods. 'Yes. If I'd known what was about to happen, then maybe I'd have taken more notice. I've gone over it – whether anything seemed significant – but honestly, I really think he was straight up. He was long gone before the morning. Before—' He doesn't finish.

'And is it true that Leo had also had a relationship with Ana Seabrook, your girlfriend?'

Fenton's laugh explodes like a cough. But there's a second when Maarten sees a flicker in his eye and the cough feels stilted. He watches with interest.

'A relationship! No, they were mates. Always have been – like siblings almost. We hung out together a bit as teens, but Ana and Leo have known each other since nursery. When we started dating they weren't as close, really. But they were never a couple. Back in school Leo had a girlfriend for a bit. But it's a small city, the schools are small. Everyone at the usual discos: Young Farmers' things, Rugby Club things... We all got drunk far younger than we were legally allowed. Lots of snogging – but not with each other.' His fingers are playing with his water cup, and he glances down at it.

'Are you sure?' Maarten presses the point. There's something Fenton's not saying. 'Brothers fighting over a girl isn't a new story.'

'Yeah, I get the brothers thing, but not for us. There was no "relationship". When I got together with Ana, Leo was living with someone in New York. It didn't last. We were solid, Ana and I. And Ana, well – she'd been through it. You know her dad died when she was fifteen? They found out he was ill, and then it all seemed to happen so quickly. She was rocked.'

He looks at his nails, bitten down and cracked. 'Losing someone is hard.'

Maarten blinks and looks quickly into the void of loss, light-headed and panicky about Liv, but she's fine. She's fine, he thinks. It's the heat, he tells himself, making him dizzy. But he knows it isn't. He knows that how close he came to losing his family has loosened something. Made him vulnerable. Scared.

Ben Fenton carries on, talking about Ana, and Maarten tunes in as he's talking about someone trying it on with her.

'Irvine?' he asks.

Fenton shakes his head. 'No, someone tried to push things with her. She mentioned it once. She didn't want to talk about it, but I got the impression he scared her.'

'What happened, exactly?' Adrika asks. Her tone has softened slightly. Maarten can tell she likes him. He's likeable. There's a quiet quality to him. When he speaks, it's like he's practising, like he's forgotten how to talk, twisting his mouth round vowels and consonants. But people react differently to being behind bars. Ben Fenton sits in shadow. And if he is indeed innocent, as the evidence presents as a possibility, Maarten can't even begin to think what the last eighteen months have been like.

'I honestly don't know. Some loser. It was Ana's sixteenth birthday and she was out of it on vodka and white cider, she said. It's no excuse for blokes thinking they're entitled, is it?'

'That's horrible. Was it an assault?' Adrika asks, placing her hand flat on the table, near Fenton's.

'I don't know really. He had a go. I know it had upset her. She said he did mumble an apology when she'd bumped into him the next day so I got the impression they'd put it behind them.'

Fenton is still fiddling with his cup. There's something going on, Maarten is sure. But what, he doesn't know. The grief about Leo is real, he's convinced. But when he talks about Leo's relationships, there's something he's hiding.

Fenton carries on, 'That's what we did at the weekends back then, we drank cheap booze, we hung out. Honestly, when I found a way to make sailing and boats work as a career, everything changed for me. I've never really been into studying that much. Uni was fun but I had no idea what to do afterwards. I got a two-two and then went abroad.'

Maarten thinks of Ana Seabrook. Losing her father so young, then she'd ended up with Irvine. But now successful, popular, clearly loved. A survivor.

Surviving is the wrong word. Surely you have to process abuse. A force that strong: he thinks of Fabian Irvine. Adrika has mentioned he has wealth and good looks. Maarten imagines he is used to getting his own way.

Ana has poise, confidence, intelligence. She is clearly bright, resourceful. She gives the impression of strength.

Women have a different map to navigate. Liv has countless stories about being in the office, and what was acceptable only ten years ago. She'd said she'd worked as a student on a factory floor when the men used to joke daily they'd like to see her wrapped up in the poly film. She'd felt like a walking piece of meat. This movement of change, of respect, was long overdue. He wants better for his girls.

'Maisie Seabrook has accused Fabian Irvine of killing their dog,' Maarten says, for Ben's reaction. He half assumes Ana has told him. But he is wrong.

'Irvine? He's back? You mentioned him earlier but I didn't realise he was back.' Ben leans forward. 'He's a real shit. When did he show his head?'

'We believe he landed in the country the day before the body was found,' Adrika says.

Ben pales, glances down. His knuckles are white. 'Then… then is it him? Do you think it's him?' He shakes his head, looks confused.

'Do you think it could be?' Maarten asks, thinking that they may as well ask all the questions now. There's no real evidence to point to Irvine but you never know what might come up.

'I… it wasn't him who was the cyclist. I would know him. He's a bully. A show-off. An egomaniac. I can see him at work in the night, if he's buried a body – if it isn't Leo, and he's done it as a mind-fuck, then yes, that's the kind of thing I'd expect of him. I can't see why he'd want Leo dead, though. He wanted to crush Ana. If he was going to do something like that, then kill me, maybe?'

Maarten takes a drink of water. His throat is dry. The room is like an oven. 'You think he might kill a dog?'

'Do you mean Jam? Jam is dead?' Ben's face falls in shock.

'Don't you talk to Ana?' Maarten is confused. 'I thought you were...'

Shaking his head, Ben glances down. He coughs. It's a dry, raspy sound. He barely notices it. 'I can't talk to her much in here. I spoke to her last week, but not since this all kicked off. I'm... I'm just surviving. I have to keep my barrier up. If I speak to her too often...'

Maarten glances at Adrika. He feels as though they've done their time with him. Fenton's looking tired, looking weak.

'Have you seen her recently?' Fenton's eyes are eager.

'Yes, we've seen a fair bit of her this week. Surely she wants to visit?' Adrika asks.

'Not in here. I've asked her not to come.' Fenton dips his head. 'I keep thinking that it will stop soon. It's like – it's like if she comes then it's real. I've been waiting for something to happen. What happened to Leo – whatever happened. It's always felt unfinished. It was too much just to end with me in here.'

'What do you mean?' Maarten asks.

'Well, I don't know. If it was a bar fight, a hit-and-run. Or a robbery, or even a straight murder – him with a knife sticking out of his chest. But it was none of those. I didn't wake up, I was drugged. And then he was nowhere.' His eyes close briefly. A tiny shake of his head. His jaw drops open and closed quickly, like a silent retch.

'Now this body... If it's him. Is it him?'

Maarten shakes his head. 'We don't have a confirmed identity as yet.'

'And you've never questioned whether Ana was involved at all?' Adrika asks. She has sat back in the chair, and she asks this quietly.

'No. No and no. Not ever. Absolutely no way.' Fenton's face closes a little.

Maarten silently praises Adrika for leaving this one until last. It's the end; they can all feel it.

'Will I get out soon? If you have enough evidence to prove I didn't do it?' The eagerness is restrained, but it's vivid. The colour of the question is scarlet, no matter how much Fenton asks it as a pale red.

'I'd suggest you stay in contact with your solicitor. We've spoken to them. It's too soon to make any promises.' Maarten smiles. 'This is new evidence. I can't really say more than that at this stage.'

On the way home, the air conditioning is turned up to the max, until Maarten can finally feel himself becoming almost too cold.

'What did you think?' he asks her. 'What's your gut?'

She flicks the indicator and shakes her head. 'Don't know, really. But if I had to go red or black, then I would say he's innocent. No motive, no body. Just not the type, really.'

Maarten glances out at the blur of fields, the sun hot on the road, a shimmer of water in the distance on the tarmac.

A sun-warped view.

29

Maarten

'This is beautiful, Maarten. I've never been to this village before.' Jane climbs out of the car, looking around, dressed in soft linen trousers and a pale blue T-shirt. After the shock of Liv's accident, Jane's energy has come flooding back and she is halfway towards the low wooden fence that looks over the fields to the Palladian church. 'That's a beautiful church – like it's standing in its own time frame. Oh, and look, they're holding an art fair there soon.' She leans to look at a leaflet and Maarten stretches, pleased he's able to loosen his shirt and take off his tie. He looks the other way, at The Frog.

The pub garden is only half full. The sun is still hot, hanging lower in the sky, and he spots a table outside with an umbrella.

'Come on, let's go over here.' Crossing the gravel to the garden, he suffers a pang of guilt at having an ulterior motive for bringing Jane to the Seabrooks' pub for dinner. But the girls are on a sleepover and visiting hours have ended. It will be a treat for them both not to cook, to sit in the sun as it drops in the sky.

'Did you say the village is called Ayot?' Jane asks.

'Yes.' Maarten nods. 'It's got some beautiful walks.'

'Oh, we should do some once Liv is out. It's such a beautiful village.' Jane smiles, looking ten years younger than she had the other night.

'Let me go and get the menu,' Maarten says, rising. 'Glass of white wine?'

Ana is behind the bar as he enters. The low-beamed doorframe is uncomfortable for him to walk through, his height making him bend. She's reading something, and it's her sister who nods a hello and looks expectant.

'I wonder if I could speak to Ana,' Maarten asks, aware that her sister narrows her eyes as she stands back.

'Someone for you,' she says to Ana, without taking her eyes off him.

'Hello?' Ana's face clouds, then clears. 'It's DC Jansen, isn't it?'

He nods, not bothering to correct his title. 'I've brought my mother-in-law here for dinner. Bit of a treat.' He's aware of the hollow ring to his words, but she smiles and rises. 'What can I get you?'

'Glass of white wine, please. Do you have Sauvignon Blanc? And a lime and soda for me.'

She moves around the bar, reaching for glasses without needing to look, nodding to a few others who enter and talk to her sister. The clink of the glasses is as warm as the air. The heat soporific. He tries to imagine the panic here the other day: the dog lying dead, the sweaty heaving of the crime scene. There are no ghosts now. The sun has burned them away.

'All quiet now?' he asks. There's no point in small talk. It falls flat for him.

Placing the drinks on the counter, she lifts her eyebrows a touch, and she nods. Her face expressionless. She glances at the other customers. 'So-so. Would you like to talk? We can sit over there?' She gestures to a table at the far corner of the pub. It's empty inside, other than at the bar. Everyone sun-seeking.

'Let me take these drinks out, and a menu. I'll be back in two minutes.'

Ana has her legs crossed and faces the window. He sits on the stool, which feels ridiculously low for his height, and she splits open a packet of crisps, taking one and gesturing to him.

'Do you want to ask me about it?' she says.

Nodding, he takes a crisp. The salt is sharp on his tongue. 'Yes. If you don't mind. Not officially. I know you've given a statement. But the abuse with Fabian Irvine...' He sees her flinch. He realises too late he's gone in quite hard. Maybe he should have alluded. She doesn't say anything.

'I just wondered if you could tell me about it. Whatever you like.'

'Well.' She takes another crisp. Its crunch is loud. She looks out of the window, past Maarten. 'He will say he was being attentive. I felt suffocated. There are different ways to look at it.'

Saying nothing, refusing to fill the void, he waits.

'I was overawed by him. To start with. Presents, dates, dinner out at fancy restaurants I couldn't afford. He knew my favourite band quickly. Got me tickets. Couldn't do enough.' She waves as someone walks past the window, nodding and smiling.

'I thought it was the dream,' she says. 'But it was overpowering, and twisted. He started to comment on my meals – if I ordered a dessert, or if I ordered a salad. Nothing went without comment. It got worse, gradually. Almost without me noticing. One day it was good, then next I was flailing, wondering what I'd done wrong, how I'd upset him. Then all of a sudden, I was in freefall. Panicking about his mood. Thinking about calming him. Trying to please him. I kept thinking about leaving but something would come up. There's very little you could prosecute him for. Nothing that sticks. Nothing that's anything more than an exaggeration of a million fights that a million couples have. Every day.'

Still Maarten sits in silence. Takes another crisp.

'For a while I wondered if this was it. If this was what it was like.'

The sun slants in the window. The glare of the evening is fading. The light catches her but doesn't obliterate her.

'For a while, I felt... I felt safe with it. Even grateful. He had still picked me. And he knew me. I knew him. Since...'

She doesn't finish. The window has her full attention. She looks through it. She looks past it.

'We don't always know what we're capable of,' she says. She shrugs. 'What we deserve.'

Glancing over her shoulder, he sees few more people enter the bar. Her sister is busy and Maarten presses for more time.

'When did it stop?' he asks.

'When he broke in. I woke in the night once to find him asleep on my floor.' She pauses, fiddles with the crisp packet. 'He grabbed me, held me up against a wall. I was so frightened. You could prosecute him for that, I suppose. Even I could see how bad it had got.'

She recrosses her legs, shifts her weight. 'After that, I couldn't even go home. I would see him on the same train. Sometimes he'd come into the pub. He'd be walking to his parents' house – and it's a pub, for goodness' sake. He had every right to come here. But I was... I was ensnared.' She lingers over the vowels, draws them out. 'I had to leave. I moved flats in London, and that's when

Ben and I really got to know each other. I'd always had a crush on him, ever since school, but as I spent more time in London, we became close. And after Fabian, he was so kind. So...' She hunts for the word. '...calm.'

Maarten sips his drink. The sun is falling further. He's been here about fifteen minutes. Jane will be looking for him.

'And now? Now Fabian's back?' Maarten asks. The end of the soda is sweet, lying with a dose of the lime that hasn't mixed. The sweet and the salt make him hungry. He thinks of the last time he ate, but he can't place it.

'I'm frightened of him, a little, but not like I was. And I'm not sure...' She pauses. 'I no longer think it's him I'm frightened of. There was someone by the graveyard, and again in the car park, and I thought I was being followed. He wore a cap. I couldn't see his face but he was somehow familiar. I thought perhaps it was Fabian, but now I'm sure it wasn't him. When I'm scared, at the moment, most of the thing that I'm scared about is...'

He nods.

Leaning forward, this time whispering, glancing over her shoulder, the shadows from her face darker. 'I'm mostly scared because I don't know what to fear.'

'Do you think it's him? The one who buried the body? The one who buried the pills and the knife? Do you think he's behind all of it? Any of it?' Maarten leans back slightly. He pushes the stool back, ready to rise. She looks tired. He sees his food order disappear through the pub, out to Jane.

'I don't think so. I've thought about it. But why would he? Why would he have killed Leo? He's capable of violence – I believed it when I was with him. He would raise his arm—' She raises her arm, like a gavel, ready to fall. 'But he never hit me. There was never anything *exact.*'

Maarten holds his breath, trying not to infringe.

'And I doubt he would fight another man. He's just not made that way. He loved me and despised me all at the same time. But murder another man? No. I don't think it's him. I think that there's something…' She shudders. Her arm has been raised throughout, and finally she drops it. Her shoulders sag.

'Thank you,' he says.

She smiles at him, her eyes warm, frightened. 'I feel like I've been looking over my shoulder since I was a teenager. There's always been something to fear.'

She reaches out, places her hand on the table next to his, taps with the flat of her fingers as she speaks. 'Please, find him. Whoever it is. Find him.'

Maarten nods. He leans in. 'Is there something else?' he asks. His voice is soft. 'My team said you had received something on your phone when you were talking to them. If it's related, you should tell me. Come in and get it on record.' It's instinct. Harper was convinced of her innocence and right now, he is too. One push. None of this is admissible, but if he can get her on side, find out what to push, it will help in untangling the knots.

She is all hollows and shade. The light is falling, and the colours under her eyes are purple dark. She holds her head still, leaning forward, and as when she had detailed her fear of Fabian Irvine, he sees the traces of fear from elsewhere skitting like clouds across her expression.

'I wonder if he's...'

Almost without moving his head, he nods; just a flicker of the eyes to encourage.

She tries again. 'I wonder if Leo. I wonder if Leo is...' She closes her eyes and sinks back against the chair, its dark wood stain curving its grooves and chiselled shapes behind her, holding her upright.

He doesn't move. He doesn't breathe.

Without opening her eyes, her lips part, and he can lip-read the last word, out in a rush of exhalation, the sound as light as the darkening air.

'I think Leo could be alive.'

30

ANA

The research facility is cool. She sighs as she enters, pausing briefly under the vents that pump out air so cold it's almost medicinal.

'I know, right!' Jack says, walking towards her with a smile. 'Every morning I do the same. I waver between cycling to work or taking the Tube. Still haven't figured out which is hotter.'

'Hi,' she says, smiling. She can feel the sticky shirt clinging to her back slowly begin to unpeel, to cool. 'I'm following up on the trial today.'

'Yes, right in here. You've just come from head office?' he asks.

'Yes.' Ana's head is still swirling. The deal is taking shape. It isn't proving too complicated. Leith hadn't been there. The grunt work is over to her for the next two weeks.

'Leith Kirwan is meeting me here, I think,' she says, glancing round.

'He's already here.' Jack starts walking her down the corridor. 'Your secret's out, by the way.'

Her heartbeat speeds. Ben?

'Don't look so worried,' he laughs. 'I had a date with Fran on Friday. She told me you worked with her. We had a lot of fun.'

'Oh, brilliant!' Ana laughs. 'I didn't want to say when we last met. Did you think I was a stalker?'

'A prospective date, maybe,' he says, smiling. 'It's amazing how frequently people don't look like themselves. You see a photo and expect to see that person. But... catfish.'

'How do they expect you to meet them, if you don't know what they look like?'

'Sometimes the photo is of the person, but they've taken the one of their best self – make-up, a wig even!' Jack shakes his head. 'They're just as difficult to recognise. I think if I bumped into someone from school on one of these things I'd never recognise them. If you really want to change your appearance, it doesn't take plastic surgery, just a few key details.'

Ana reflects on her teenage podge, her acne. The fringe that had definitely been a mistake. 'I had a perm once, I think I was fourteen,' she whispers, miming talking behind her hand. 'Don't tell a soul.'

He is laughing as they enter a large room with yellow sofas laid out around pale coffee tables, like a Danish spa.

Leith looks up as they enter. He raises an eyebrow. 'Something funny? Do tell me the joke.'

'We're laughing about teenage mistakes,' Jack says.

A shadow passes over Leith's face. He glances at Ana. She curses that he has seen her again laughing with Jack. That he might think her unprofessional.

Jack walks over to the coffee machine in the corner.

'The meeting went well this morning,' she says, spilling the words out quickly to cover any stain.

He nods, stands quickly, gesturing for her to sit. He sits as she does, and lifts the iPad he's been holding. 'Yes, thanks for sending through the figures. It's looking quite promising. Fingers crossed. The next meeting will be the big one. Looking at staff outcomes is always tricky.' He looks up at her. 'You won't speak about this to Jack?'

She can feel herself blushing. The red heat rising quickly. 'No, of course not! We were only joking on the way in. It wasn't anything—"

'It's fine. Just remember that some of these people might be on the list.'

'Ready?' Jack says, returning and putting down a tray of coffee and biscuits. 'It will be about five minutes now.'

Stepping out onto the road, visit finished and almost back to her office, crossing between St Pancras and King's Cross, she doesn't see the motorcyclist.

The bike runs close; her bag is whacked and falls into the road. Her lipstick, her keys spill out, part crushing beneath the wheels of a car.

There's a shout and just before the lipstick dies, Leith pulls her off the road, onto the pavement. The traffic had been beeping, swerving. She had stood, blinded by shock, in the road.

'Ana!' His voice is tight. He holds her wrist for a second, and the pressure reminds her she is safe. She trembles.

After a second, he waits until there is a break in the traffic, and then picks up her keys and her bag. 'Are you OK?'

The shock of it, the suddenness, swamps her. She feels the tears coming before they hit. She shakes as she dusts off her handbag. Scuffed and wheel-marked, the leather is war-torn.

'Ana, are you OK? Did the bike hit you?' Leith says. He stands, arm out for her to take if she wants – a fraction from putting his arm around her.

She doesn't fall on his chest crying, but manages a 'Could we sit down?'

He leads, walking to a plaza. Fountains burst upwards in the centre, small vans dot around, painted in cobalt blue, granite grey; one has retro metro tiles running along the side. All selling gourmet coffee, pizza and wraps. One with artisan beer. A pop-up eatery. Pop-up drinkery.

'Here.' Gesturing to a concrete seat that looks out on the fountains, he vanishes for a second. She takes a breath. Looks at the blue sky.

He returns holding coffee. 'Americano, white, right?'

Nodding, she can't even sound a thank you, swallowing sobs, choking on them. It's harder than it should be. And from nowhere, the image of Jam's face springs up, and the cries come louder.

Finally, it slows. They sit in the sun. People stretch everywhere, like a sea of cats, spread long and wide under the sky. Ana still doesn't trust herself to speak: the speed of the motorbike, the handle had skimmed her arm.

'I brought ice creams, too. How much does "industrial chocolate" appeal to you? Sounds more like a floor cleaner to me. But let's give it a whirl.' As well as coffee, he carries two waffle cones and scoops of almost black chocolate ice cream, which spill over the sides.

'It might kill us, but no better way to go,' Leith says, smiling, but looking out at the fountains, where a small dog yaps crazily.

The chocolate is bitter and rich. The sun behind them, Ana closes her eyes as the ice melts in her mouth. She feels herself calm. The sun unfurls the tension, dries the tears.

'So,' Leith says after a minute. 'You're sure the bike hasn't hurt you? It was going at quite a speed. I didn't see it either, until it was on us. Here are your things, by the way.' He fishes them out of his pocket, and she opens her bag with trembling fingers.

She shakes her head. 'My dog died at the weekend.' She gulps back a sob. It's so much more than that. All her energy is focused on staying calm. Not on grief, and she has tried not to think about Jam. The bottomless pit of daily grief that is living without Ben. She misses cleaning her teeth with him shaving over her shoulder; the toast he would leave out for her as he left the house; the touch of his fingers on her neck at the end of the day; his breath up against her cheek. They'd locked him in a cage and they'd locked her up too.

'Oh no!' Leith says. 'I'm not surprised you're upset.'

'We've had her since I was a teenager,' Ana says, desperate not to cry again, but wanting to talk about it to someone who is outside of it all.

'I was worried that Jack has been bothering you. I'm pleased it's nothing to do with that.'

Ana rushes out a 'No! God, no. He's...' But she doesn't want to say he's dating Fran, because that's Fran's news to tell. She peters out. Then finishes with, 'He's friendly. That's all. Nothing else.'

Leith nods.

As they finish their ice creams, a small boy on a skateboard skims close to their toes, and Leith says, 'Nice moves!'

The surprise of being spoken to makes him look up, and he loses his balance, falling, turning a somersault. His wail is loud, and his mother runs over.

'Shit,' Leith says. 'I might be in trouble here. Let's scarper.'

They stand and walk away quickly, laughing once out of earshot.

'I don't think he was too badly hurt,' Leith says, grimacing. 'Only trying to pay the little dude a compliment.'

'Seems fine to me,' Ana says. She peeps over Leith's shoulder, back at the boy, who is headed towards the same ice cream van. 'Looks like the healing power of frozen milk is going to work its wonder on him, too.' She smiles at him. 'Thank you.'

'No worries,' he says. His eyes bright blue under his blond hair, his skin tanned. If he were not in a suit, she could see him on a surfboard. For a second, she wonders what he would look like on a surfboard, and realises the thought is appealing.

'Tell you what,' he says.

'Yes?'

'How about I buy you a drink, then you go and take the afternoon off. When I say off, I obviously mean write up the report from home, and don't stop until midnight.' He winks. 'Seriously. This is your station. And there are no meetings planned for the day. You can go home, sit in the garden, think about your dog. Think about the deal...' He grins. 'Aperol Spritz first? There's a lot of vitamin C in all that orange...'

31

MAARTEN

The flowers are huge and they make him sneeze as he carries them into the room.

'Happy birthday,' he says.

'Oh, Maart, they're lovely! Lilies as well.'

'Your favourites, and chocolates. You need to keep your sugar levels up in here.' He produces a box of Belgian truffles. Kissing her, he finds she smells more like herself. The tan from the early hot summer has faded, but so have some of the bruises.

'I've not got long. I'll bring the girls in later. They've made a cake.' He smiles. Nic and Sanne had decorated the cake, casting handfuls of sweets like seed to a hungry earth. Dolly Mixtures were what Liv had craved when she'd been pregnant, and he'd ordered a huge box of them to be delivered. It was a Dolly Mixture spectacular.

'How are you feeling?'

'OK. Not a great night. Poor Aggie was upset. They've taken her outside for a walk. She's still calling me Katie, but now she's distraught – keeps telling me she couldn't save it, she's so sorry, she knew I loved it. I think she must be confusing me with one of her patients. Perhaps someone who lost her baby? She seems so sad.'

There are shouts from the hall. 'I'm fine, fine, I tell you! Get your hands off me! I can walk on my own, so I can…'

The voice stops as Aggie comes into the room, and she freezes as she sees Liv. 'Katie. It's you. I'm so sorry.' She seems distressed, and her head shakes involuntarily. 'I haven't told anyone, no one at all. You must take care. You need to rest.' Tears leak at the corners of her eyes. She wrings her hands. 'Katie, I'm so sorry. I wish I'd done more. I could've done more if… It's over now, though. The worst is over.'

She begins to cry, and her tears are like a child's. They fall from her eyes in a steady stream and she makes no move to brush them away. Great gulps come and the nurse with her mouths, 'Sorry', in their direction and helps her into bed, pulling the curtain around the cubicle, Aggie gradually quietening.

Maarten drops his voice. 'Are you sure you don't want me to try to get you a private room? I can pay if you like.' He grins. 'Call it a birthday present.'

Liv shakes her head. 'Much as I'd love a few nights in a fancy room, save the cash for the summer holiday. She's quiet most of the time and sleeps a lot. I'll be out soon. My temperature has steadied. I can't wait, Maart.

I honestly can't wait to get home. They never really turn the lights off in here. I just need sleep.'

He peels open the box of chocolates he'd brought in. He doesn't really like chocolate that much, but he offers one to her and takes one himself. 'Well, it can't come soon enough. We miss you. I miss you.' He reaches out for her hand. Her lips stain dark and sweet like expensive lipstick, truffle-dressed.

'Love you, *liefje*.'

'You'll have to take them flowers home with you,' the nurse calls on her way out. 'They're banned in hospitals.'

Fabian Irvine sprawls in his chair. Long legs crossed at the ankles, back slouching slightly, even his hair hanging out – swept over to one side, casually, carefully. He wears a T-shirt, dark shorts and flip-flops. If he were styled by *Vogue*, it would be hard to get a more picture-perfect look of a beautiful man dressed for the ideal summer. He half stands as Adrika enters the room to join Maarten for the questioning, not sitting until Adrika does, and, smiling, leans forward to shake her hand: 'Fabian Irvine. Good to meet you. We didn't really get a chance to say hello the other day.'

Adrika shakes his hand and catches Maarten's eye, pulling out her notepad.

'I've not been back to the UK for a while. Can't believe this weather. I've been up in the Hamptons for a few weeks before catching the flight, but I swear it's hotter here.' His smile is white teeth and charm. Even his slouching is appealing, making the room feel more relaxed. Maarten is used to interviewing people who are tense, nervous, sad... Rarely are they as at ease as they would be in a bar, or on a beach.

'I just have to make you aware we're taping this interview...' Maarten begins, gesturing to the camera, and Irvine gives his consent and his name clearly, in vowels like English crystal.

'Would you like to tell us a little more about the disturbance in Ayot at the weekend?' Maarten says.

Irvine laughs, chocolate sweet. Rich. 'I think you're better off talking to Maisie Seabrook about that,' he says. 'I honestly have no idea why she thinks I've killed their dog. Jam was a great little mutt.'

'Well, we have spoken to Maisie, and to Ana, and they believe you might have reason to wish them harm.'

Slowly, as though considering carefully, Irvine shakes his head. 'Well, I have no idea why. My relationship with Ana finished years ago. I live in New York – I'm in a relationship there. It's quite serious, actually.' He tilts his head, as though confiding. 'Ana's last boyfriend is doing time for murder, you know?' He shrugs, smiles. 'Maybe she is casting back to better times, trying to get my attention.'

'How did the relationship end?' Maarten asks this casually.

Irvine offers a shrug, a smile. 'So-so. It's rare that anyone comes out of these things completely unscathed. But it was a few years ago. We've both moved on since then.'

'The sisters have both claimed it was, how should we put it, "somewhat acrimonious" at the finish?'

No one speaks for a second and Maarten smiles. Irvine shakes his head a little. Maarten waits it out.

'I was upset. Who isn't upset at the end of a relationship?' he offers easily.

'We have spoken to the festival you attended. Your alibi checked out for the first night up to about 10 p.m., but not past then,' Adrika says.

'What?' Irvine scowls. 'You need to account for my every minute? I was tired. I'd just flown in. I held the hand of my act who was going on, then I checked in to a hotel. I've had enough of tent living. I went along the next day for a meeting, but the band I was due to meet didn't turn up. Too drunk, probably. So I left and came back to Ayot. I pretty much slept for two days.'

'So you were in Ayot the night that Jam was killed? You sure you didn't do it? A final kick when your ex-girlfriend was down? The body that was found has been all over the news. You knew the details of the first case. It wouldn't take much to scare her, to sneak into the garden and to kill the dog, to make it look as though it was something else.' Adrika has gone hard, driven it home, and Maarten watches Irvine's face. The man shows nothing. The scowl darkens but it could be anger or guilt. His eyes slip easily into anger; his long fingers flex. His arms, tanned and smooth, cover broad muscles. Their definition is sharp.

Irvine cracks two knuckles, sits up slightly straighter.

'I can't quite remember the ins and outs of our break-up. It was a while ago. But to be honest, I don't really see how that's got any bearing on a dead dog.'

Maarten ignores this last statement. 'Apparently Ana Seabrook woke early one morning to find you asleep on the floor next to her. In her flat in London.' He tips his head slightly to one side, still smiling. 'That's illegal.'

'She makes it sound much worse than it was.' Irvine's voice is colder, yet it still sounds reasonable. Maarten doesn't buy it. Doesn't believe him. But the temptation is there. It's his tone: steady, honest. Unperturbed.

Irvine continues. 'She'd told me where she hid the spare key. She'd gone home drunk. I used the key to let myself in and check on her. I was worried about her. We hadn't quite broken up then. You don't leave an upset, drunk girl on her own.' Chivalrous.

You do if she asks you to, Maarten thinks. *You don't break into her flat.* Ana Seabrook had been believable because she had been reticent, embarrassed. She should have been angry – but instead she wanted it in the past. Irvine, in contrast, is confident, forthright. He is convincing, when the embarrassment should be all his.

Vicious, Maarten thinks. *Dangerous.* That he believes his own words; he can't see he crossed a line. Chivalry – you save the girl and you lock her in the tower.

'Well, Ms Seabrook asserts that you had indeed broken up. That in fact you continued to "let yourself in" until she changed the locks. That she saw you near the flat on a number of occasions. And that in the end, she moved to get away from you.'

'London isn't as big as everyone thinks it is,' Irvine says. 'Bumping into your ex-girlfriend is bound to happen. It's not my fault if it makes her jumpy. I can't avoid her completely. It doesn't work like that. And I still don't see why all this is relevant. I didn't kill her dog.'

The problem, Maarten thinks, is that the lack of evidence means he's right – they've pushed him, but he doesn't really seem as though he killed the dog. He can justify his past actions to himself, he can't see his flaws – dresses them in silk. But if he didn't kill the dog, break in, then there's no point in holding him.

And it's not murder, which at the end of the day is the big question here. But it's interesting to rattle him slightly. To see what falls out.

'Look, DCI Jansen.' Irvine manages perfect pronunciation. 'I'm a busy man, you're a busy man. Neither of us wants our time wasted. I didn't kill the dog. I'm sorry Ana feels our relationship ended badly. But that's over now.' He pushes his chair back, stands and offers his hand. The smile has slipped back in place. 'Do let me know if I can be of any other service.'

Adrika hisses by his side as Irvine walks ahead of them towards the exit. 'Vile.'

Maarten nods, but knows there is nothing they can do. Nothing to charge him with. He feels deflated.

'Sometimes you let them go,' he says. 'I don't think there's anything here. Time to examine Ana Seabrook a bit more closely, I think. Can you check the Proof of Life on Leo Fenton? And I think we need to have a look at Ana Seabrook's phone. See what text she received that spooked her in your interview. Get a warrant to search the pub as well, just in case there's any resistance from the Seabrooks to having a look around. If she's hiding something on her phone, she's capable of keeping other secrets. If there is anything to hide, I don't want to have to pause to give them time to do so. We're changing tack.'

32

BEN

Irvine, was it Irvine who killed Leo? Is it Irvine who has buried the body? It would make sense that he buried it in Ayot – to bring it close to Ana, to make her feel it. But why would he kill Leo?

'Tabs,' he nods as the Scotsman walks alongside. They are outside, heading over to the gym. They're both on good privileges at the moment, and there's only a few of them. Macca's nowhere to be seen. He's lost the gym for a few weeks.

'Aye, lad, how goes it?' Tabs falls in line with him.

'Irvine. Fabian Irvine. You said you remember him?'

'The one we talked about the other day? Yeah, I remember him from school. I was head of Year Seven. I had to bring him in for detention – bullying some of the younger kids. His parents moved him to a private school after that. They came up to protest but I wouldn't move an inch.'

'He was in the UK the night before they found the

body. He used to go out with Ana. She left him in the end because he bullied her. He was a real shit. You think it's a coincidence? You think there's any mileage in it?'

'Woah... hang on. You think he's the killer? You think he set you up in here?'

'Might have done. To get back at Ana. To get back at me for being the one who was with her? Bit handy he comes back the day before all this starts.'

'What do the police say? Tell you what, let's chat in a bit.'

They're almost at the gym. Now the group is closing up it will be easier to be overheard.

Ben glances around, whispers. 'They mentioned it. To see what my reaction was, I think. I didn't know what to say.'

They filter in, get ready, start on the machinery. Ben and Tabs are used to falling in side by side. They work quietly to start with, stoking up a sweat.

The equipment is old, but looked after. The officers use the gym in their lunch break, and the sauna – an old wooden slatted one, but it does the job. Inmates behave in here. No one likes to lose this privilege. Weights fill most of the room. Ben picks up some dumbbells and starts the exercises he'd been advised to do by a physio he'd seen in here. With all the sitting in the first month, his nerves had become tingly, his hands bursting with pins and needles. He does the same set of exercises three times a week to strengthen his shoulders and keep his body moving. He'd never needed the gym before. With all the chest infections, it's getting harder and the weights are getting lighter.

'I can ask around. See if anyone knows what the background is, if there's any whisper of anything. Bodies don't move themselves easily. If there's anything to know then someone in here might know it.' Tabs lifts heavy. His barbell is stacked, and Ben wonders at the weight: he'd be crushed.

Tabs's arms strain, and the veins from beneath the edge of his T-shirt bulge.

The mat is threadbare in patches, the colour scrubbed out where Ben stands. There's no air con and the smell of the men's sweat gathers quickly, sitting in the air. It makes Ben gag, but he pushes through it, enjoying the feeling of his body working hard. It keeps him alive.

'You know, it's a shame you didn't stay longer at the school,' Ben says. 'Bet you were a great teacher. You must have been young – I had a science teacher who was as old as the hills.'

Tabs barks a laugh. 'You always think that when you're young – bet he was only forty or something! Yeah, I was a young 'un. Started out with my teaching practice there and stayed on. I was only twenty-two. Wet behind the ears.'

'Come on, lads, got the next lot in soon,' the guard shouts, checking the clock on the wall.

'I'll get back to you if I hear anything,' Tabs says on the way out. The planes in the sky scratch the roof of the Earth, leaving criss-crossed lines like white chalk against the cloudless blue. 'Someone must know something. Bodies don't stay hidden for too long without someone noticing. I wish I'd known your brother.' He lands his hand on Ben's back in a clap, and Ben swallows hard.

33

ANA

'Come on.' Maisie pulls her hand.

Ana, in vest top and shorts, doesn't feel ready for something new; it's too late. 'Where are we going, Mais? It's 11.30. I was off to bed.'

'Maybe bed, but not sleep. I heard you last night, up and down. I can't rest here. I've been thinking about Leo.'

'Leo?'

'Yes. Jess was telling me this morning about how this body was discovered. I knew they'd found it, but I didn't know *how* they'd found it. Did you know she's Charlie's mum? Wasn't he in Ben's year at school? Such a small world.'

Maisie is carrying something. There's a jute bag; items poke from the top.

'You've got candles and flowers,' Ana says. 'Why are you carrying candles and flowers?'

'Well.' Maisie has now successfully pulled her

downstairs, pushes flip-flops into her hands, unlocks the house front door. 'When Jess told me – I love her, by the way, she's great – when Jess told me about the fact that this body was discovered in a grave, it made me think. It's like his resting place. I know they've exhumed him and taken him off for the autopsy, but he was actually buried there. And we're all hoping it's Leo. So let's give him a goodbye.'

They now stand outside; the night air is fresh. The dense skin of heat Ana wears during the day has fallen away, the warmth more like a cardigan, like cashmere against her skin. The night is wearable.

'Mais, please don't tell me we're going—"

'To the temple graveyard, yes. Yes, we are. He needs a send-off, Ana. You need to send him off. He was your best friend for years. He's part of your history.' She takes Ana's hand and squeezes it. 'What if when we're buried, we lay our souls to the earth. What if his soul is resting now, and no one has said goodbye. There must be a reason people all over the world stand by graves and weep. It's for a goodbye.'

'But for us, not for them. Not for the dead! You don't think Leo's soul is lingering in Ayot, do you?' Ana whispers furiously. What if someone sees them? Whoever it is: the picture, the text, the body – what if *they* are here now, skulking? She still hasn't told Maisie that she wonders if Leo ever died at all.

Maisie has pulled them off the road. They walk

along the path in the field that leads up to the Palladian church. The marble pillars gleam white under the moon. The fields are quiet, the sky cloudless. Stars are bright and Ana looks up; the heavens are open wide.

'Who knows if he's here or not. But if he is, then I'm lighting a candle to tell him he's not alone. That we miss him. We never really cried for him, Ana. Your crying for Leo muddled with crying for Ben, and then crying for you. One big ball of grief. Leo deserves some candles, some flowers. Leo deserves our tears.'

They step through the kissing gate. Its wood is still warm from the heat of the day. Wood and stone soak up the heat, Ana has realised. When she stands next to the old stone walls of the pub in the evening, it's like someone has lit a fire beneath them. Residue of the day. She strokes the wood as she weaves through the gate, letting it fall behind her, softly.

She thinks of coming here with Leo when they were young. Planning their futures, discussing school, plotting band tickets. Leo is knitted in her memories.

The graveyard rests, empty.

'This must be it.' Maisie has stepped up to a mound of earth that is grave-size. The police tape has disappeared. The hole has been filled back in, but it takes a while for the earth to settle.

'Leo,' Maisie says, 'Leo, we've come to say goodbye.'

Maisie unloads the contents of her bag. She shakes out a rug, laying it next to the grave. There's wine, complete with picnic glasses – tall plastic stems. Ana laughs, quickly covering her mouth.

'Maisie, for God's sake, it's not a picnic!'

Maisie hisses, 'Red wine. Like blood. We're doing it properly. Dust to dust and all that.'

'Where's the dust?' Ana shakes her head, but pours the wine. Maisie lays flowers on the earth and picks up a handful of dirt, and Ana thinks less of who might be watching, and more of Leo.

Maisie is right. She's never cried for Leo without also crying for Ben. She's let him down.

Maisie hands her some earth. It's hard and crumbles quickly beneath her fingers. The sun has banished all the water.

'Dust,' Maisie says. 'Dust to dust.' Maisie starts to cry, and holding the earth over the grave, she speaks quietly. 'I'm sorry, Leo. We forgot about you. In all the police investigation, the court case – all of it – we forgot to cry just for you. We loved you. We all loved you.'

Tears flood Ana's eyes. Rubbing the dirt between her fingers, she thinks of him at the start, in her class at school. Clever and quiet. Then a clown as he grew. The funny geek. She'd told him about her first kiss. He'd been the first one she'd told – of teeth gnashing, with James Blunt blaring away in the background at someone's birthday party. He'd been the first person she'd told everything to, back then.

Then she thinks of New York, and her eyes squeeze shut.

Even when she'd been with Ben they'd been close. They had all gone sailing a fair bit; he and Ben had taken her. The boat had caught the wind; it flew. She'd hung on to the side, and the boat had tipped slightly – she'd clung harder and he'd shouted, his eyes bright beneath his cap, 'It's OK! It's called heeling!' His words had arrived on the wind and the spray. The boat had tipped further, and she'd clung, white-knuckled, as she rose high out of the water. 'You're on the windward side,' he'd said. 'Amazing, isn't it!'

And it had been amazing. The whole bloody time had been amazing.

'I'm sorry, Leo,' she says.

Maisie throws in a flower she'd kept back, giving one to Ana. 'I've heard that the Greeks started the throwing of flowers onto graves. If they took seed and blossomed, then it meant the souls had passed to the next world, and found happiness.'

Maisie's face is streaked with tears. She must have had glitter on at some point today, as there are sparkles that catch the light.

Holding her sister's hand, Ana whispers, 'Is that true, Mais? Did you find it out for tonight?'

'Probably a complete pile of shit,' Maisie says, grinning through her tears, wiping them with the back of her hand. 'But I like the sound of it.'

Ana throws her flower and it lands on the dry earth, petals falling to the side, splayed. 'Bye, Leo,' she whispers.

Sitting on the rug, stretching out, Maisie passes her a glass of wine. It's warm, slipping easily down her throat.

'I smelt booze on you when you got in today,' Maisie says. 'What were you up to this afternoon?'

Ana smiles. 'Funny one… I almost got knocked down by a motorbike after a meeting. With the partner for this deal, and I ended up crying all over him and telling him about Jam. He took me for a drink.'

'A motorbike? Ana, are you OK?'

'Yes, I was fine. I just dropped my bag. I mustn't have looked properly. But he was… kind.'

'Hmm, over and above the call of duty?' Maisie raises an eyebrow.

'Oh, I don't know… I was all over the place. He's one of the youngest partners at the firm, or something like that. He didn't freeze when I started to cry – he was… nice.'

'Nice doesn't buy you drinks. Nice checks you're not injured and asks if you need a taxi somewhere. Ulterior motive. Your time pays his wages – is he fit?'

Ana shrugs, offering her glass for a top-up.

'Do you fancy him?' Maisie asks.

'I don't think I fancy people any more. I'm dead inside,' Ana says, deadpan, then laughs and chokes on her wine. She gasps for air as wine sprays down her nose, and Maisie slaps her back hard. 'Ow! I'm coughing! I haven't swallowed a grape!'

They laugh, falling back on the rug, and Ana feels her sides hurt, like she might snap a rib. She hasn't laughed like this since...

When they quieten, the wine is almost gone.

'Not even a little bit?' Maisie says. 'Not even a glance into his eyes, and a mild stomach flutter?'

'Maybe a tiny flutter,' Ana concedes. 'He is *very* fit.'

'To Leo.' Maisie raises her glass, the last of the wine swilling at the bottom, sediment black in the moonlight.

'To Leo,' Ana echoes.

They sit for a moment. Ana can hear the sound of crickets, something rustling in the grass of the field; a light wind passes over the temple. The candles flicker against the marble of the nearby headstones.

'Night, Leo,' Ana whispers.

34

Wednesday 20th June

MAARTEN

'What?'

Sitting suddenly, Maarten grabs his pen and starts scribbling.

'Can you say it again? Give me all the details.' He scratches out the information, mutters a thanks and moves quickly into the open-plan office. His tread is quick and heavy. Heads turn as he enters at speed.

'Meeting!'

Maarten hands the pen to Adrika – no one has ever been able to read his writing. He sits on the edge of a desk by the window. His tone announces the excitement of his news before he speaks.

'I've just had a call from Peckham. A payment was declined this morning. The name on the account is Leo Fenton. Our Leo Fenton. The attempt at payment was made from a mobile phone, linked to his credit card. The card is no longer active, but someone has tried to use it.'

'Does that mean he's alive?' Sunny asks.

The team mutter. Adrika writes furiously on the board, holding the notes Maarten has passed her. Maarten waits for them to settle.

Adrika glances at him. 'Did they detain the person?'

'No. The card machine asked the retailer to keep the card, but as it was a phone they let the customer go. They were gone by the time it triggered on the police watch. Can you send someone to look over CCTV? Get a description?'

Adrika nods, staring at the board as though secrets may unearth and leap out.

The muttering has slowed.

'It's a bit…' Sunny doesn't finish.

'Convenient?' Maarten offers. 'Yes. Yes, it is.'

'If he is alive, then… Well, who is the skeleton? Have we got an ID back yet?' Adrika asks.

Sunny shakes his head. 'No, not yet. Robyn is trying for a bone marrow sample, but it's taking a while; it's all they've got at the moment. If we can find the location where the body has been stored then it gets easier. Medical records have been retrieved and checked, and they're cross-checking with a broken bone. They think they'll have more of an idea tomorrow, or in a few days.'

'*If* he's alive. This is the big question. If he's alive, then who is dead? If he's not alive, then who is pretending that he is? And why? Why? Why to all of this – none of this is making sense. Sunny, when that report comes in, can you read it and take the details? And I think our warrant on the Seabrook house must have come through. Can you organise a sweep, and get Ana Seabrook's phone?'

The muttering has started up again. Maarten glances at Adrika and asks, 'Anything else?'

'No, not from me. I need to process this. Give me ten minutes to run through a few things. I'll come to your office?'

'Good plan. Thanks, everybody.'

Maarten leaves Adrika to assign tasks and heads back to his office. He glances out of the window. The sun is reflecting off the car windows as they pass. They flash like lights. It's impossible to see the faces of the drivers.

The sun hangs a haze over things. A film.

What had he said the other week – what had his hunch been? The car crash has distracted him. He's had other things to think about. He's normally more focused. Flicking through his notes, he finds what he's looking for. The location – the location of the burial. It must be significant. Certainly as important in all this as the body and the killer. Could it lead to both?

Adrika knocks and enters. 'Where do we go from here?' she asks, sitting in the chair opposite him.

'I think we go back to the grave. Let's go for another look around. I have a feeling we're missing something we're meant to see. Can you get Sunny to release some past photos of Leo Fenton? Show them around. The CCTV is likely to be poor.'

Tapping his list, he glances down at the thick black lines that have underscored the question: *Graveyard significance?*

'Let's head over to the Seabrooks' later, at the end of the search. First,' he says, 'let's see if we can unearth something else.'

35

Wednesday 20th June

BEN

'Oi, Benny.' It's Mr Burke. He calls as Ben is finishing work on the bookcase he's building. He has a few jobs in prison.

'Yeah?' He stands up, pulling his shoulders up and back, soaked in sweat.

'Heard something you might be interested in. Top secret, like.'

Ben takes a step closer. His release leaps to his mind, making his blood quicken.

'Only hearsay, so don't get your hopes up. But I'd want to know if it was me. You're in here for killing your brother, right?' Burke is leaning in, and glances round to check no one can hear.

Didn't kill him, Ben thinks, but he nods.

'Well, I've got a mate who's a copper in south London. Your brother's name and photo flashed up in their station this morning. I don't know much, but something's triggered it, and they're doing a Proof of

Life. I was telling him about you, after that body was found in that grave and it was in the press. I was telling him you was one of my wards. Think on, eh.'

It's not that Ben doesn't have any questions, but he can't speak: Leo could be alive?

Dizzy, he sits on the bench at the side. There are wood shavings all over it but he doesn't brush them off. He clutches the lathe, and he can feel his skin prick, but he doesn't look at it. If Leo's alive, and he can really talk to him again? Go sailing… They'd let him out for sure. It would be like a bad dream – could this all really just lift?

'I can have an ask around if you like.' Burke is still there, glancing at the floor. Swings his keys.

'Could you? That'd be—'

'Cost you, though.'

Ben stops. Takes a breath.

'Cost me?' he says.

'Yeah, not your money, Benny. You can keep that. But you're looking to get out soon if all this proves right. And we're a bit stuck at the moment. Macca, he's getting a lot of supplies in right now, and we're not sure where it's coming from. I'm not asking for much. But if I ask about your brother, could you keep your eyes open? Let me know if there's something I need to know?' He pauses, scratches the back of his neck. 'Someone I need to know?'

Ben finds himself nodding. Grassing in here is a death

sentence. But he can agree to look. He doesn't need to say anything to Burke.

He needs to find a way out of here.

'Catch you later.' Burke walks off, fluting a low whistle.

They had held a memorial for Leo, but by then Ben had been behind bars. Their parents dead, it had only been Ben and Leo for a few years, before it all happened. Ben had sat in his cell the morning of the memorial and ached with the loneliness of Leo hovering over his own service, with no body, no parents, no brother. The loneliness had crept like a cat between the bars of his prison cell and Ben had wept.

The memory lives behind his lids.

That morning, an overpowering stench had assailed him as he woke. He had called out for Leo, but there had been only silence. The tent had been ripped at the top – not enough to drag a man's body out – and the front of the tent had been flapping. The tent would heat up

in the summer, and usually they woke and unzipped it immediately, so the flapping had not been a surprise. But normally Leo would be nearby – cooking bacon, making coffee, even opening a morning beer. Ben had called a few times as he dragged his eyes open. 'What's that fucking awful smell?' he had shouted, pulling his fleece over his face as it lay next to his side.

But nothing had answered him. And when his eyes

had fully woken, and adjusted to the glare of the sun, he had seen the blood.

It had been everywhere.

Even now, when he thinks of that moment panic eats him. 'Leo! Leo! Where are you? Leo!'

He couldn't get out of the tent fast enough. His fingers, trembling, unable to work the netting zip. The main door flapping back into his face, catching his eye and making it sting. He had stood up once outside and made to run, but had fallen immediately. Rising again, he had stumbled, and he had screamed as he ran. 'Leo? Leo! Can someone help me! Can I have some help?'

He misses his brother. He misses his brother with a gnawing ache. If this is Leo, and he finally does manage to get out of here, then maybe they can both finally begin trying to work out what really happened that night.

He hadn't killed Leo. Had someone else? Or could he really be alive?

It doesn't feel real and his numbness is creeping back in.

He doesn't believe in fairy-tale endings, not any more.

36

ANA

'Ana!' The shout is loud up through the house. Getting ready for work, she thinks of the document, about visiting the trial again.

'What?' Shaken, she drops her make-up brush and runs, feeling all her nerves jump up at once. 'Maisie? I'm coming.' She scrambles across half-packed boxes, trips over old clothes, old books.

Slipping on the stairs, she grabs the rail and sees Maisie at the bottom.

'What is it?' she asks. Just looking at Maisie, she can see it's something. Maisie's wired.

'It's Ben.'

'What? Has something happened?' Ana's breath comes quickly, in gasps.

'No. Ana, he's on the phone. He might have news.'

Ana shakes her head. She feels caught out. He'd not called for over a week, and she'd missed the stilted half conversations they have – that are all she has. This last week has been the longest of times.

Gulping back the tears, trying to compose herself, she leans on the wall.

'Are you OK?' Maisie asks. 'I know there's so much to say right now. Look, Mum's out front and I'll give you some space. You can be on your own. Here. Sit. I'll bring you a tea. I told him you'd be a minute.'

Sitting in the overstuffed armchair, curling her legs under her, the sun hot through the window on the back of her head, Ana picks up the phone receiver.

'Ben?'

'Ana…' his voice cracks. Immediately. She can hear him gulp tears. 'Ana…'

'Ben, bloody hell, Ben…' she cries.

A minute passes. The sun begins to burn her neck. Maisie puts down a mug of tea and vanishes. The empty space that is Jam, in front of the fire grate, catches her eye.

'Ben… you might be out soon – Ben, I've missed you. There's so much…'

He doesn't speak but isn't silent. There are chokes, gulps. She can imagine his face, crumpled. The photo of her and Leo together, smiling, flashes up, and she thinks of whether she's going to have to tell him. She's hidden it from him for so long.

She wants to touch him. She wants to reach out and hold him. Be held by him.

'Ben, did you hear about the body?'

'Yes. I saw it on the news. And there's something else.'

'The knife and the pills? I called Harper.' Ana is slotting together the Ben she holds in her memory, always the first to dance at a wedding, his insistence at holding a BBQ on Boxing Day, with this tired voice, this new Ben, watching TV in a prison cell.

'Knife? No, not that.'

'Oh, did you hear about Jam?'

He stops. 'Yes… I'm so sorry, Ana. Christ… What's going on?'

Ana says nothing. She can't tell him everything.

'Fuck,' he says quietly. 'There's something else too. I was told today, and I have no idea how true it is, but one of the guards in here told me that Leo might be alive. There has been some evidence.'

'Alive?' Ana's heart beats quickly and she thinks of the text message: *Are you missing me?*

Can this really be happening? 'But that's… That can't be true! Do you think it's true? What's the evidence?'

'I don't know anything. That's why I'm calling. I don't know who is in charge of the case, but they should know. If my prison guard knows, then the police will know. Can you look into it? Ana— Ana, I've been holding on. Barely holding on in here. You have no idea. I'm sorry I've kept you away, but I think if I saw you in here…'

'It's OK, it might be nearly over. I've been thinking about Leo, and the past. I've been trying to think of who might be doing this. I've raked up all sorts of memories. But I've spoken to Harper. And there's another detective from St Albans who's in charge now. He's Dutch. I'll speak to both of them. I'll find out what I can.' She takes a breath. If he says no to this, she thinks she might break, but after hearing his voice, it's too much... 'Ben, can I come and see you? Please. Let me come.'

'Ana...' There's noise she can hear. Wherever he is has become busy. Loud male voices hammer down the line, echoing and vibrating. The noise bounces round, like it's in a steel can. Ben's voice drops even more. 'Ana, look, has there been any evidence of Leo? Anything?'

'I've had a text,' she says. Then she pauses. She hasn't told the police yet. It might be nothing. She starts immediately to backtrack, changing tone with, 'But I can't believe it's from him.'

'From his phone? Fuck. They never found his phone. We assumed it had been lost at sea.' Ben's voice is dry.

She thinks of Leo, leaning back off the boat, his cap damp from the spray. 'There's more. I've been seeing someone... at least I think I have. Anyway, the one thing that draws it all together...' Is it a reach jumping to such a conclusion? 'Whoever it is always wears a cap. And I know it's probably just to cover their face but there's something...'

'You think it's Leo's cap? You think you've seen him?'

'I don't know.'

'Ana, you've got to be careful – this is serious. There's a body, there's a murder. You can't take any chances with your safety. If someone is pretending to be him…'

'Please, Ben. Please let me come and see you.'

Another shout in the background. Swearing, laughter and Ben says quickly, 'I'll call again soon.'

And then he's gone. Just like that.

Ana holds the phone, light in her hand. Its whiteness catching the sun that now glares from behind.

She looks at the clock on the mantelpiece – it's 10.30 a.m.; she has to be out of the house soon.

Her mouth tastes dry. Her lips are sore, and she runs her tongue round them. She hasn't drunk the tea Maisie brought, and she picks it up, still warm.

The tea spills, and she sees her hands are shaking.

Dressed, Ana gets ready to leave. She'd taken longer, called Leith and said she'd work from home for the morning. There's noise behind her as she finds her phone.

The knock is loud and she curses. There is little time left to get to work.

'Ana Seabrook?'

She opens the door to an officer she hasn't seen before. There are three of them, waiting patiently. 'Yes,' she says.

'We have a warrant to search the premises. And we'd like to take your phone. Please...'

Colour drains from Ana's view. She knows what they will find.

37

MAARTEN

'Is it something about the church itself, maybe? Did it reject someone? Refuse burial?'

Maarten shakes his head. The flies are back. These fields, the cows nearby, they pull them in like a magnet.

Adrika is wearing a yellow top. It has very short sleeves and a V-neck and the wasps have made a beeline for it. They hover. She swats them, and they return. He flinches each time they get close to her neckline – one is hovering now, and she's unaware. He wants to wave it away. His teeth on edge, it flies closer still.

'Maybe it's something to do with who built it? Some kind of lifelong vendetta,' Maarten says, refocusing. 'Did someone die in the building of it? Can we get some background on the build, any accidents?'

Adrika scribbles notes as Maarten walks around the graveyard. There aren't many graves here. 'I wonder how you do get buried? There must be hoops to jump through.'

'I'll look into that, too. I'll get a list of anyone who has been turned down. See if anything turns up,' Adrika says. She pauses and leans to look at something on the ground. 'Who's been drinking by this grave?' She pulls out a plastic bag and, slipping her hand into it, holds aloft a blue plastic wine glass, the kind you take on picnics. She sniffs. 'Red wine. Someone's left it by mistake, it's not a cheap one. And by our grave. Who's been celebrating this?'

Maarten considers. 'Probably just kids. Let's get it checked for prints. You never know. Someone might think they've got away with something?'

Adrika speaks into her radio before heading up the steps to the entrance. She pushes the heavy doors open and Maarten can see the chequered floor leading down to the altar, beneath the patterned dome. The squares are tilted for a diamond floor. The ceiling is tall; the white inside is startling.

'Built to imitate the columns found in the temple to Apollo on the island of Delos. Greek revival style, not technically Palladian.' Adrika is reading from a printed leaflet stacked on a side table.

'Apollo had a sister called Artemis, the goddess of hunting, protector of young girls. Think there might be something in that?'

Adrika pulls a face. 'I have no idea.'

It's cool as they enter.

'I can see why they built these in Greece,' Adrika says.

'I'm sure it's even hotter today.' She fans herself with the leaflet and shakes out her brown bob.

Maarten sits on one of the wooden seats. He knows he's about to ask a question that might be inappropriate, or might veer slightly outside of the scope he's used to when talking to Adrika, but he's realising more and more that with her previous involvement, Harper Carroll's clear offer of help with this case might be what they need in the next few weeks.

'What is the problem with DI Carroll?' he asks. He doesn't look at her – he looks instead at the high, white ceiling, where a huge circle sits inside the stone lattice pattern. A bit, he thinks, like a large, intricate waffle.

Adrika hasn't answered, and Maarten doesn't speak. Minutes play out, but this heat makes it easier to sit. The warmth seems to absorb the silence.

'We used to be in a relationship,' Adrika says finally. 'We were together for a few years, and then it ended. It ended badly. I haven't – or hadn't – seen her since. The first time…' Adrika pauses.

Maarten gazes upwards resolutely, listening, counting the squares in the ceiling.

'Well, when I turned up at the station for the crime scene at the Seabrooks' house, there she was. Exactly the same. In charge, in control… Well, you've met her.' Adrika shrugs.

'I see,' Maarten says.

He drops his gaze to the left of him; Adrika sits on his right. Tall arches hang over the windows. It really is an extraordinarily beautiful piece of architecture.

'Would it be too hard if I asked her to come back and join us for a briefing? I've got a feeling there's something very obvious, something we already know, that just isn't seeming relevant. I think her expertise on this case…' He lets the end of his sentence trail away.

'I'd be fine, sir,' Adrika says. 'It was such a shock to start with. But of course she was fine. She would sail through—' She stops, shrugs.

A fly has found its way in, and it hovers near Maarten's face.

'She was the sun, really. She was the sun.' Adrika shrugs again, and Maarten looks at her.

Her eyes are dry.

'Come on,' he says. They stand and walk out. Maarten thinks of what she has said as the heat hits them full force, stepping back down to the gravestones.

Blinding, bright. The hot rays burn.

Maarten's phone rings just as they're climbing in the car.

'Got something.' It's Taj.

'Yes?' Maarten stands stock still.

'A photo, found under her pillow. It's a photo of Ana Seabrook and Leo Fenton in a kind of embrace. They've clearly had too much to drink. We've run the details of the bar mat and the name of the place – you can see it on a pile of matchbooks in a glass jar on the bar. It's in New York. They were there together. From the angle of the photo, I would say it's a selfie.'

'Anything that gives us a real lead?' Maarten asks, thinking that the photo was under her pillow, and Ana Seabrook hadn't mentioned anything at all. Who keeps a photo of the dead brother of your boyfriend under your pillow?

'They're holding hands, Maarten. We'll do the fingerprints now. But the phone is in too. And there's a text on there. From Leo Fenton: *Have you missed me?*'

'I'm heading in now.'

38

BEN

'Got some news for you.' Tabs jogs alongside Ben.

They're doing a few circuits of the exercise run.

Ben breathes in and out, stretching himself, coughing. He's wasting away. This news has given him a new lease of life. But if it comes to nothing he's not sure how much life he'll have left to live in here.

'I asked around; I don't have many contacts but there's someone on G Wing I get on well with. He seems to know everything that goes on. There was some mention of a van, needed from Norfolk to Hertfordshire. That's all I know, but it was the week before this all kicked off. It needed a proper clean after, so there was word out.'

Ben shakes his head. The sun and sweat compete to irritate his eyes.

'From Norfolk to Hertfordshire? Does that mean...' He's not sure what it means. He pulls up, leaning over his knees, coughing. His chest aches.

'What does it mean, Tabs?'

'Well, like. If I wanted to move something that shouldn't be moved, then I might go after a van like that. And if I was going to bury something that I'd been keeping in one place and wanted to bury in another, then that might make a lot of sense to me.'

Ben rises. Phlegm sits in his mouth, and he turns, spitting it as far as he can.

'So the body was kept in Norfolk? All this time? Leo's body?'

Tabs shrugs. 'No idea, mate. But you know what I know.'

He runs off.

Ben is dizzy with knowledge, with heat, with thirst. He needs to tell Ana, to get her to tell the police. He feels himself tip back. The security of the world he knows is vanishing, the ground is soft, the horizon hazy.

39

It's late. Dante is back. His top jaw resolutely still for the last few hours, despite his answering question after question. The bottom works hard, grinding out the words. Ana watches it, fascinated, as she scribbles the notes.

She'd handed her phone over, left for work and not looked back. She carries the weight of Ayot like Sisyphus; so close to getting Ben out, then back to fear and terror. They will find the text message on the phone. They will find the photo. She hasn't told anyone, least of all the police, and there's no hiding from it now.

There's an offer for the buyout on the table and so far, everyone seems happy. It's been a relatively easy deal. They've almost finished working through the details. Tonight will be late, she thinks. It's her job to work on the document. She needs to turn the heads of terms around to the buyer and selling shareholders before tomorrow's meeting. The focus on work will be a relief.

Alex, the boss, again says little. She only interrupts Dante if she needs to refine a point, and Leith appears to have matched her silence.

This grunt work is her role. To be honest, she's surprised that Leith has stayed for the whole time. He will charge these hours back to the client. He bills out at over £600 per hour. This meeting has been over three hours long so far. It's not like him to overstaff something. The rates go up but he's a fan of clear and sensible billing.

Maybe he's checking on her.

Maybe, says a tiny voice somewhere in her head, *he's checking you out. Like when you used to hang around the gym lockers after football because you thought Andy Miller would be heading that way.*

She jolts, stung, and she sees Leith's eye cast her way, then back to Dante, who's talking about forecast figures.

Andy Miller.

She hasn't thought about him for... Well, she opts not to think about him.

Back in school it was different. She'd fancied him for ages. They all had. Three years older, and he'd had a car. She thought she'd landed gold when they'd ended up chatting at that party. She'd been hammered. Vodka-soaked. Cider-soaked.

Her teeth set slightly, jarred, she shakes her head and tunes back in to what Dante is saying.

'Could you just go over how you reach that number?' she asks.

'Well, I'm basing it on...'

'Went OK?' Leith says.

She nods, checking her watch. She has some drafting to do on the document before she can pass this to the other side for discussion for the meeting tomorrow. The shareholder adjustments aren't too bad but they'll take a while. It's almost 9 p.m.; eating will be a stretch.

'Look, I'm going to head out to dinner,' Leith says. 'I've got a client thing. It'll end late. Can you courier me the document once you've finished? I don't want to read it on an iPad after a late day. Still like paper.' He smiles. 'I'll walk back to the office to pick up my stuff around midnight, so if you're finished then, I'll collect the print-out. We're only over the road.' He names an expensive restaurant on the same street.

Ana calls in sushi takeaway as she sits at the desk. She'll need something to pick at to keep her going and she hates cold pizza.

She types, the words swimming before her eyes. She's exhausted. Andy Miller swims up again; she sees his name in the words she types.

Why is she thinking of him again? Now?

She'd spoken to Maisie the next day. 'I slept with Andy Miller last night.'

'You didn't!' Maisie had been wide-eyed. Agog. Had it been awe? 'Are you going out with him? He's like… wow. Did it hurt?'

She'd managed to move on quickly. She was trying it out for herself. Selling it to herself. Trying to turn it into a trophy. When what had she felt… stupid? Ashamed. She'd been so… naive. To think he liked *her*. The kissing part had been fine.

It had been the usual affair. Small disco floor, lots of booze drunk first. In that way where you knock a lot back quickly and it only hits you later, dancing in the heat. Then it slams you. She'd had a small bottle of vodka, syphoned off the supply at home, and she was adding it to her Coke. Leo had got himself a girlfriend. And he'd said he had the flu that night. Ana was on her own.

She was always on her own. The heaviness of her dad's death kept her walled away. She was tired all the time. Even when people spoke to her she found she could only react, not really engage. She relied on social reflexes. Her classmates were kind, but they gave her a wide berth. No one seemed to know how to talk to her. Not about death.

Andy Miller had come over. He'd sat down, checking his phone, and she'd offered him some of the vodka. A song had come on – some muso song – and she'd made a comment about it. Leo had told her about the band a month or so before. Andy had looked again at her then. Asked her what kind of music she was into.

At some point they'd kissed, and the vodka bottle had been empty.

She'd almost popped out of herself inside the room to look back at herself, at them. Andy kissing Ana. The knowledge she was kissing him had almost been better than the actual kissing, which had been... Too much vodka. Cheap crisps.

But outside. It had been hazy. It was still hazy, in her memory. She had drunk so much. One thing had led to another, and she's sure, she's still sure that when he'd tugged down her jeans, she'd said, 'No. Please, I don't think...' But had she said it at all? Had she said it loud enough? She'd drunk so much. She'd never thought it would go that far. She'd only ever kissed a boy before.

She doesn't drink too much any more. She's never overdone it on the drink, really. Unless it's with Maisie or Fran and they're at home. Watching a film. She's always made sure that when she's out she's 100 per cent able to get home. She never gets into unmarked taxis. Doesn't take the night bus alone. Walks in the dark with her keys splayed between each finger, ready.

Afterwards, she does remember that she'd said she needed to go to the toilet, and he'd looked sheepish.

She'd gone round the back of the club into the prefab toilet block and Alice Sheppard from her class had been in there crying about a boy.

'Bastard,' Alice had said, through snot and tears. 'Bastard!'

Then Ana had cried too. It *had* hurt. 'Andy Miller just had sex with me,' she'd said. And she'd had to grab the sink to stop the room swaying. Leaning forward, she'd thrown up.

Alice had rubbed her back. 'Everyone fancies Andy,' she'd said. 'How was it?'

'I don't know. I told him I didn't want to, but I think I said it too late. I shouldn't have gone outside with him.' Ana cried and cried, and threw up again in the sink.

Ana heard another girl come out of a cubicle and say the word *rape*, but Alice was firm.

'It's not rape if you've already started – especially if they don't hear you say no.' Ana's head was bowed over the sink, and Alice rubbed her back again. 'Honestly, if you hadn't wanted to do it, why did you go outside with him?' The other girl left the loos without another word, and Ana had been weighted with the knowledge that she was really to blame.

She had thrown up again. All over her jeans, her shoes. And in the end Alice had called her mum for her on her phone.

Her dad had died only nine months earlier, otherwise he would have come.

She did see Andy waiting for her as Alice helped her to the car. He'd started to walk towards her, but had stopped when her mum had got out of the car. He'd hovered at the edge of the lawn, and then she'd thrown up in the car on the way home.

She'd practised telling Maisie in the morning. But she couldn't do it properly. She couldn't sell it to herself. And then later, Andy's sister had died, and they'd moved house. He'd gone to a different school. She'd never seen him really after that.

Why was she thinking about Andy Miller now?

She'd almost told Ben, in the end. She'd almost told Ben everything.

Except it doesn't even help to think about Ben now. Ben won't see her.

She understands why... It must be so much harder for him. But the rage she feels with him sometimes. Shutting her out. She is in this too.

The city skyline is lit and buzzing. There are black cabs sailing down the street and groups of drinkers moving in packs on the pavements.

London drinks al fresco in this weather. Pubs spill out, and many have put up tables along the pathways. She can make out the river from here, too. She does love it. The feeling of there being life outside. The peace she'd had with Ben broke into tiny, tiny pieces – trying to fit them back together will be like one of those million-piece jigsaws; maybe they'll never manage it. And sitting

at home, in Ayot with her mum, in her childhood bed…
The vibrancy of London is the antidote to her thoughts,
her aloneness. She's stagnant. There're no plans to be
made. Just counting days.

Her email flashes: 'Just heading back now. I'm
guessing you're not finished so send it over with a
courier when you're done. I'll read it before tomorrow.
Thanks for the work. Leith.'

She realises, as a bubble pops somewhere, she'd been
hoping he'd come back. That she'd get to see him again
tonight.

Stretching, she flexes her fingers and turns back to
her screen.

'Forecasting for…'

40

MAARTEN

'Is Ana Seabrook here yet?' Maarten puts the phone down after talking to the Super. Stretched thin at the moment, he's managed to get himself off a course he'd been due to attend. He feels as though he's failing in every direction. The Super had been fine, but he's behind in a string of postponed meetings and paperwork.

The tiredness is starting to pull at his edges. The heat doesn't help. The girls are sleeping OK, all things considered. But Sanne's cast is itchy. And even with all the windows open, and with only a sheet on the bed, she is uncomfortable at night.

'Mama, Mama!' The cry had come in the night, and he'd crawled in beside her.

'Papa's here, *schatje*. Do you want some water?' She'd had a sip, then curled into him. Her arm stuck on the top of her body, looking heavier in the dark.

'Is Mama coming home soon?'

'Yes,' he'd said, stroking her brow. Her hairline sticky with sweat. 'Very soon. She's just getting stronger. Like you need to. Papa will stay here. Shhh.'

He'd woken with his arm in a cramp an hour or so later, and had managed to slide out without disturbing her. His own bed vast with its emptiness.

Thankfully, the case is picking up. Ana Seabrook is due in this morning.

'Yes, she's downstairs. How are we playing it?' Adrika asks. She puts a coffee down on Maarten's desk and stands ready for the interview. 'Are we accusing her? Seeing what falls out?'

He shakes his gaze, picking up the coffee and taking a sip. It's his main fuel at the moment, and his head starts aching with withdrawal if he misses a cup.

'No, we're going softly. There's no identity on the body and no results back from the knife that prove conclusively it has any relation to Leo Fenton. We're not in a position to charge anyone. We'll go in gently, but we need to ask about the photo, the text and the presence of the knife and the zolpidem. Sunny's taken a brief statement, but more background will help. We need to get a feel for it. Whatever happens, let's keep the tone calm. Harper's convinced she's innocent and we're more likely to get something from her if we go gently.'

Entering the room, Ana Seabrook is crying. Her eyes are puffy and she keeps pulling at the edge of her brow, running her fingers along and upwards at the side. She looks much younger, he thinks. It's not being dressed for work. And she looks tired, pale despite the sun. Most of his younger staff have been soaking up the warmth, colouring like chameleons.

'Good to see you again, Ana,' he says as he sits, smiling.

She nods, her hands trembling as she places them on the table in front of her. She reaches for a cup that someone has given her, and she lifts it, but doesn't drink. 'Yes, I understand why you want to see me,' she says. 'I'm sorry. I can't seem to stop crying. I have no idea why, I've been holding it together pretty well so far. I think it's the interview room. It brings back a lot – all those times with Ben when Leo died.'

Maarten nods. It's not a home from home. Her tears drip and fall. She will know what they have, and maybe it's fear, that he will press her and that she will be found out – if she has something to hide.

'You know that we found a knife buried at the bottom of your garden? And we also found a batch of drugs that were the same kind Ben had in his system after Leo's death. There's certainly some cause to believe that the person involved in the murder of Leo buried these. We're looking into it, and we're also checking to see if Jam died of an overdose of zolpidem.'

The tears don't slow, and she nods, clutching a tissue and shaking her head. 'Poor Jam.'

'The other things we found of interest are a photo hidden beneath your pillow, and also a text message on your phone, sent from an account you have listed in your contacts as "Leo". We checked the number and it's the last number we have for Leo Fenton. His phone wasn't found at the scene of his disappearance.'

She's still crying, quietly, and Adrika looks at him, opening her eyes wide for a second, rolling them up and back into her head, and then switching back to blank.

He feels the same. It's so hot outside, and she has withheld this information. It's in all their interests to just get on with it.

'Ana, why didn't you tell us that Leo had texted you? If there's a chance that he might still be alive, didn't you think we needed to know?'

She begins by shaking her head. 'I don't know. I know how it looks – the photo...' There are fresh tears and Maarten firms his tone up.

'What's happening in the photo?'

'It was—,' she begins, and her hands tear at the tissue she's holding. She picks up the cup and drinks this time, swallowing loudly, appearing to calm a little. She shakes her head again, looking down and twisting her fingers. 'It was something that shouldn't have happened. I was in New York with work. The company has its head office over there and they throw these huge elaborate conferences every few years. Five-star hotels, big meals, long days listening to speeches – a lot of booze. Anyway,

Leo worked over there, so he came along one night to join us for a drink before we went for dinner. It was in the W bar – cocktails, lots of cocktails. I had a drink with him, and he chatted to a few of my colleagues...'
She fades out.

Maarten watches the sag of her shoulders. Her speech slows. Her words come slowly, as if digging for them exhausts her.

The case shifts as she speaks. He feels the layers beneath the surface rising, shaking off the dirt and sand.

41

She has to tell them. There's no holding this back now, but it's important she get it right. She needs to be clear and give them the facts correctly. Not cloud Leo's name, not darken his memory or scribble over his truth.

'He was upset.' She remembers the heat in the bar. It had been June and New York had sweltered in a heatwave. This part seems important, and she adds it in. 'When New York gets hot, it's like the air changes – the mood. It's like a different city.' Thinking carefully, she remembers Leo drinking quickly, like he was thirsty, but it wasn't water he was knocking back and he was normally more of a beer drinker.

'We were both drunk,' she says. 'The heat seems to make you drunker somehow. Is that a word?' She shakes her head. He had held her hand, and she'd been surprised that when she'd looked at him, there had been tears in his eyes.

'He was upset,' she says, and now she looks at Maarten Jansen, implores him to understand. 'He was crying in the bar and Leo doesn't really cry – at football sometimes; when his parents died, but he's not a crier. I was worried about him. I'd been on a bit of a session after the conference, and it threw me a bit. My office had dinner planned but I said I'd catch them up.' She thinks of who she'd spoken to. Probably Fran. They'd all been drunk; no one had given it a second thought. She'd sat with Leo in a booth and he'd ordered more drinks. He'd gripped her hand tightly and he'd cried, saying something she couldn't hear. The music had been loud.

'Go on,' Maarten Jansen says.

The room here is hot, and both the officers sit very still. The heat makes her head thick, takes her back to that hot night.

'He was upset. He said that something had happened, a while ago. That he'd got someone pregnant.' There's not a flicker on the faces of the police, but her stomach plunges just thinking about it again. She'd reeled back, surprised. The beat from the music had thumped in her stomach; she'd felt sick. 'I knew he'd had a long-term girlfriend for a few years, over there, but a baby... I had no idea. Anyway, he shook his head and said no, it wasn't his American girlfriend. But he wouldn't tell me who it was. Only that there was no baby in the end. That it had come to nothing, but that he should have behaved better.'

He'd slammed his fist hard on the table. The glass had tipped and the bartender had given them a warning look. More drinks had appeared, but she couldn't remember whether she or Leo had ordered them.

'He said he should have been a better man, a better human being,' she whispers, thinking of the noise in the bar, how she'd strained to hear him. There had been a group of girls screaming at the bar in laughter, and she'd leaned right in to Leo to listen to what he said. She'd had to ask him what he meant.

'What did he do?' Maarten Jansen asks gently. She hears him from a distance, feeling Leo's hot hand as he'd looked at her with eyes swimming in shame.

'Ben had told him to walk away,' she says slowly. She still can't believe he would have done it. The anger and shock she'd felt. 'He'd been young, Leo said, but still. I couldn't believe it. I just felt... betrayed. Like it had happened to me.'

'His brother?'

She nods. She looks down at her hands and remembers that she'd been wearing black nail varnish, that her fingers had gleamed like black diamonds.

'They'd been young, and Leo said he was going to change his mind, go back to her, but it all came to nothing anyway. It had been taken out of his hands and he hadn't had another chance. He never saw her again.' She thinks of how exhausted and beaten he'd looked when he'd said this.

What, never? she'd asked, and he had cried afresh, dipping his head down. There had been something she hadn't wanted to ask but she can't remember it now. She looks at Jansen. 'He said he thinks of it, around that time, mostly. Each year.'

He had leaned in to her and his breath had been sweet – the strawberries from the cocktails had stained his lips, and they had been an inch away as he had whispered his secrets: *Ana, I would give anything to have said something different. What do you think of me now?*

There had only been him and her. His breath, soft; his hand holding hers so tightly, and she wasn't sure who had tipped first, but the kiss had been soft and familiar. His tongue had been laced with vodka and the sweat in the bar was on their skin. She'd been wearing a thin, strappy top, and the bare skin of his forearms had brushed up her arms and snaked round to the skin on her back. She had felt naked, dressed only in him.

'We kissed. One thing led to another. We were drunk,' she says. Her head bowed. 'You have to understand that it wasn't about betraying Ben, it was about comfort – and spite. We both let him down. But Leo was angry with him... and so was I, in that moment, in that night. I think we did it a little to spite him; but we were both to blame.

'Ben had been young too, looking out for his brother. Not much more able to deal with the seriousness that a baby can bring than Leo was. It was Leo's decision, at the end of the day.' She's not crying any more; the fear of knowing she would have to tell the story passes as it hits the air.

The room is still. The face of the DI, who had looked so cold at the start of the interview, is alive with listening, bent forward, ready to catch the truth in the story.

'We spent the night together. In the morning, it was like it was finished, all by itself. We had breakfast together, and by the last coffee, it was gone, buried. I don't think we agreed out loud, but we weren't going to tell him.' She thinks of ordering the pancakes, of the blue of the sky outside the hotel she was staying in.

She catches her breath for a second as she thinks of the night. He had been... She had tasted his skin. She won't say it aloud, but she had wanted him. She had been on fire with wanting him – drink, New York; once he had touched her, she couldn't reason it with words, but she had known exactly. If he had hesitated at any point, she hadn't. Skin on skin, simple desire. It had been another life.

'I think that because of our friendship – we'd always been so close – it was easy to compartmentalise, to tuck it up and place it out of time. It was about comfort. And we never told Ben.'

She loved Ben. In the morning, when she'd walked the blocks to the office, sailing in her heels, she had felt painted in guilt. But it hadn't really changed them. She and Leo had slipped back into friendship in a way that, if anything, she felt had strengthened them all. One secret was out. The other one buried.

There had been times in the past when she'd been jealous of their relationship, of their closeness. And now she'd sunk herself into the fractured cracks of their brotherhood.

'And the photo?' Maarten Jansen asked. 'Have you always kept a photo under your pillow?'

'No!' She speaks quickly, the shock of the photo a reminder of where they are. 'I was sent it the day the body was found. It came to my office. Leo had taken it on his phone, and I'd always assumed he'd deleted it, to be honest. He'd taken it in the bar. But someone sent it to me, which means that someone knows. Someone knows about that night. I thought the only people who knew were Leo and me.'

This time the DI speaks, and she does so slowly, with a layer of anger brimming somewhere. Ana understands; she's been withholding evidence. 'What if it was Leo? You have a text on your phone from him, and a photo that you say only he has. Hasn't that made you think about the possibility that Leo himself is the one sending these?'

Ana thinks quickly, trying to put it into words, but it's hard making it sound clear. 'Initially I thought Leo wouldn't have sent me that text, I didn't think it sounded like him. Do you see? It's never come up. It's never been something that we talked about, or even thought about. I assumed he wouldn't ask if I was missing him. I thought it must be someone else – someone else might see it as something very, very different. But now I don't know. I'm not sure of anything any more.'

Maarten Jansen looks at her for a minute, and no one speaks. Then he nods slowly. 'You mean that someone else might see the photo as evidence that you and Leo Fenton were having an affair. And that by faking his death, and setting his brother up, he manages to get rid of the man he is so clearly angry with and get his girl, all in one swoop.'

'But—' Ana says, stopping, knowing that this sounds plausible, but it's so far from the truth.

'And the reason you might not want to tell the police about it is that it would seem very possible that you were an accomplice. That you buried the knife and the drugs. And that your dog found them and dug them up. Do you think Leo's alive, Ana?' He leans forward, and Ana is so dizzy now there are dark spots in front of her lids, patterning the room.

'Is Leo alive, Ana?'

The room swims, swims with a head in a cap. Could it be Leo? Nothing is clear any more. Nothing makes sense. As the black spots bleed into a curtain before her vision, she thinks of Leo's touch, his scent. The cap half turns. Is it him?

42

LEO

'You fucking what?' Ben's voice is loud. The volume and anger in it eases Leo's tension a little. Like bloodletting. Like scratching a mozzie bite.

People look up. The mother nearby frowns as their card game pauses. She is dressed in a blue-and-white striped top. Breton, Leo thinks. The pattern is Breton. He looks back at her, but doesn't apologise. He's unleashed it. It's only going to get worse.

Slowly, he turns his gaze back to Ben. He deserves this. He needs to take some kind of retribution. He is owed it.

'You did fucking what?' Ben repeats, slightly quieter this time, but not necessarily because of the background. He stares at Leo and the look is one that Leo hasn't seen before. Like he doesn't know who he is.

'I slept with Ana. Just once. A year ago,' Leo repeats. 'I'm so sorry. I'm so sorry.' He scratches his arm. He doesn't know if he is sorry. He knows it in his head, but he's numb. He just wants to feel again.

'Why the absolute fuck would you do that?' Ben holds his pint still, holds his head still.

'I didn't plan it. It was in New York – she was over for work and it was June. It was... the anniversary of... you know. I wasn't holding together well. I got upset, we were both drunk and it kind of... just happened. I'm so sorry.' There he is again, saying he is sorry. He had sworn to himself he would never tell Ben. It would never happen again. It hadn't happened because he'd intended it to. He'd fallen down the rabbit hole. He had stopped feeling after June 2010. He would have done anything to feel.

It's the same thing. He's doing something he will regret in a few months, once the cloud has passed. He knows it already, even as he goes in deeper – he knows it's not the thing he means to do. He's setting fire to the things closest to him.

'She's my girlfriend, Leo. And you're my brother. Why would you ever do it?' Ben shakes his head. He puts his pint down undrunk, untouched. He gestures with his arm, like he's illustrating a point. 'And why tell me now? I've just told you I've bought a ring! Why tell me at all?'

Ben's voice is rising, and people are looking now. Everyone is looking. The anger vibrates round the bar and there is no sound other than Ben's voice. Leo sees the barmaid looking over and she's worried. She disappears out the back.

'What am I supposed to do now!' Ben screams, and knocks his pint from the table. Leo doesn't think he intended to knock it, but his fist is flailing round. He realises that Ben might be about to hit him. Part of him anticipates the feeling of relief this will bring.

And he wonders what it will feel like to hit Ben. He screams back at him, 'I wanted to go to her! You told me to walk away!'

He looks at Ben, untouched by the guilt.

Ben stands, and he leans forward, poised.

Nobody moves. The pub holds its breath.

Out of the corner of his eye, Leo sees the barmaid return, and she's brought with her the manager. He moves over, hands parted and raised in a white flag gesture. 'Lads, I don't know what this is about, but I think it's time to head outside. People are getting upset.'

Stepping on the glass, the crunch is loud to Leo, the crackle of glass and the squelch of the beer into the carpet.

'I'm going. I'm going RIGHT NOW.' Ben leaves with a shout and his chair falls behind him. His fists are clenched tight. His face beetroot.

Leo knows he has broken his heart, and part of him feels better.

43

ANA

Exhausted from the interview, Ana is working from home for the rest of the morning but can't get anything done. Instead, she's clearing out. The boxes from the previous life are starting to drive her mad. Baggage. Heading downstairs, she hears the bang of a bucket.

'Right, that's me done for the day.' Jess pulls off her Marigolds and lays them on the bucket, hefting it up and walking through the back of the bar to where the toilets and cupboards lie.

Ana can hear her closing the door.

'Thanks, Jess,' she says as the cleaner comes back in the room and picks up her bag. 'Thanks for staying later today. Mum's not feeling too well, so it's been a real help.'

'No problem. Nothing serious?'

Ana shakes her head.

'Want me to have a clean upstairs as well? I do domestic cleaning too. Might be nice for your mum, not to have to think about it for a while. And for you.'

'That would be great. We're having a clear-out at the moment. I've got all my schoolgirl stuff in there with all my adult stuff I brought back from London. Lots of boxes.'

'Charlie could help with his van, if you like? I'll ask him; he's picking me up.'

Ana smiles. 'That would be great. Off anywhere nice? Enjoying the sun?'

'This heat?' Jess shakes her head. 'I'm off to hospital. My sister's in there. I don't go much as she doesn't really recognise me. We didn't get on that well when she did recognise me neither.'

'Oh, but that's sad.' Ana thinks of Maisie and how lost she'd be without her. 'Has she been in long?'

'A bit. She's used to hospitals. She was a midwife for years. She might have brought you into the world, you never know. She's done her time in Ayot and St Albans.'

Ana grins. 'Bet she has some stories!'

Jess rolls her eyes. 'Liked her drama, did Aggie.' Jess shrugs. 'Some real sadness though, among all them happy mums. She entered one of those charity races for suicide ten years ago with someone's name on her back – Caitlin, I think – she's buried in the graveyard here. Hung herself.'

Hanged, Ana thinks. *Hanged herself.* She remembers something about that. A girl at her school had been found hanging in the woods She hadn't known the girl well, but she had heard afterwards that it had been Andy Miller's sister. She feels a sudden wrench of pity for him, but bats it away. He of all people doesn't deserve her pity.

'No doubting Aggie has courage, and could be kind. Walked that five k, in some heat. Never forget it.'

Ana hears the crack in Jess's voice. She moves quickly to the older lady, putting her arm around her shoulder. 'Here, come and sit down. Let me get you a cup of tea. You've been working for hours. You must be exhausted.'

Bringing a plate with biscuits and tea, Ana watches Jess shrink before her when she sits.

A dark male head appears at the window and there is a knock. Ana opens the door. 'Charlie?'

'Yep. Just come for Mum,' he says, nodding.

'Come in, she's just finishing her tea. Can I get you one?'

'No. Thanks.' He stands in the doorframe. Glances around the pub.

Ana tries again. 'Maisie, my sister, said we were at school together?'

He nods. 'Yep. You don't remember me, I suppose. I remember you. You were best mates with Leo Fenton – I heard he'd died. Sad case.'

Offering nothing else, he holds his hand out to Jess as she rises. 'You'll come back and collect some bags from here in an hour or so, for the tip, Charlie?'

He nods and her pride at him beams like a beacon. She's such a powerhouse when she's cleaning but she looks tiny as she smiles a goodbye.

This rapid life. Speeding by.

This fragile life.

44

Thursday 21st June

MAARTEN

'DCI Jansen, I was hoping you'd call. Any news?'

Maarten sketches around his list of notes as he hears Harper's voice. He'd been on hold for a few minutes. The interview had been exhausting. They'd all emerged like ghosts – Sunny had done a double take, asked for an update.

The idea of the coast this afternoon is both necessary and so appealing.

'Some news. Yes. We have a possible sighting, or possible evidence, of Leo Fenton. He might be alive.'

He waits for some reaction, but Carroll bypasses that and moves swiftly into details. 'Where was this? Could you email me through the report?'

'I was thinking,' Maarten says, 'of one better than that. How about I come up with it? I'd like to see the original site. I feel I need to get a grasp on the whole of this case.'

'Good plan.' This time there is a pause. 'I never

thought it was him, you know. Ben Fenton. I would have sworn blind on anything you handed me that he didn't do it. But everything pointed that way. It was my first case. In the end, I was a part of the machine – it wasn't up to me. If you think you can compile a case to get him out, then I'm on board.'

Maarten looks out of the window. He sees Adrika pulling the car round to the front. She'd said she'd come, that she'd be able to do her job. Adrika is excellent police.

Harper speaks again. 'I watched him. I knew he wasn't lying. More than that – I knew he was telling the truth; the two things aren't necessarily the same. But the weight of evidence…

'My team were convinced he was guilty, and in the end the Super called me in. Asked me what I was waiting for, Christmas? Fenton sat there. White-faced. The charge sounded convincing: he woke, that morning, to find his brother gone, but his blood all over the tent, all over him. The sheer volume of blood implied severe trauma, some kind of fight, assault. He saw no one, didn't wake up. They were both alone and nothing was missing. He was asking us to believe they both went to sleep and the assault occurred in their tent from a random stranger, in the middle of the night – so secretive as to disguise any prints, any clue that there was anybody else there at all…

'No sign of Leo; he hadn't touched credit cards, bank accounts – a life departed.'

Maarten listens. He'd been in situations like this before. As police, they were there to investigate the evidence. You didn't always like the outcome.

'I charged him. I knew he would go down. Even without the body, the barrister was like a steamroller. But if Leo Fenton is alive. If he's been alive all along…'

'See you in a few hours,' Maarten says. 'We'll leave now.'

'Great. Bring walking shoes.'

The flats of Blakeney stretch out to the distant sea. It's hazy on the horizon – boats sit like dots. The harbour is quiet mid-week. When they'd bought a ticket from the guy in the parking van, he'd said that the weekend had been busy, would be once the summer holidays started.

There are boats everywhere, and the harbour is at low tide. Mudflats rise like tiny islands. Children slide down the mud banks straight into the water. They look like seals, slicked with the thick, oily mud.

'Morning!' Harper strides over. Her red hair is twisted up in a knot and she wears sunglasses, and running shoes on her feet.

'Adrika.' Harper smiles warmly at Adrika, nods to Maarten. 'It's quite a walk along the coastal path. I thought we could do that first. I'll get someone to pick us up on the other side of the site. They can bring us back. It's worth walking the whole stretch, to get a feel of how isolated it would be at night.'

Maarten welcomes the breeze that arrives as they walk the path leading out of the harbour car park. It's narrow, but he can see it widening as it leaves the village and bends round to the right, curving an arc through the flats.

Harper gestures. 'The beach lies up that way. We've got just under an hour's walk to get there. That's the pub up on the high street.' She looks out, the heat on the sea, the salt in the air. 'It's so quiet it feels unlikely it was a random act of violence. Yet I'm sure he didn't do it.'

They walk past an old abandoned rowing boat, lying in what must once have been a pool of water. A couple approaches with a dog trailing, and they nod. 'Morning.'

Maarten nods and Harper remarks on the day.

He notices how she and Adrika fall into step. They speak of the weather, of the case. They speak on first-name terms quickly.

He thinks of Liv as he walks, how she would love the space up here. She gives him space. They had been planning a break. The girls would love this too. They could run. He'd grown up on a farm, just outside Rotterdam: its ports sailed out to the world. He could handle a boat. The peace up here – he breathes deeply.

He thinks of his parents. They flash and blink in his brain. Their loss had been an enormity – just waking each day had stirred a numbness in him. He'd become quiet at school, come home to work on the farm. Avoided parties. Cafés. The numbness had slicked itself over his skin – like an oil. Impenetrable. Liv had peeled its edges, seeped underneath.

He misses Liv. Dizzy from the lack of her. The crunch of the car metal, pinging amid all the noises of the day. He doesn't know if it's her car or his parents', thinking of him as they closed their eyes.

Drifting out of his reverie, he finds the walk has been like a drug. He feels lifted. It's been almost an hour and Carroll stops.

'Up there, that's where they pitched the tent.'

They have arrived at a point where the coastal path has risen up; close to the sea on high ground, peering down on the blue.

All three of them look up at a flat-ish patch of land, tent-sized. A small cluster of trees mark a path upwards, and a gate into the trees highlights that there's private land behind there, with notices there should be no camping in the woods, no dogs, no fires.

They scramble off the coastal path. Standing at the site, Maarten looks out at the sea, still before them. So calm, mirrored, you'd be tempted to walk across it. Its horizon seems limitless.

'Perfect spot for camping. It's so quiet,' Adrika says. 'Like private grounds.'

'Yes, not many people, and the kind you do see are walkers, cyclists. It's too far to head out just to get drunk if you're a group, and no one would come here to try to mug someone. It's very unlikely someone just randomly came across the tent, and you can't see it from the main path. It all pointed to Ben Fenton.'

Maarten makes his way up to the gate, which lies hidden in the trees.

'This is locked,' he says. 'Who owns the land?'

'A family who live in London. We looked into it, but there was no one home at the time. It's rented out every now and again, but the management company who run it said it was empty that week.'

'And how far to the road from here?' Adrika asks.

'From this coastal path, if you're walking, about half an hour. It's faster through the property, as there's a private driveway that leads down from the road. The nearest car park to here is about a twenty-minute walk. We've come this way to retrace the last steps from the pub to the camping spot, but we'll head home from the car park.'

Maarten, still standing by the gate, looks out over the sea. It's stunning. There's shade by the trees, and he suddenly feels tired. The heat is setting in. It's close to three.

'Tell you what, I'd like to look at the house. Why don't we head out to get some lunch? Could you speak to the management company and see if we can have a look around the grounds of the property afterwards?'

'Of course. I'll phone and get a car to meet us at the car park.'

The sun is bright on the sea, reflecting back the heat, which has become sticky and thick. Maarten wishes he'd brought more water.

Adrika is standing facing the sea, her hands on her hips and her arms akimbo. He can see the sweat on her neck. Carroll finishes a call and smiles at her, taking a step towards her, holding out the last of the water from her bottle.

45

ANA

'Yes, sure. Give me a call later.'

She knows the voice. Standing still, as if in an ice bath, she sees Fabian leaning on the fence, finishing his call. It's almost lunchtime, and the gnawing hunger she'd started to feel turns to nerves. She couldn't eat now if she tried.

The earth is hard, she is hardening. Everywhere needs rain. There must be some respite soon. She is lambasted by heat. And the threat of Fabian.

'Ana!' He sees her, smiling and walking over. 'So good to see you before I head off.'

She wonders what he is thinking behind those eyes of his; what is he calculating? She is in no doubt he's been waiting for her.

Ana feels his hand on her wrist. He leans in to pull her towards him.

'Ana, let's talk. Please...'

She knows him. She knows this feeling. She feels herself

wanting to calm him, and it floods back to her, why she had stayed. It was because it had always been the easiest option. Baby steps. Micromanaging each situation.

'Ana. You and me.' He smiles, stepping closer. 'You know there'll never be another one like you. I don't know what happened to us. I'm with someone, but really, if you said the word.' He smiles, his head comes closer and his hand tightens on her wrist. 'My flat in New York, you'd love it...'

His breath hot. His smell familiar. His touch makes her skin crawl.

But losing Ben – the *grief* of that had been the worst thing she'd ever endured. What can Fabian do? What power does Fabian Irvine have over her?

His hand has risen up her arm and his fingers trace under the strap of her dress. Just his fingers. They travel lightly, tapping gently.

'Fabian.' Despite his size, he's such a little man. Why has she never noticed it before?

'Ana?' His fingers feel like gorillas' digits might feel. Thick. They tighten slightly at the base of her neck. His eyes are brown and they smile at her. Dark.

'Enough, Fabian. Enough.'

She can feel the pull on her neck. His hand now a vice and his grip steel.

'Ana, you don't mean that.' Whether it's a statement, question, threat, she has no idea. But, she realises, she no longer cares.

'Oh, but I do.' She pulls away from him.

He's not what scares her now. Once, she would have been sure it was him, following her in the dark. Now, she knows it is not. What a relief to find he's lost his hold over her.

The thought that it could be Leo...

She turns to him, drops her tone, stares him in the eye. 'It's done. If you ever speak to me again, I will go to the police and I will sing loudly about you.' She hasn't raised her voice but she drips scorn. 'It's a crime, you know. Emotional abuse. And I don't care if they don't convict you. But I'll sing. I'll sing loudly, and you—' She speaks clearly. '—you wouldn't survive the shame.'

'Ana.' This time it's smaller. She turns, lifts her chin as she speaks. His eyes have narrowed. Like raisins.

'Ana, you don't mean that. You and I... you can't avoid it – us.'

Stepping forward, she can see her mum and Maisie up ahead, loading the van ready for the tip. The clear-out has been cathartic. Clothes, old coats her mum had kept for years that she'd never wear again. Maisie had boxes of saved comics, yellowed and curled at the edges.

Women are good at adjusting, she thinks. *We can tread water and stay afloat. We don't always swim for shore.*

He's still talking.

'Bye, Fabian,' she says, walking forward. Turning her back.

'Ana Seabrook!' His voice carries down the road and she sees Maisie glance up, with a box in her arms.

She doesn't need to look back.

Charlie is up ahead too. He's been round a bit lately, helping Jess, looking after his mum. It had been kind of him to offer to help them. Offer to help Maisie.

He scowls at Fabian, or at the sun in his eyes, turning back to Maisie, helping her with the bags.

46

Thursday 21ˢᵗ June

MAARTEN

The house is old and painted white, but he can see there are patches that need a retouch. The management firm have sent someone to meet them.

'Hello,' says a tall, dark-haired man. He walks towards them, his hand outstretched. Maarten sees him do a double take when he looks at Carroll. He offers her his hand first. 'John Jablowski.'

'I'm Harper Carroll. Thanks for coming out. We're interested in the grounds, as well as the house. Could we start there?' Carroll says. She glances around, gesturing to the woods that lead down to the sea. 'Maarten, shall we start at the bottom and work up?'

'Good plan,' Maarten says. He smiles as he watches John Jablowski forget to shake his hand, or Adrika's, instead smiling at them and trotting eagerly off behind DI Carroll, who strides over the bumpy field. They'd given the dates of the week two years ago when they'd called but Jablowski hasn't mentioned it.

The ground is uneven. There is a track that runs along the field edge, and they pass a cluster of play equipment: an old red slide, faded to pink by the sun. There're some swings and a football goalpost.

'This rents out quickly during the summer. It's a great space for families,' Jablowski says, panting to keep up with Carroll. 'I can show you inside as well.'

'Pretty remote,' Adrika comments. 'Lovely spot to get away from everything. To get up to something.'

'Yes.' Maarten and she walk side by side, following the scrabbling Jablowski.

Adrika calls to him, asking about the week of the murder.

'It was empty that week. It had been booked out, but the customer was a no-show. Unusual, as it was all paid for.'

Maarten speaks to Adrika. 'Interesting. Can you track down the booking? If someone did book it out, but apparently failed to arrive, it would be a good way to keep it empty.'

'And easy access to the tent,' Adrika says.

'Hmm.' Maarten imagines walking through this cluster of trees in the dark. Imagines creeping up to the tent.

'The thing that really gets me is Ben Fenton not waking,' Adrika says, swinging her arms as she walks. The sun flashes on her watch. 'If he didn't do it, and if it really was zolpidem that made him sleep, then at which point did an intruder drug him? This potential cyclist we haven't managed to find. If he really exists, then surely it can only have been him who drugged him. Failing that, Ben Fenton must have given it to himself to cover his tracks. Or Leo Fenton is alive. And that is how he managed all of this.'

'I know – if Ben's innocent, someone's planned very well. The zolpidem would explain him not waking, but it would take a while to work. It feels…' He grasps for the words. 'It feels like shards of different cases, thrown into one.' He looks out through the trees. They have arrived at the other side of the gate they had stood at that morning, and the sea lies sleeping. It's like a postcard. Nothing stirs.

'The gate is always locked. Each family renting the house is given a key, but as we've said, no one was here the week you've asked about.' Jablowski is chatting quickly, nodding at Maarten and Adrika every now and again, but his eyes return to Carroll. She spins, oblivious. 'Could you take us to the house, please?'

'Of course, this way.'

Through the door, Maarten notes the traditional holiday cottage dressing. Woven baskets, pale wood furniture. Pictures of the local area and seashells hang round the house, signs with quirky messages about the beach.

'How much would something like this cost?' Maarten asks.

'To rent? About £3,000 a week in high season.'

'And you say a family own it as a holiday home?'

'Yes. We don't see them much. The house runs itself. A profitable holiday rental. They've actually put it on the market quite recently. It's been on for a few months. There hasn't been much interest but it's expensive.'

They do a quick tour, but there's nothing to see. Maarten has no idea why, but he feels it's important somehow. It's like a square peg for a round hole. There are too many separate parts to this. If this report about Leo Fenton being alive is true, then that will shift everything. If Leo Fenton didn't die, but managed to arrange for his brother to be charged with his murder, then it almost makes sense. There is real spite in this case. Tangible spite, wound round the whole thing. This is a case where he can smell the revenge.

Yes, that's what it is. That's what lies bitter on his tongue. It tastes like revenge.

'Are there more grounds? Any more buildings?' The blood trail had led over the cliff. There had been items found on the seabed. There had been no trail to follow up the hill and into the unoccupied house. But he has a feeling. An itch. He looks out to the sea again. The watch had been found on the seabed. Could the body have gone down, then maybe taken to land further up the beach? If it was as well organised as it seems, then it could be possible. And there were plastic fragments found with the soil and the body in Ayot. There was no reason the body couldn't have gone into the sea first, then been brought here. And if it was wrapped in plastic, and there was no DNA trail...

The estate agent half rolls his eyes. He's sweating now. 'We've walked over most of it,' he says.

'Maybe we could do it one more time?'

There is a cluster of sheds right at the bottom by the trees.

'Can we look in here?' Maarten asks.

The agent looks at his keys. 'I've only got keys to the main house.'

'I bet they're kept in the house,' Carroll says. 'I'll run back.'

Without waiting for an answer, she jogs off. Maarten sees the agent follow her with his eyes.

Through the windows, there are bikes, a boat, a wheelbarrow... Nothing of any note.

The sun is fierce now. Moving to the shade of the trees, Maarten spies another shed. Darker wood. This one has tarpaulin covering it and he tugs the corner, revealing the whole. This one has no windows. The locks aren't rusted.

There is a shiver, a tiny run of excitement. It tastes metal in his mouth.

'Adrika, can you keep this area clear?' He raises his voice. 'Mr Jablowski?' He doesn't take his eyes off the shed, but he moves backwards, to prevent the agent coming closer, contaminating the scene. 'Can I speak to the owners? Get their permission to thoroughly search the sheds? It might involve some disruption to the shed itself.'

'Well... I could...'

'Mr Jablowski?' Maarten looks at him, down at him. He can feel his tone formal, authoritative. He steps towards the smaller man. 'When you speak to them, can you mention it's a murder investigation?'

The grounds are full of movement. Jablowski stands at the side of the fence, cowed by the sight of the police force in action. He keeps shaking his head.

'Here?' he says again. 'You think there's been a body here?'

Maarten and Adrika stand with him, drinking weak tea that someone has supplied. Jablowski had called the owners, asking for the whereabouts of the key. It was the only outbuilding for which there was no key provided. Maarten had known for sure then.

It's late now. The sun is heading down and everyone is here working overtime. Taj has come straight up. The press have got wind of it and there are a few journalists parked out on the road.

The blue sky is darkening to a purple, knitted with pink and orange.

'Oh, we rent that one out,' the woman had said,

on the other end of the phone. Maarten had asked Jablowski to make the call on speakerphone, so that he could chip in.

'To whom?' Maarten had asked.

'I can't remember. My husband dealt with him, all done over phone and email. There was someone who said they'd like to keep some cycle equipment in their own shed up here. Said they wouldn't bother us at all as they could make their way up from the cliff path. I think Pete said he sounded quite posh. They paid up front for three years, just over two years ago. A shed arrived one day, was erected on the space he'd rented, and that was that. We've never seen him since. He's kept very quiet. Paid very generously, too. We had to tell him that we were selling the house about four months ago, so my husband's trying to arrange a rebate. He wasn't too pleased, by all accounts.'

Maarten heard the part about selling the house as though it came through a megaphone. That would have sent someone into a spin, forced them to rethink their hand. Of course they could have just disposed of the body elsewhere, but sometimes acts of revenge don't provide the expected sense of peace. Appetites for revenge were difficult to sate. If a change of plan was needed, then maybe Ayot became Plan B? For someone. But who?

Adrika had taken the number of the husband and called Sunny, who was heading into London to take a statement. Maarten has asked them to trace the email and the bank account.

'We investigated the house,' Carroll had said, shaking her head. 'But there was nothing – no sign of anything. The path of blood led over the cliff. The dogs led us there too. We searched for the body in the sea and found traces of Leo's effects. His watch, his clothes. We checked the house and driveway, but there was no sign of anything. I suggested a wider DNA search, but with the evidence the Super wouldn't sign off any more spend. It seemed clear-cut. God, if only I'd pushed...' Carroll is silent.

'Sir?' A uniformed officer approaches him. 'The CSM is asking for you. Forensics have found something. The floor in the shed has been cut out in the centre. Looks like something's been buried. The soil is freshly turned. There's DNA all over in there. Signs of blood residue coming up under the scanner...'

Maarten nods. His head is aching now. If the body was kept here, then that makes a lot of sense. Three unanswered questions: Why Ayot for the burial? Who rented the shed? And are they the mysterious cyclist?

47

ANA

The hardness of the mirror, its coolness, offers her no judgement. She looks to it desperately, painting, colouring in. The cracks of sleeplessness need crayon, the red eyes need drops – like watercolours.

This misty presentation of herself is real. It's painted over, and yet it's still real. It's the face she can point at the world, like an Instagram filter for skin. It's no less real than the ragged face she had peered into that morning. Lack of sleep, red from tears.

Ben hasn't called since. She'd hoped that he would be able to call, but he hasn't called.

Red lipstick. She had put some on earlier but the coffee had lifted it. Draw in the outline and shade in the middle. Not too dark. Only a shade or so stronger than your actual colour. Don't do lips and eyes, one or the other.

It's not just anger, it's sadness. This grief that had stirred up within her, swirled around like a pit of smoke, has burst into flame. Because who is she to him? Who is she to be ignored? Of all people, by Ben?

Contouring. She'd thought it a load of crap when she'd first heard about it, but if you do it gently enough then you can pull it off. Bronzer under the brow bone, under the chin. The edges of the cheeks.

Why was he shutting her out? There must be a timeline for grief. You mourn and then you eventually move on. Yet she wasn't mourning, she was just stuck in this perpetual cycle of sadness. Of anger. Of rage. Of heartache. Then it all fizzles up. It wants to explode from the top. From her mouth. She had spent the last day and night thinking of what she'd say when he called again. What she wished she'd said at the start. It's not like he can't see her. He's not locked in isolation. It's less than an hour in the car.

Eyelashes, eyebrows. First colour, then sweep upwards. Expands the eye. Opens your look.

There. She stands upright. The heat of the train, the Tube, the packed underground had melted it all since leaving the house. She'd been called in for a meeting in the end.

She sometimes feels she's glued together by artifice.

You can only paper over the cracks for so long.

She's going to have to tell Maisie about Leo, about New York. Although after their evening in the graveyard, she suspects she has already guessed. At some point, she's going to have to tell Ben too.

But part of her has always been scared that maybe Ben already knows. That Leo might have told him on that camping trip. She's scared still.

She's always been sure of Ben's innocence, but in her darkest of moments, in the dead of night, she worries if he had found out about their night together and they had argued – what if it had got out of hand? This tiny fear has wormed through her for two years. If Leo is dead, or even if he decided to disappear, did she cause it? Did she lead to all of this?

Hurriedly she adds face powder. Covering the guilt.

48

MAARTEN

'It's a match, sir,' Sunny says, almost jogging into Maarten's office. 'Taj just called up. He put the soil through the tests first and it's a match – there are traces of blood and some form of plastic in the soil from underneath the shed, which match those found in Ayot in the Palladian graveyard. He needs to do more testing, but he said his best guess at the moment is that the body has been wrapped in some form of plastic sheet, then buried under the shed. What it does is confirm for us that the body reburied in Ayot can feasibly be linked to the site under the shed in Norfolk. It also tells us the murder was planned. Plastic sheeting, there probably to keep the DNA from being found, to avoid leading a trail to the shed, where the killer didn't want us to follow. I wouldn't be surprised if he'd been dressed in a plastic suit too, to minimise evidence. We found spare pairs of plastic gloves at the scene.'

'So we now know where the body was kept, which implies that this sighting of Leo Fenton is fake. It's smoke and mirrors. The initial briefing this morning said they've found at least two lots of DNA from the shed. One is Leo Fenton's and the other is only in traces, and identity unknown. It will need some work. We still have a suspected murder weapon, the fishing knife discovered at Ana Seabrook's.'

'Have we got anywhere on the trace to the renter of the shed? Do we know who it is?'

'Not yet.' Sunny shakes his head. 'The email account isn't coming back with anything. It's like it's been shut down. And the initial emails were sent from an Internet café in London, the kind used by backpackers. The CCTV doesn't go back far enough.'

'If we draw a line from all of it, where do we get to?' Maarten stands. He picks up a pen. The whiteboard on his wall is blackened slightly with smears. But his markings are clear.

'Sir?' Sunny asks.

'Well, we draw a line from all of this. And where does it leave us? Really, if we find the body of a murder victim eighteen months after the murderer has been put in jail. What will you tell me?'

'That he didn't do it,' Sunny says. 'He could have got someone else to move the body, but arranging all that from prison would be hard. Unless it's Ana Seabrook.'

'Exactly.'

Maarten stares at the board. 'The central figures in all of this are Ben Fenton and Ana Seabrook. Let's assume Leo Fenton is dead. And then let's assume his body was moved, but not by Ben Fenton. So what about Ana Seabrook? Let's not forget that evidence connected with Leo's murder was found in her garden, and the plastic wine glass from the graveyard we found had her fingerprints on it – strange to go back there. She could have moved the body, to make Ben look innocent. When the skeleton wasn't immediately identified as Leo's, she could have changed tactics and sent herself a text from Leo's phone, to make it look like he was alive. It's possible that, with a good lawyer, it would be enough to at least get Ben an appeal hearing.'

'Really? You think they pulled it off together?' Sunny crosses one leg over the other and leans forward. He pushes his hand through his hair.

'Do you?' Maarten asks.

'I think... I think the planning would be immense,' Sunny says. 'And it's a confused way to go about it. If Ana is involved, why would she bury a pack of pills in her compost if she knew her dog rooted around in there? And then there's the photo and the text, supposedly sent from a man who we now know Ana had a fling with. Why would she do that? Why would she bring that secret to light?'

'The planning *is* immense,' Adrika says. 'It's the mad thing about all of this. The planning is huge. It's the linking. It's the linking that's the problem. The thing is...' She shakes her head.

'Go on,' Maarten says. He leans back against the window ledge. The window is hot against his back.

'I suppose the thing is that I just don't think she did it. I can't see her digging a grave. I *believe* her when she sits there frightened. She seems so spooked by the whole thing. I believe that she's distraught about her dog. I just *believe* her.'

Maarten nods. 'Yes, I believe her too. But there must be something we're missing. Did anything turn up on the graveyard? Is there anything about that graveyard that is telling us it's a site of interest?'

Adrika shakes her head. 'Not so far.'

'Well, let's go one further. Can you run a search on the people already buried? See if anything turns up.'

Adrika makes a note.

Maarten stretches, the sun competing with the air con. 'Whatever it is we're missing, we can't deny that all the lines, each one, lead back to Ana Seabrook. They lead back to her,' he repeats. 'And it's our job to follow it up. So, let's do our job.'

49

Friday 22nd June

ANA

'Hey there!' Jack calls, walking down the corridor. His trainers make no sound on the floor, whereas her heels clip-clip in response. 'Not in my white coat today.'

'How's it going, 812? Get to spend much time in head office?' She smiles, falling into step beside him. She's joining him to observe the progress report meeting on the drug's development. The head office has as clean a feel as the research facility.

'Well, ya know.' He smiles, affecting an American accent, and raises both hands, mimicking a shooting action. 'Hear you nearly got blown away on your way back last time?'

Ana smiles, despite flinching at the thought.

'You normally take the piss out of near-death experiences, do you?' She raises her eyebrows.

'Nah, I'm just crap at empathy. I use humour to demonstrate concern. Seriously, you OK?'

She nods. She is wearing a pale red pleated silk skirt, falling just below the knee, a pale yellow silk T-shirt, tucked into the skirt, and heels that lift it from casual to office wear. It's cool, it's chic, it's a uniform that screams how together she is feeling. She had chosen it carefully. Her hair is tied up, in a loose topknot. It had taken many hair pins to achieve, precisely, the desired loose effect.

'You're reporting on the follow-up today?'

'Yes, the drug should start to show effects over six weeks ideally, so now we're in Week One of the follow-up. We take blood pressure, blood samples et cetera. My report is positive. The drug looks like it's going well. They're keen to sell, I've heard – you should have an easy deal, I guess.'

'How right was I?'

The update had gone well.

She laughs as he catches her up after the meeting.

'Fancy a coffee before you head off? They've got some cakes in today.'

Ana nods. She collapses on a sofa in the corner of the room. The yellow of the sofa is as cool as the puffing air. Five minutes before hitting the heat of the sun and the Tube, then the heat of Ayot.

'So, has Fran mentioned me much this week?' He grins.

'I see! The real reason you're offering me coffee.' She smiles. 'A bit. A little bit. And you know I'm going to tell her you asked.'

'Here, carrot cake,' he says, pushing out a plate containing slices of cake thick with icing. 'Consider yourself sweetened up when you speak of me. Then if you wait five minutes, how about I take the Tube back with you? I told Fran I'd meet her for a drink after work and I've got the rest of the afternoon off. She said she might be able to get out early – I'll try to get her to come out and play.'

The station platform feels ten degrees hotter than the air outside. The sweat on her neck soaks the top of her shirt, and she's dizzy. She takes a drink from the water bottle she carries. Jack is pushed up against her as the crush from the Friday footfall intensifies due to Tube delay.

'They wouldn't transport animals like this,' he mutters, his mouth pushed up against the top of the back of her head.

Someone stands on her toe, and she winces. The rush of hot air through the tunnel signals the arrival of the train, and from somewhere there is a shout. Turning instinctively, she feels Jack fall onto her and he swears.

They tumble, crashing to the platform, beyond the yellow line, and Ana tips forward. Slow motion kicking in, until she dangles head first over the edge of the platform; she is half on and half off. Her bag falls on the track and she looks left to see the Tube train screaming towards her.

A woman cries; there is a surge of panic.

She grabs the side of the platform to try to push herself back up, but she doesn't have enough time. It's hurtling; fractions of a second away, whining its way forward, brakes screaming.

She relaxes, and closes her eyes.

Then jerked, suddenly, she is back on the platform. Her head lands with a bang on the concrete and she rolls to the side, her legs twisting beneath her. Her skirt billows as she comes to rest, caught up around her knees. Graceful, a single slow movement, the arc of the air beneath the silk like a collapsing tent.

The alarm is ringing and there are screams. Blood races in her ears. She thinks of her bag, crushed beneath the wheels of the Tube, lying down with the rats beneath the rails.

'Fuck, Ana, are you OK? Ana? Ana?'

And her world fades. The dizziness already taking hold, the heat of the platform a force she can't fight.

There is blackness.

'Ana! Ana!'

It's noisy. So hot. Her head hurts.

'Don't move her!'

'Where are the police?'

'They're on their way. Please stand back.'

Lights flash. Her neck aches. She tries to move her head but there's a pain shooting down her left side.

'Lie still.' The voice is soft, warm. It's a woman's voice. She opens her eyes and looks into brown eyes, a face a few years older than she is. 'I want you to try to lie still. Please, just lie still.'

Ana drops her head back down onto something soft. She can't think where she is, but this heat. This overwhelming heat.

The train, coming towards her... 'What happened! Did someone fall?'

'Hello, Ana – it is Ana, isn't it? My name is Petra and I'm a doctor, I'm going to check you. Can you lie still for me, Ana? Can you tell me if it hurts anywhere?'

'Did someone fall? Did I fall? The train...'

'You're OK. Can you take a breath for me? Can you take a deep breath? You fell and almost landed on the tracks, but they pulled you back up. Just in time.' The woman is working quickly. A light shines in Ana's eyes and she blinks, seeing spots of black among the bright sheen.

'Ana, does it hurt anywhere? Can you tell me how many fingers I'm holding up?'

She's crying, she can feel her limbs shake, her hands shake. She tries to lift them, to wipe her eyes, but her back screams when she lifts her arm.

'Ana, don't try to move. We're going to lift you in a minute. We need to wait for the paramedics. Can you tell me how many fingers I'm holding up?'

'Four,' she says. The light hurts her eyes. She closes them, tilting her head. 'I think there are four.'

Petra lays a blanket over her. Ana is shivering now, despite the heat.

'My back hurts, it hurts.'

'You've jolted it, it might be bruised. Don't try to move.' Petra leans forward and takes Ana's hand, smiling. 'You're looking OK. I've checked your reflexes. The shock is making you shake. Just lie still. We'll get you sorted in no time. I'm going to stay with you. It's important you don't move. The paramedics will get you to hospital.'

Who had she been with? Jack, that was it.

'Ana! Ana!' The shout again. She can't see; it's only on the edge of her vision, but is that Jack being held back?

'Police are here!' someone calls.

'It was him, he pushed her!' This time a man's voice calls out. 'I saw it, he pushed against her and she fell!'

'I didn't, someone pushed me! I pulled her back up on the platform. Ana, are you OK? Ana!'

Pressing down, the heat is too much. It's hot and cold. She's still shivering. Her neck aches. Her head hurts.

'Ana, try not to sleep. Can you take another breath for me? Try to squeeze my hand. Tell me where you were going, were you on your way to work?' Petra says, but all Ana can do is close her eyes.

Like falling backwards, sinking beneath the surface of a swimming pool, she has the impression of immersion, of dipping into the darkness. Being swallowed up.

'Ana, can you press my hand? Take a breath. Try not to sleep.'

All she can do is allow the blackness in.

There's a face, at the edge of the crowd. Is it Jack again – calling? Her eyes flicker as her lids fall.

It's the cap again. The same cap.

Is it Leo?

50

MAARTEN

'So, she fell on the tracks?' Adrika looks incredulous. 'People don't survive that, surely. They get electrocuted?'

'Not the tracks,' Maarten says, shaking his head. 'She half fell off the platform. The Tube train was coming, and someone pulled her back just in time. Lucky – she wouldn't have stood a chance.'

'And this Jack Thurbridge allegedly pushed her?'

'That's the story. We have a witness statement sent over from the police. They were called, and she was taken to hospital. They've dropped her off by ambulance. There was concern about her spine, but they checked her and they've let her go home. She's suffering from concussion. She banged her head at some point, and there's been some trauma to her back. But nothing serious. Mainly just bruises.'

Adrika turns the engine off and they step out of the car. The evening air is still hot; the sun relentless. Noise chatters from the pub garden.

'Friday night, sir. I bet the pub itself is empty. Everyone will be outside in the beer garden when it's like this. God, we need rain. Do you think she's up to talking to us?'

'Who knows. But any threat to her ties in with our case. For all we know, Jack Thurbridge could be our missing link. It's best to get her statement today. Who knows what she'll remember on Monday.' He checks both ways and steps across the country road. 'I told her mother we'd use the side entrance,' Maarten says. 'Come on.'

Ana Seabrook is pale against the sheets on her bed. The window is wide open but it brings little breeze, and the noise from the pub garden sails in clearly. Maarten would hate it. He thinks of Liv still recovering in hospital, and how little disturbance Aggie offers compared to this.

'We're just here to hear your side of events. If it was just this incident, we'd wait,' Adrika says, 'but we're investigating any possible links to the body in the graveyard. You seem to have been at the heart of a number of recent incidents. If Jack Thurbridge pushed you then he's a suspect.'

Ana lifts herself up, leaning back against the pillows, and takes a drink from the glass near her bed.

'Ana, they can do this later, you know,' Maisie Seabrook says.

'She's right,' Maarten says. 'We can come back later

for all the details. We really just want to know if you think you were pushed. What you saw.'

'I don't know,' she says. 'All I know is that one minute we were standing on the Tube platform and it was hot. There was a crush, you know, busy. The train was coming and I heard Jack shout, and then I fell. The train screamed down the track – I was scared. The lights were so close, glaring.' She sounds exhausted.

'Did you feel him fall, or did you feel a push?' Adrika says.

'I think more a fall, but I can't really say. I thought maybe someone had fainted – there are always people fainting in this heat.' She shakes her head, as though clearing water from her ears. 'I don't know him that well. But he seems nice. He could have pushed me. It was the weight of him that forced me to fall. But then wasn't it him who pulled me up? No one's told me yet.' She looks tired. She lies back and rests her head on the back wall behind her bed. 'I can't think why he would push me. What would he have to gain? I've only known him a week.'

'Did you see anything? Anything at all that you want to tell us?' Adrika leans forward, her notebook open on her knee.

'I might have seen...'

Maarten watches her glance at her sister before she speaks.

'I might have seen Leo.'

'Leo Fenton?' Adrika is scribbling furiously in her notebook.

'Yes, but not really him. I don't know what it was…'

Her sister has gone white, and she clutches the arm of her chair for support.

'I know, it was the cap. He, whoever he was – surely it can't have been Leo – he was wearing Leo's cap. The one he always wore.' She looks to Maisie. 'You know.'

Laughter comes in from the pub garden and enters the hot bedroom, hanging in the air like smoke.

51

ANA

'Can I come in?' Fran pokes her head round the door.

Ana isn't asleep. Her head has a dull ache, but other than that she's just tired. It's her mind that fizzes, flicking quickly from one thing to the next. Won't rest.

'Of course, do. I didn't know you were still here.' Ana sits up, lifting her hair to tie up.

'I've just had dinner,' Fran says. Then grins. 'With The Leith himself. Who knew the lengths you'd go to in order for me to have a bit of one-on-one time with him. You're a good friend.'

Ana smiles. 'And how was he? Small talk scintillating? Masterful?'

'We talked about you, Ana. He feels really guilty. He said he thought there was something funny about Jack… He's downstairs. Going to drive me back. He won't come in here, but he wanted me to say how sorry…' Fran shakes her head, reaching out and holding Ana's hand. 'I had no idea. He seemed so… nice.' She shrugs.

'Crap word. Crap judge of character.'

'But honestly, Fran. The things Leith is talking about weren't anything. I recognised him from your photo. Awkward – but he joked about it. Asked about you. He was looking forward to meeting you for a drink. I honestly don't know if he pushed me. I wouldn't have thought… I mean, I couldn't see what happened, he certainly fell on me. But pushed me on the track?'

'Really? Is that what you told the police?'

'I just said I didn't know. Why? Why would he do it? It just makes no sense. But then again, nothing does.' She lays back on the pillow. Her head throbs.

'He's with the police now. I haven't spoken to him,' Fran says. She traces her finger up and down the inside of her arm, looking out of the window. 'First man I like in a while, and he turns out to be a lamb with shark's teeth.'

Ana squeezes her hand, shaking her head. 'It might be nothing. He might have nothing to do with any of this,' she says.

'What, with my luck?' Fran says. 'Nah, just your average Friday night out.'

52

MAARTEN

'Anything?' Maarten asks, speaking quietly down the phone in the corridor of the London police station Jack Thurbridge had been taken to for questioning. Due to the link, he's been allowed to question him with the officer here. But Thurbridge is protesting his innocence.

'I just can't tell, sir. I've stared at this CCTV for hours, and it's just not conclusive. He stands right up behind her, then falls forward. He could be pushing or could have been pushed himself. There's such a throng of people on that platform. I'm surprised they don't have more accidents.'

'And the cap? What about that, any sightings?'

'It's there. There's a man, at least I guess a man, but you can't see the face. We've looked at his gait and height, and given the find in Norfolk, we don't think it's Leo. Someone is trying to give that impression, though. Dressed in T-shirt, jeans. All you can see on the CCTV on the platform is him standing close to our two. The interesting thing is that once the incident occurs, and the crowd forms – gruesome as it is – then this person with the cap lingers for a minute and walks away. It's interesting only because he doesn't seem interested. Unless he was trying to get away.'

Maarten leans back against the wall, nodding to a uniformed officer who squeezes through. It's late, and he wants to see Liv. They'll let him in late, but he hasn't managed to catch the girls before bedtime. Jane is still here, saving him. If he were on his own, he just wouldn't know how to do this job and have children. How do other people manage?

'Look, the golden hour is long gone. There's no point carrying on tonight. Are there any leads following the cap outside? Any glimpse of his face?'

'Zilch, sir. Zero.'

'Right, then let's call it a day. I'm done here. He outright denies pushing and it's not our case anyway yet. If we can find some link to Leo Fenton, then we can call him back in. But it's late on a Friday night. It's time to go home.'

Heading out of the station, Maarten breathes in the cooling air. London lights are bright all around. The city is out drinking on the pavement. It feels like a different city in the heat. Tomorrow he will take the girls up to the forest for a walk, picnic, a swim in the river. And see Liv. He misses her, like a thirst.

The country needs drenching. Everything is parched. Even the air is brittle now – the news had reported six fires in the last twelve hours; a message to the public urged vigilance with cigarette ends. The heat has stuck at over 30 degrees Celsius for the past week.

Ana Seabrook has been very lucky today. Or very unlucky, however you viewed it. These close brushes with death: his family, Ana Seabrook. The summer has weaved mortality into its heat. This earth, the grass, the drying river beds – they are all weaker, and he is weaker too. When the heat is close and sticky, he just wants to sit with his arms around his family, their warmth running like blood between them.

Time for a glass of red wine. And a family weekend. Ana Seabrook and Jack Thurbridge can wait until Monday.

53

MAARTEN

'Monday morning, anything new for me?' Maarten settles back on the edge of the desk, coffee in hand. Liv had been a lot better at the weekend. Aggie was quieter and so Liv was getting some sleep. Almost out, almost home.

'How's Liv doing?' Adrika asks as the team grab pens, iPads, start settling down.

'Nearly as good as new,' Maarten says, smiling. 'The hospital thinks she'll be home by the end of the week. It's been tough.'

'Bet the girls are pleased,' Adrika says.

'Everyone's pleased.' Maarten thinks of his mother-in-law. She'd had a break over the weekend but she is exhausted. He is exhausted. Liv's absence is marked in the house: the shower screen has clouded over in the last few days, the post has built up by the door. The washing basket spills over. He feels guilty, realising all that she does. They both work, but she clearly carries the lion's share at home. Luckily, she is between projects at work. That, at least, had been easy. She hates letting anyone down.

'Where did we get to on Jack Thurbridge? Anything?' he says to the team.

'Well.' Sunny steps forward. 'I had a bit of a turn-up. I did some digging, and turns out Leo Fenton was at the same university as Jack Thurbridge.' He doesn't wait for an answer, but writes on the board as he speaks. 'They were a couple of years apart, but there's a chance they may have crossed paths. Leo received a chunk of money from a pharmaceutical company after a buyout, didn't he? If there's any work jealousy or some story there, it could be a possible motive. It's quite a coincidence. It's worth pursuing.'

'Good job, Sunny,' Adrika says. 'You must have been working the whole weekend!'

'A part of it,' Sunny says, grinning. 'I couldn't take the sunburn any more so I knuckled down for a few hours.'

'It would be useful to talk to Ben Fenton again, to see if there's any link. There's no mention of Jack Thurbridge in the files from the original investigation,' Maarten says, looking down at his notes. 'What about Leo Fenton? Any word on him?'

'The Proof of Life hasn't turned anything up. A credit card, Ana Seabrook thinking she recognised his cap... Not enough,' Adrika says. 'And with the soil samples matching between Norfolk and Ayot, we're working on the assumption that it is Leo Fenton's skeleton that was buried in the churchyard. The man Ana claims she saw must be somebody else.'

'Yes, let's keep going. Widen the CCTV around the station from Friday? Let's see if we can find the cap and if we can get a face shot at some point. Let's try to get to the bottom of this one. Suspects: Ben Fenton is doing time for the murder. Ana Seabrook had a fling with the victim. They could be working together, but the recent attack on Ana makes that seem less likely. Ben could have discovered the affair, killed his brother out of jealousy and now be orchestrating a campaign of terror against Ana to spook her. Difficult to do from prison, though. And now we have Jack Thurbridge, who could be acquainted with Leo Fenton, and is a possible aggressor to Ana Seabrook – though we can't see any motive. And lastly, we have Fabian Irvine. He's looking far less likely. He might want to punish Ana for breaking up with him, which would explain the photo and the text, but I don't see why he would want to kill Leo. Even if they did have a romance, it was after his relationship with Ana.'

Maarten taps his notebook, finishes his coffee. 'There are still two missing links here. One is the cyclist, and the second is why choose the graveyard to leave the body? I still think there's something there. If we can get to the bottom of that, then I think we'll have more of an understanding of where we should be looking. Adrika, anything from the burial applications, or the bodies already buried?'

'Not yet, but give me another day.'

He scans the room. 'Adrika, I want to head back over there to do a walk round, and then let's call in on Ana Seabrook and see how her memory is doing. She must be feeling better today, and things might have fallen into line a bit more. Finish up here and meet me downstairs in a few minutes. I've got a meeting with the new Super.'

Back at the graveyard, Maarten walks under the sun, letting his eyes fall from each headstone to the next, letting them drift in and out. He'd studied them harder last time, but still, there were no surnames, no family members that seemed to be related to any persons of interest in this case. He comes to a stop by the grave of the young girl, Caitlin Miller, that they'd noticed the day the body was recovered.

'You think this one might be important?' Adrika asks, coming to stand next to him. She's wearing shades and a hat, and she lifts the shades to lean in and read the writing carefully.

'No idea. But she would be a similar age to Leo Fenton and Ana Seabrook now. Perhaps they knew each other? It's a long time ago – ten years since her death.

But we need everything we can get. The background will be ready later?'

She nods.

He turns and sees a single cloud, hovering in the sky. More a puff than anything substantial. 'They were saying on the radio it's been almost forty days without rain,' he comments.

'Scary really, if you think about it too long,' Adrika says. 'We're not set up for it. Crazy country. Two snowflakes and the trains grind to a halt. This sun and no one can sleep, the ground turns yellow. My mind overheats by lunchtime. My thoughts roast. Burned on the outside, pink in the middle, BBQ brain.'

Watching the cloud as it floats away, with its promise of rain, Maarten nods his head. 'We could be more productive right now. Inertia is heat-bred.'

Ready to get out of the sun, he heads back across the hard ground. 'Come on, let's visit Ms Seabrook. There's nothing new to see here.'

54

ANA

The pub is closed until 6 p.m. today and Ana stretches, lazy like a cat, flat on the grass. She's missed her run for a couple of days, and her limbs feel heavy. The heat has unwound her muscles, already softened them. She flexes her foot, testing herself, then she pulls her body up in a yoga move, arching up. It's a bridge pose. She breathes into it, feeling the muscles down her spine locking. She's downloaded some app with daily ten-minute workouts. Her back is getting stronger. Physically, she's almost whole.

'Is it OK if we come in?'

Ana sees the police entering the pub garden. They must have knocked and spoken to her mum first.

She lowers herself, sitting up, waiting for the pull in her back to fade before she stands. She's light-headed.

The very tall one, the Dutch DCI, comes in quietly, and the DI is the one who talks, chatting as she enters: 'It's lovely here – how amazing to get all this space.'

'When I'm not sharing it with the rest of the village,' Ana says, drinking from her water bottle, uncurling her legs and rising carefully to sit at one of the wooden tables.

The benches either side of the table have no back support and she pulls in her stomach.

They sit, baking in the morning sun, facing each other. Sweat sits on the brow of the Dutchman. He is upright and melting. He looks like he exercises, though; he's not flaccid in the heat like some.

'We have no evidence that it was a push rather than a fall,' the DCI says, his soft accent laying out the facts clearly. 'But we have found a link to Leo Fenton. It's far from proof, but he and Jack Thurbridge were at the same university.' He pauses, allowing this to sink in, looks at her then looks away.

Despite the heat, he seems comfortable, relaxed. He doesn't tell her this with any sense of eagerness. Seems oblivious to her hands, which close tight on the wooden table of the beer garden; her knuckles, which pale beneath the sun and the burn of the news.

His eyes swivel back to her. 'We'll follow this up. We wondered if it rang any bells.'

She shakes her head as she looks at him. He has dark brown eyes behind the thick black frames. He must be about ten – fifteen? – years older than her; he's handsome, in a geek-chic kind of way. She can imagine him drinking red wine, at film festivals... She wonders if he takes delight in his cases, in this case. Like he might seek the delight of finishing a Rubik's cube. Turning her upside down, slotting her next to the reds, easing out the yellows. She thinks of Leith's energy, which rallies others to please him; of Ben's humour, which can hold a crowd in a pub on one story easily for half an hour.

And of Jack812, who possibly tried to push her under a train.

'You think he might have killed Leo?' she asks. 'You think it's been him all along?'

'We have no idea,' he says. 'We're looking into it.'

'We looked for the face of the man you saw wearing a cap, but there wasn't enough CCTV to get a clear image.' The DI speaks, and she leans forward, placing her hand close to Ana's. 'He might be completely unconnected. Have you remembered anything else?'

Ana shakes her head. Her mind is filled with the rush of hot air as the Tube sped towards her. Her fingers had almost brushed the tracks as she had tipped down. A jerk from behind. The billow of her skirt.

A cap.

'There's no chance Leo might be alive?' she asks. 'That maybe it was all one big fake?'

She is dizzy now. The back of her neck burns under the sun. Ben is in jail. Deep down, she knows Leo wouldn't have left him in there. Even if Leo had wanted to get away from something, he wouldn't have left Ben in jail.

Jansen shakes his head. His eyes are kind, she decides. Noticing the kindness makes her feel as though she might cry. It's only her fingernails, digging into the wood on the old table, that keep her from tipping backwards, from giving in to the dizziness that makes her head spin. She hasn't eaten, she remembers, she's eaten nothing at all since last night.

He says, 'We don't discount anything. We'll follow up on it all. We have fairly solid evidence that Leo is dead. It's the lead we're pursuing at the moment. I'm sorry.'

'Can Ben get out of prison soon? If you're convinced that this is all the hand of someone else, you must be sure now that he didn't kill anyone. So, can he get out? Can he come home?' She longs for Ben, for what they had, like the country longs for rain – seeking the familiar, wanting to ease this dryness, this burn.

DCI Jansen nods. His face is impassive. There is no hint of anything. The kind eyes, the face that gives nothing else away. Rod-straight, he sits beneath the sun and is unmoved. Melting, but unbothered by it.

'If the identity of the body is confirmed as Leo's then it's likely Ben will be released. We have no interest in keeping an innocent person in jail. Can you think about any Jacks that Leo might have mentioned? Sometimes it takes a reminder to bring things to the surface, a catalyst.' This time he smiles. 'If anything occurs to you, you have our number.'

'Hopefully, it won't take long, Ana,' the DI says, leaning further forward. She smiles, and Ana finds herself smiling back, trusting her. Trusting both of them. 'We want Ben to come home to you. And we want to give you all some closure with Leo. We know how hard it is for the families when a body is missing.'

Maarten Jansen smiles at her. 'I did want to ask if you knew a Caitlin Miller?'

Shaking her head, Ana tries to banish the fog of heat that is closing in. She thinks for a minute. She'd been thinking of her earlier. Who else had mentioned her? 'Caitlin Miller? She was Andy Miller's sister. She hanged herself – depression, they said. We were all given sessions on how to handle the stress of GCSEs. They moved away afterwards. It was very sad.' She thinks of how sad it had been – no one had really understood it. 'But I wasn't sorry to see Andy Miller move.'

'There was no relation to Leo? To Ben?' Jansen asks.

Ana looks down at her nails. One has ripped, and there's a darkening pink underneath. It will bleed, she thinks. The dizziness increases. The heat cannot be fought. She lifts her nail, aware of the sting of it, and as she does so, her vision melts into a landscape of grey. Her head becomes soft and the muscles in her stomach, holding her back upright, release.

She shakes her head again. 'I don't think so. I was a bit of a recluse around then. Dad had died. I wasn't coping. I think Leo went out with her for a while, boyfriend and girlfriend, but I don't really remember… He was always in love with someone. He was a charmer.' She smiles. Laughs. 'He pulled you in. The Fenton boys have something.' Her smile disappears quickly and she thinks of Leo, and thinks of him lying in a grave. So young. So unlived.

As the sound of her voice fades along with the faces of the police, Ana hears only one word as she tips backwards, back towards the hard ground, the odd cigarette butt, the patchy earth. It comes from her mouth, but it could come from anywhere.

'Leo.'

55

MAARTEN

'Mama, we brought balloons!' The girls rush into the room, a vent of energy, a gust of colour. The balloons snag on the doorframe before pulling down and up again. Vivid, they fill the space, rising up towards the ceiling; thin twisted foil ribbons catch the light as they dangle down, grabbed by tiny hands.

'Thank you!' Liv, dressed and waiting in the chair by the bed, hugs them both – still moving cautiously, Maarten sees, but her colour is normal, and she stands on both legs equally, solid again.

'Thank God you're coming home,' Maarten says as he kisses her, smiling. 'We can't do anything without you.'

'Bloody can't wait,' she says. 'Can we have pizza takeaway tonight? And wine?'

The girls collect the drawings that they've given her, pinned around the bed in frames; they clutch trinkets. Sanne wraps up the picture she'd made for Liv. She lays it carefully on the bed, wrapping it slowly in the tea towel she'd brought.

Maarten wonders if they've grown too fast in the last couple of weeks. They have had to show him how to plait hair, explain who the parents were who'd offered play dates, lifts to swimming, to ballet, to football. Cried because they remembered the crunch of metal, called for Liv in their sleep.

'Must be a special occasion if you've let them bring me helium balloons,' Liv says, her arms full of a rainbow-coloured one; she pulls it down and watches it float up again.

'I had no choice. It was all they wanted to bring. You know there is still a helium shortage? We will run out. And MRIs, they don't know—'

'I know, Maart, I know. Thank you. It's made their day.' She laughs at him, and he shrugs, pleased everyone is smiling, almost ready to cry with relief.

The bags are wheeled to the door, arms full of hospital bric-a-brac.

'I can't believe all this stuff!' Maarten says.

'You're the policeman, aren't you?' The voice comes from behind.

He swings round, and it's Aggie. She's shuffling back in from her walk, on the arm of a nurse. Her lined face is scrunched up – in fear, he thinks. She looks frightened. She leans in and squeezes his arm. Her fingers are strong, and they pull him towards her.

'You're not taking Katie?'

'It's time for her to go home. She's all better,' he says, smiling. He speaks gently, bending slightly so that he can look clearly into her eyes; her pupils are like beads now, almost black. Her terror is writ in there.

'Don't take her. She's done no wrong. It wasn't her fault!' The hand on his arm shakes, the fingers dig tight in sharp trembles – she pulls him closer still. Her breath is tea-scented, with sour milk. 'It wasn't her fault. I know it's a crime, but she wasn't hurting nobody. She doesn't deserve to be taken by the police!'

'Aggie, come on, into bed,' the nurse says, trying to steer her away.

But her hand is locked on his arm.

'It wasn't Katie's fault!' Tears are running down her face. The nurse glances at Maarten, and she nods to the door, indicating that he should leave. But Maarten can't move, he'd have to peel her fingers away. He sees the girls' faces, confused; Sanne takes a step towards them.

Aggie turns to Liv, addressing her with a voice that is light as air, rising in tone, quivering with grief. 'Katie, I never told them. I never told any of them. He wondered if you'd come to see me, before. I don't think what you did was a crime. You was just sad. It was his fault, that's what I told him. I told him he was to blame. Not saying sorry for what he did to that poor girl! Of course you'd be upset. If he hadn't shouted at you, hadn't gone off like that… leaving you. Upset. In your condition… But I never said. I never told no one.'

She collapses on the nurse's arm, crying, muttering.

Maarten's arm pinches where the fingers dug deep, and his brain ticks over once. Stirring.

Katie.

Caitlin. A crime. Is she talking about suicide?

He steps forward to ask her, but the nurse is already leading her to bed and Sanne's face, tiny and tight, looks to him for explanation.

Nic clings to Liv's hand, and Liv is already reaching to stroke Sanne's hair.

The room waits for movement, the balloons holding their height in the air as though stilled for a picture.

'Is she OK?' Sanne asks. 'What's wrong?'

'She's just old, sweetheart,' Liv says. 'She's confused; she thinks I'm someone else.'

Maarten hunkers down, smiling at them all, whispering. 'She's remembering something, but her brain isn't working quite right. Look, she's fine now. It wasn't about Mama. And you know, we haven't told Mama how many ice creams we've been eating since she's been in here. Shall we pick some up on the way home? Chocolate?'

Aggie is quieter now. The curtain round her bed is pulled closed, and Maarten steps through the doorframe before swinging Sanne up on his shoulders. He will need to come back. He needs to settle his family first.

'Ice cream?' Liv says. 'With waffles cones?'

Maarten glances back once. Yes, he'll come back, he thinks, once he's worked out the questions. There are questions forming. Something is tapping its way into shape.

56

ANA

There's definitely a presence.

She runs through the field. The sun is hot and the ground is hard. There's a patch at the edge where the local cricket team play and a sprinkler lifts itself up and arcs back and forward across the bowling run. It's the only green thing in the whole yellow landscape. She makes a beeline for it and her legs and arms catch the drips as she leaps through the falling spray. She imagines rain, thinking of it as something historic, a fabled tale. Everywhere needs rain. The world as they know it is burning beneath their feet.

Running round the edge, she can feel it again. It's like eyes on her neck. She runs faster, lengthening her stride. Her chest burns as she pushes herself but she feels strong. She will outrun this. Real or not.

Landing on the road, she runs up on the verge as a car passes, and then back on the tarmac. She's almost back in Ayot.

Still, that feeling that there are eyes, that someone follows her. It's like a bag she carries now. One she can't leave the house without.

Slowing as she reaches the pub, she allows her arms to swing wide in windmills, then bends, catching her breath. She walks across the gravel of the tiny car park and stops outside the door to the pub entrance to stretch. She glances at Jam's bowl, which has not been moved. No one can bring themselves to take it away. The image of her lies in the garden whenever she closes her eyes.

'Ana?'

Her name lands with the crunch of gravel, sharp and biting. She spins, her heart racing quickly as though she's running again, preparing to flee.

'Jack?' She steps backwards, glancing left and right.

'Please.' He holds up his hands and stops. Stands stock still. 'Please, I just wanted to talk to you. And I thought if I did it in the morning, when it was light…'

'How do you know where I live?' Ana shakes her head. Why would he come here? He looks the same. Friendly, unassuming. He is paler, though, slightly gaunt round the gills. Slightly haunted.

He steps forward and her heart pounds.

'I knew the village when you mentioned it ages ago. I tried the other pub first, then I came here. Look, Ana, I'm not trying to frighten you, I just wanted to say that it wasn't me. I didn't push you. Of *course* I didn't push you! One minute we were standing there, and I felt a bump and fell. I was the one who pulled you back up on the platform.' He runs his hand through his hair, takes a breath. Looks like he's trying to compose himself. Another step.

'But why come here, Jack? Seriously. What's wrong with the phone?' Ana says. She bangs her fist on the thick glass of the pub window behind her. She retreats backwards towards the door. 'You know what you've been accused of, and yet you come here, find me on my own. Who does that? Don't you blokes get it? Don't you get it at all? Every new man Fran goes out with, for the first three dates we have a rule, she calls me from the loo so I know she's safe, that she's not meeting a psycho. I don't know you. I'm sure it's hard for you—'

'Hard?' His voice rises in volume. 'Ana, I can't go into work. They told me to take some time off until this is resolved! Hard? It's my reputation, Ana. My fucking reputation is in tatters.' Spit lands from his mouth on the gravel. She doesn't recognise this face, twisted in rage.

She shakes her head. She believes him, she had never really thought it was him. What investment does he have in all this? He doesn't know Ben, her. But she's scared. His coming here like this is it in a nutshell.

'Your reputation? That's it, isn't it. You're scared of what other people will think of you, and I'm scared I might get raped or murdered. That about sums it up. You've come here to salvage your honour, and found me on my own. You think by holding up his hands, a man accused of pushing me under a train won't seem to pose any threat? You just don't get it.'

The pub door opens to the left, and Maisie sticks her head out.

'Ana, you OK? I heard banging.' She sees Jack on the gravel, not moving.

'What's going on?' Maisie comes out, suspicious. 'Who's he?'

Ana wonders when she will go back to not being afraid on her own. At which point will she stand on her own with a man and not feel as though she should know where her escape route is? Ben had given her that. Ben alone had taken nothing from her.

'This is Jack. The one from the deal at work. The one who was with me on the Tube when I fell.'

'The one accused of pushing you?' Maisie comes out. She walks between Ana and Jack and puts her hands on her hips. 'If you're not gone by the time I've counted to three, we're going to call the police. Ana, go and get the phone. One.'

'But what else can I do? I just wanted to tell you it wasn't me. I just wanted you to know...'

'Two.'

'This is ridiculous! Why would I push you under a train? For fuck's sake!'

'Three.' Maisie takes the phone from Ana and presses the buttons, calling the numbers out loud: 'Nine, nine, nine.'

'Alright, I'll go. I'm sorry.' His shoulders sag in defeat.

Ana would feel sorry for him, but for the fact that she's sick of feeling sorry for men.

'Ana, call me when this is done. Please. I'll leave it for you to call me, but please do. This can't be how it ends. I want you to know I wasn't trying to hurt you.'

As he disappears round the corner, Maisie's shoulders drop a little, her head softens and she shrugs. 'Loser,' she says.

'I don't think he did it,' Ana says.

'No, I don't either. But since when did how he feels about this become more important than how you feel? You're the one who almost bloody died. And if it wasn't him, then who was it? He wasn't backing down there, not without a threat.'

'Girls, you OK?' their mum calls.

'Yes, Mum, just coming,' Maisie calls back.

Ana squeezes Maisie's hand. 'Love you.'

57

LEO

'Are you there?' Leo calls. The tent is zipped partway. The sun is falling and the colours of the sky are red, violet, blue, silver and gold.

There's a sound from inside the tent.

Leo bends. Ben's face is red with weeping. He sits in a ball, smoking. He hasn't smoked for years.

'I'm so sorry,' Leo says, and this time he feels it. What has he done?

Ben doesn't speak immediately, the silence uncomfortable. Leo tries to read his face, to gauge where they're at.

It's slow when he does speak. Ben's voice is raw. 'Mate, I've been thinking. I know how you get. I get that you two were best friends. I get it. I never thought it would be a problem.' He takes a drag and blows smoke up and out, drinking from the beer that sits by his foot. 'You know she's never said a word?'

Leo shakes his head. 'She loves you, Ben. She loves

you. It was stupid. We were beyond drunk. It wasn't even real. I was a mess.' He drops to the floor, crawling into the tent, tying up the flaps and letting in the night air, which drifts around them.

'Did you tell her about Caitlin?' Ben asks.

Leo looks out over the sea. To be honest, he can't even remember. 'I think so. I think I told her what happened with the pregnancy. I don't think I said who it was.'

'Well then, no wonder. If she thought I'd told you to ditch your pregnant girlfriend, I can imagine how she might react. She probably hated me that night. I hate myself sometimes.'

'You do?' Leo is surprised. 'I didn't realise you thought about it.'

Ben laughs, like a shout, like a car backfiring. 'Of course I fucking do! You don't think I blame myself? You were only fifteen, for God's sake. What the fuck were you supposed to do? You came to me and I let you down.'

Wrapping his arms around his knees, Leo tucks his chin on top, feeling fifteen again. 'It was still me. It was still me who let it happen. I should have been better. You were thinking about protecting me. I should have been thinking about protecting her.' She had been his first girlfriend. He'd held her hand nervously on their first date.

Ben looks at him. He passes him the cigarette and

Leo takes it, the sharp burn of smoke catching the back of his throat.

'How do we move on?' he asks, and Leo shakes his head.

The sound of birds calling, of the trees moving with a sudden burst of wind – Leo listens as he thinks of the future. 'Will you tell Ana what I've told you, that we slept together?'

'She already knows, mate! You mean tell her that I know too?' Ben's laugh is sardonic. He shrugs. 'Probably not. I need a bit of time. I need to let it settle first.' He looks at Leo. 'Just the once?'

Leo nods. 'Yes. It won't happen again. It wasn't about the sex.'

'You still angry with me?' Ben asks.

The stillness of the evening is loud. It must be about 10 p.m. now. Leo nods slowly, like he's confessing to theft. 'Yes, I think so. I think sometimes I'm blind with rage. But it passes. It doesn't last for ever. I can't seem to shake it. I don't know how to get rid of it.' The last words are a whisper. He's not sure Ben's heard, but he sees his brother nod.

He'd been fifteen, almost sixteen. Katie was about six months older and he thought maybe she was hung-over when he'd watched her vomit after school, when he'd held back her hair and asked her why she was so sick again.

'I'm pregnant,' she'd said between hurls, her skin

clammy and her face grey. 'I'm pregnant, Leo.'

He'd dropped her bag and run home. Chased by the idea of a loss of future, of a vanishing youth. Ben had been in and he'd cried in the kitchen. He'd had a few missed calls from Katie but he'd just stared at the phone, frozen by fear.

'What is it?' Ben had said, coming in to get Coke from the fridge and opening the biscuit tin.

'Katie's pregnant,' he'd said, before sitting at the kitchen table, his hands shaking.

'Shit.' Ben had sat down, pulling a chair round and sitting astride it. 'It's yours?'

Leo had shrugged. 'I guess so. I didn't wait around to ask. Fuck, Ben, what am I going to do?'

Ben had shaken his head, drinking Coke and tapping his foot furiously on the floor. 'Fuck. Well, first of all, give her some space. Whatever you do, don't go over there offering marriage or anything. You only did it once! Why didn't you use a condom? I told you to use a condom!'

'I did! We did!' Leo was crying now. 'I bought them from Boots. How can she get pregnant from one time, with a condom?'

'Fuck, Leo. Did you fuck it up?'

'I don't know!' Leo had cried and cried. He'd ignored all of Katie's calls for the next two days. He hadn't gone to the disco that night. The whole school had gone and he knew Katie was still going. He couldn't face her.

Finally, after three days of feigning the flu, he'd imagined his baby. He thought of Katie going to a clinic on her own, and he'd called her, but it had gone straight to voicemail.

He'd got dressed and headed downstairs. He had to face her.

It had been then, just as he passed through the front gate, that their neighbour, Alice, had come running out of the house in tears. 'Leo! Leo!' she'd screamed. 'Have you heard?'

The dread that had hit him then hits him now. The idea of Katie, hanging in the woods. He'd killed her. He'd abandoned her.

'I'll get you a beer.' Ben begins to crawl past him.

'No, I'll go,' Leo says, suddenly needing the air. Outside, thinking of the guilt he can't shift, Leo stares across the sea. The ocean is flat, unmoving, like time has stopped.

There's a shout below, and Leo shakes himself, forcing himself out of his reverie, seeing a cyclist fall from his bike, coming fast down the coastal path.

The sea is flat and indigo. Long boats lie still on the edge of the horizon.

58

MAARTEN

Maarten taps the desk. The coffee in front of him is now tepid, with a swirl of white forming across the skim of the surface. Although Transport has closed the file on Jack Thurbridge, with the CCTV not conclusive either way, some idiot who had been at the Tube station had given a press interview and had released Jack's name. He'd heard it during all the furore. There would be questions soon. No one liked the eye of the media staring at them – the station would be under fire to either confirm or deny.

Adrika had updated the team that morning: 'We've got the identity on the body finally. Leo Fenton, as sure as they can be.' There had been gasps, but they'd been expecting it since Norfolk. They just need the final pieces.

Maarten isn't sure if Thurbridge pushed Ana. But it still feels significant. The act of Ana falling was more than a coincidence. There is too much here, too many happenings for this to be an accident, a simple trick of fate.

And the cyclist. They had got nowhere with it. The only person who had seen the cyclist was Ben Fenton. There are circles around his notes, doodles and question marks.

'Adrika?' He leans and taps the glass wall of his office, mouthing her name.

'Yes?' she says, walking in.

'Do we have a photo of Jack Thurbridge? Not a police one, where he looks guilty, but any other one? One where he looks natural, like a cyclist you'd invite for a drink.'

'He's got a Facebook page. I could print one off, but he's wearing some kind of hat dress-up – like a photo booth picture. It's not great for ID. I tried to call earlier, but I can't get hold of him. I tried his flat and his work. I hope he's not taken himself off somewhere with all the press attention. Be useful to ask him for a photo.' She purses her lips. 'Wait a minute, Ana Seabrook sent something through. She'd shown Sunny a picture she'd taken of the trial group and he'd asked her to send it over. Hang on.' She disappears.

Maarten drinks the coffee. Why is it you can buy iced coffee and hot coffee, and they both taste perfectly reasonable, but lukewarm coffee tastes like bile?

Sunny enters. 'Alright, sir. Adrika says you want the photo of Thurbridge. Here we go. Seabrook showed it to me during her statement about her relationship to Thurbridge. I wondered if it would be useful.'

'Sunny, you are doing really well at the moment. You're going over and above. Could be time for you to think about your next set of exams.'

Slipping his hands in his pockets, Sunny reddens under the praise. His blond hair flops forward as he nods his thanks and steps backwards out of the room.

The photo is of a group of people in hospital gowns, with Jack Thurbridge in the middle. There's also another man, the lawyer from Seabrook's office, looking stiff and slightly uncomfortable, but Thurbridge is front and centre, smiling widely. It's a great photo.

'Sunny!' he calls.

Turning and coming back in, Sunny nods. 'Sir?'

'Fancy taking this up to Ben Fenton to ID first thing tomorrow? The drive's not too bad. Could you get him to have a look at this? See if he recognises Thurbridge as the cyclist? It's a bit of a long shot. Head home afterwards. No need to come back into the office.'

'No problem.' Sunny disappears and Maarten takes another sip of the coffee, gagging. He puts the mug down and looks out of the window. A vague theory forming in his mind.

59

BEN

'Oi, why does he get out and I have to sit in this oven? Not fucking fair, innit. I'm only asking for what he gets. Fucking special is he...'

Kiz's voice rattles on as Ben is led down the platform, gradually fading as he moves further away. He can see over the barrier on his left, and Macca is down there, looking up at him. A sneer on his face, in his eyes. Ben is being watched.

Ben doesn't blame Kiz. The cell is hotter than an oven. There'd been an item on daytime television about how hot it needs to be in places of work before you should be able to be legally sent home. Apparently, there is no current limit but this heatwave has produced calls for a limit to be set. What about in here? They sweat and sit. Lethargy seeps in. Frustration, anger – both fermenting. Brewing.

Ben is also pleased to be out of the cell just to be moving. The news that morning had reported a man allegedly had tried to push Ana under a train. He still hasn't quite calmed down. He'd spoken to her over the weekend and she'd told him about the incident, but had played it down, said that she'd fallen only on the platform. But a murky phone-video has been released to the press. She'd fallen further than the platform. He burns with rage. That he's stuck in here, and can't go to her.

'Police in here, Benny. Best behaviour, eh.' Burke nods as he opens the door.

A blond man in plain, dark clothes stands. 'Hello, I'm DS Atkinson. I work with DCI Jansen, who you met last time?'

Ben sits as the man explains he has a photo, that they have a possible picture of the cyclist. Is it him? Ben's stomach growls like it's hungry, his blood hot. His senses on red alert.

He tries not to grab it as the photo comes into view over the other side of the table. He stretches out his hand for it prematurely, before the officer has finished speaking. Pulls it from him a little.

'Here, is this him?' The policeman nods to the photo on the table Ben holds. There's a group of people, some look overweight, all dressed in their gowns, with their arms around each other.

Looking down, he sees the face, and his pulse quickens further. His head shakes, his hands shake. He can see the policeman watching him. He tries to speak but it takes a moment.

'Fuck,' Ben says, lifting the photo to his face. 'Fuck.'

He goes to speak but the face... The face is burned in his brain, the whole night is branded behind his lids, pressed into his memory in hot reels on the end of a blacksmith's iron.

'That's him. I'm sure that's him. The cyclist. I mean, he's quite distinctive, he stands out. It's him.'

'Really?' The policeman pulls out his phone, pressing a number. 'You need to be sure.'

'Yes, I know him. The one in the centre of the photo. It's not a face I've thought about, not on purpose, but it's been in my dreams. I can't shake those twenty-four hours. They just appear.' He feels dizzy, but also alive. This must be it, this must be the thing that sets him free. No, he'd never really thought of it before, not from that angle. 'And he's the one who pushed Ana under a train? He tried to kill her?'

'There's an allegation.'

The policeman smiles at him, then leans to the side. His phone is lit. 'Adrika, it's me. He's confirmed. Can you let the guv know when you get the message? On my way back.'

'You.' Ben lifts it again, looking closely. He taps the centre of the photo, wiping a tear from his face, rubbing his forehead hard with the base of his hand. 'But why?' he asks, staring at the face. 'Why would he do it?'

60

ANA

'Is he here?'

'Who?' Ana says, smiling at the DI. It's the one she likes, with the brown bob, who had dealt easily with Fabian.

'Jack Thurbridge. The last sighting we have is his car heading towards Ayot, heading towards your pub.'

Ana notes she's not smiling today. She's not angry, but she looks official. Less sympathetic than she has been. Ana is hot. She's just back from a run and she hasn't even had a drink. Her mouth is dry, and she's sticky with sweat, her head light. She's been running off the demons.

'Oh, yes. He was here the other day. He came early in the morning. I'd been for a run…' Ana lets the sentence trail away. The expression on the DI's face is unchanged. She already knew he had been here. That hadn't been the real question.

Ana opens the door wide and stands back. 'Do you

336

want to come in?' she says, thinking it seems like there's something serious to say. Thinking she needs a drink, her throat parched.

The DI looks left and right, like she's checking for someone. But there's no one else here. She doesn't move.

Ana can hear Jess inside, putting the bucket away. The door to the cupboard under the stairs closes. Her footsteps sound on the stone floor.

She tries again. 'Look, the cleaner is just finishing. I'll be on my own if you want to speak privately about something. Is it Ben? Is there news about Ben?'

'All done,' Jess says. She's wearing a T-shirt with Wonder Woman on the front. She changes into her purple trainers beside Ana, putting her inside shoes into her bag. 'I'll be off, then.'

It will be all over the village later, that the police were here again. That something's brewing.

'Thanks, Jess,' Ana says, smiling, willing her to just leave. The DI has brought a tension with her and dread lies across Ana's stomach. The DI hasn't smiled once. If Ben were ill, surely she'd be looking sympathetic. It's something else, but how many more things can there be?

'Off to the hospital?' she asks Jess.

'Yes, looks like Aggie's getting out today or tomorrow. Going to put her in a home. She can't look after herself any more. Can't face the prospect of any more home fires. At least I won't have to make the trip to Stevenage any more. Costing me all my favours in lifts and spare change on the bus.'

The DI steps back, allowing Jess to pass. They both watch her walk over the gravel, exit under the sign for the pub.

'Please,' Ana says, 'what is it? Please tell me.'

'Jack Thurbridge hasn't been seen for a few days. The last known sighting we have of him is on his way here. You've confirmed his arrival. Ana, can you tell me what happened?'

Ana can hear a buzzing in her ears, at first faint, but it grows louder. She rubs her right ear with her hand, batting away an imaginary bee. It grows louder still.

The DI seems to take her silence as refusal to speak. Her face hardens further. 'Ana, we need to get a full statement about Jack's visit.'

The buzzing is loud now, and the heat, as heavy as it has been for the last thirty days, becomes oppressive. It weaves around her, threading itself, kneading her legs, her arms. Ana just can't stand it any more. Her knees are soft, and the picture of the DI, standing at the entrance to the pub, becomes blue, and then a hazy grey, and then black.

And then nothing.

61

MAARTEN

'No sign?' Maarten asks as Adrika returns.

'Ana Seabrook has nothing. She said he left.'

'Sunny has his car abandoned nearby, I've sent him out with a team to follow up searching the local area. He's our number-one suspect now. We need to find him.' Maarten is at the board ticking, crossing, making notes. 'We need to find Thurbridge and find the identity of whoever rented the shed. As we have identified Thurbridge as the cyclist, we're expecting them both to be the same person, but then we can charge him. Particularly as we have DNA from the shed. But to do all this, we need him.'

He turns, feeling warm even with the air con. This heat has reached baking point. Something will break soon. The seat belt had burned his neck this morning as he'd got in the car. The country is browning, melting, wilting and they need rain soon.

Adrika sits behind her desk. She begins saying, 'The

graveyard, there was something,' but a door bangs at the far end of the room, and Maarten hears the clip of heels.

'I've got permission to work here for a couple of days. We're quiet up in Norfolk and the Super's nervous about PR since your find in the shed.' It's Harper, sweeping in. She drops her bag on the desk next to Adrika, and Adrika smiles at her.

'Great. Can I leave you two to run this for an hour? I need to prepare quickly for the press conference.' Maarten checks his watch. 'Adrika, check in with Sunny, and let me know the moment we hear anything.'

Nodding, Adrika smiles. 'Of course.'

Is it just him, full of gratitude that Liv has come home and brimming with love at her being safe again, that sees Adrika's smile much warmer than it has been? Her eyes are bright. As he walks towards his office, he sees Harper pull up a chair and put her hand on Adrika's arm. She says something, and he hears Adrika laugh as he closes the office door, leaning in to Harper.

This heat has burned something away between them. It hasn't taken the life out of everything.

The press release is read and rehearsed, containing an update on Jack Thurbridge, communicating his disappearance. He's almost at the doors to the stairs when Adrika shouts across the room, 'Sir, we've had

Ana Seabrook on the phone. The desk sergeant's on the line now.'

'Put it through, would you?' he says, picking up the nearest phone. 'Yes?'

'Ana Seabrook is feeling better, and she wanted to let us know that when Thurbridge was at their house the other day, she had felt watched that morning.'

'Thanks,' Maarten says, replacing the phone. He thinks for a second. 'Adrika? I'm doing this press conference quickly, then I'll head out to Ayot. Ana Seabrook's remembered something. The car was near there so I'll coordinate the search for Thurbridge with Sunny after I've spoken with her.'

'We're close – I think we'll have news soon.'

'Good work.' He turns as Harper bends to Adrika, her head near.

They're the two best officers he's got. They will sort this, he can feel it in his bones.

62

Friday 29th June

MAARTEN

The road narrows as Maarten approaches Ayot, and the tips of the trees meet over the passageway, like a bridal arch. The sunlight is filtered through the leaves. Blackberries have started to sprout early. It's the heat, Liv had said. It was the heat signalling an early harvest. The trees in the back of his garden have brought the first apples to fruit. Nothing is moving as it should. This heatwave has disturbed the natural order.

He parks his car out on the road by the pub. A handful of press are gathered around the house. Someone flashes a camera as he makes his way through. Maisie Seabrook stands guard at the entrance to the gravel car park, not letting anyone past. She steps aside to let him go by. 'They arrived earlier. That video of Ana being pulled off the tracks has gone viral. Fucking leeches.'

He smiles as he slips through, saying, 'Good work.' Ana Seabrook is in good hands.

She is waiting for him by the door to the pub garden. She looks drained, in running shorts and one of those sleeveless mesh sports tops, falling in scoops under the arms. She wears a chunky running watch, the kind he uses when he goes out on his bike. Her face is washed clean, paler.

As the sun becomes intense, as the heat from the walls threatens to topple him, he nods quickly.

'Let's go inside,' he says.

Her movements are jerky, and she pushes her fingers across her brow repeatedly, smoothing tight new furrows.

'You told the station you'd been watched. Was it Thurbridge?' he asks. They stand by the bar. The blinds are lowered and it's stifling. He feels the walls closing in.

'Yes, I'm sure there was someone watching me, and then Jack came to visit. It could easily have been him. I didn't really believe it was him at the time. He's always seemed so nice…' She drifts off, and her fingers rub her brow again. There are red marks appearing, and like when he watches Sanne scratching her eczema, he has the urge to lift her hand away from her skin.

'I'm telling you this, but it's not for general interest – Ben has confirmed that Jack Thurbridge was the cyclist.'

'Christ!' She looks ashen, leans back against the bar. 'I can't believe it.'

'Look, I'm going to have to go. We're searching for him now, but this is the last place he was seen coming. You're the last person to see him.'

Maarten's phone buzzes. He answers, swinging round as some gesture of privacy.

'It's A. Miller!' Adrika's voice vibrates with excitement down the phone. 'We've got the bank account from which the payments were made and found a link to an A. Miller. We had to go through a few steps to find it. The first name on the account was John Smith, but we managed to follow the money put into the account, and that came from A. Miller. It took some finding – Harper made the final leap. Jack Thurbridge must be Andy Miller.'

Maarten glances at Ana, unwilling to share this just yet. She would have mentioned it a while ago if she'd recognised him, but it wouldn't take too much to change your adult identity from your childhood one. Andy Miller's name has come up more than once.

'Adrika, this is great work. We need to find him. Meet me with Sunny? I'm leaving now. Can you send Harper to The Frog? She knows Ana Seabrook well and it would be useful to get a formal statement from her, now she's feeling better.'

If Andy Miller is Jack Thurbridge, then it all makes sense.

He turns back to Ana, who is ashen against the bar. She looks like she might faint again. He feels a stab of sympathy for her. 'You know Harper Carroll well, don't you? She's on her way here to be with you. I'll need to check on the search so I'm going to have to leave but she'll take your full statement. You're going to be safe now, Ana. We're going to find him.'

She nods. *Brave*, he thinks as he makes his way to the door. Trusting the truth and your instincts in the face of such a campaign of terror is as brave as you get.

What will be uncovered today, before the sun cools and the moon brings its gentle relief?

On his way to the car, he glances at the Palladian church across the field.

Caitlin Miller. Caitlin Miller. That name. The graveyard.

The image of a headstone: 'Beloved daughter and sister.'

There's something else. What had Adrika said? She'd read it out on the very first day. She had died on the day they had uncovered the body, ten years ago, but the same day. And Adrika had remarked upon the coincidence.

Caitlin. Katie.

'Adrika?' He picks up his car keys as he speaks into the phone. 'That gravestone we saw on the first day, Caitlin Miller. You were going to tell me something about the graveyard earlier. What was it? Was it to do with Caitlin Miller?'

'She was in school with Ana Seabrook, sir. And you remember Ben Fenton told us about Andy Miller, who he suspected had tried it on with Ana in some way? He was her brother.'

They are back near the Palladian church, on one of the walking routes.

'Over here!'

Maarten runs over to where Sunny is standing.

'It's his car keys. He's dropped his car keys. He must have come down here. He must have left his car and run for it.'

Maarten looks down at the keys. He can feel the excitement in the team. He might not be far.

His phone buzzes. 'Yes?' he says, answering.

'Sir, we've got some more CCTV in. It shows Thurbridge swerving to avoid a press van, then pulling off the main road just out of Ayot. He must have been spooked, gone to ground.'

'Brilliant.' Maarten looks down the path, the ground hard, and the sun is fierce. 'Let's move quickly. He could easily have hitch-hiked, or walked to the nearest station. If he's still around here we'll have to be fast. Can you get me a list of hotels and B&Bs around here and send it over?'

'On it.'

Maarten looks out across the sparse yellowed grass

and gestures ahead. 'He's somewhere down here. If he's left the road, he must have gone down here. Maybe he thinks he can hide out and get away once the attention has died down.' He takes a step forward, raising his hand to shield his eyes from the glare of the sun. There's a farmhouse further ahead, and a cluster of cottages. 'Adrika's sending a list through. Can you start door-knocking? He might have found somewhere empty. Check no one's away on holiday in those cottages, and get the farm buildings checked. If he's panicking, he could be anywhere. We need DNA confirmation before we charge him. Make sure you keep it calm.'

Maarten is on the phone to the Super, under the shade of a tree, when the shout comes.

'Got him, sir! He'd broken into an empty cottage, claims he's innocent but was hiding from the press. He'd seen your statement, knew he was chief suspect. He's in a bit of a state.'

Telling the Super he'll update him soon, Maarten pockets his phone and shouts back, 'Good work. Get him to the station. Make sure you get him checked by a doctor – dehydration et cetera. We'll interview him soon. Can you let the station know you're on your way?'

Maarten leans back against the tree. The shade is a welcome relief. It might be almost finished.

The sun burns in the empty sky, but there are clouds appearing too. There might be relief all round.

63

Friday 29th June

BEN

The cyclist. They've found him.

But there's something else. It's niggling away at him. What is it?

That face. There's something about that face.

What was it? What was it about the photo?

Fuck. But can it be him? Surely he had brown hair, not blond.

It was him.

It is definitely him.

He bangs on the cell door. 'Hello? Hello?'

'What's up?' It's Mr Burke. 'Kiz gone under again?' He looks behind Ben, into the cell.

'No, I've remembered something. The police who were here. They showed me a photo, and I've remembered something.'

Burke tips his head to the side. 'Now, now, Benny. Not like you to cause a scene. You asking me to get the police back up here? You know that will take time.'

'Can I just speak to him? To the officer who was here? Could you please just let him know? I'm not messing around. I know what it looks like. Wanting special attention, wanting to get out of my pad for a few hours, get some...' He shakes his head. 'Please, Mr Burke.' Desperation now. 'What we said. Remember. Please.'

Burke turns round slowly. Ben knows he's suggested he has something to share. Of course he knows how Macca gets the stuff in. They all know. His sister soaks the pages of the magazines in spice, then she brings them in. Macca sells them like candy in a playground. The young uniform turns a blind eye, doesn't get the magazine checked like all the reading material is supposed to be checked. If he tells Burke, he's dead in here. Or maybe this gets him out.

'OK, Benny. As you're asking. I'll see what I can do.'

The slow gait of the retreating man stirs Ben. Makes him aware he needs to throw the watching inmates off the scent. They need to know it's about the case. It can't seem like grassing.

'It's important! About the photo they brought!'

Burke lifts a hand to show he's heard, but doesn't hurry.

Macca is nearby, shouts out. 'Look at 'im! Knows something, does he. Needs a bit of guard time. Aye aye.'

Ben spins, stands with his back flat to the wall. Eyes closed.

He's sure. The cyclist is Andy Miller from school. He'd bet his freedom on it – bet his life.

64

Two Years Earlier
June

LEO

'Christ,' says the cyclist, extending a hand. 'Ow, shit. I came off good and proper.' His accent has a twang and Leo takes his hand, helping him up.

Leo had been walking out to get another beer when he'd seen the bike tip and had run down to help. The man had still been crumpled in a heap when Leo had reached the coastal path.

'That was a bad one. Bike OK?' he asks as the man rises.

'Think so.' He lifts it and drops it down on the tyres, looking at the wheels, spinning the back one round. 'Yeah, fine. I'll just catch my breath for a minute then I should be OK to head on. You walking the path? Lucky for me.'

Leo shakes his head, gesturing up the bank. 'Camping.'

The cyclist looks up. 'Any chance you've got some water? I'm out.'

Leo hesitates for a second. It's not what Ben or he needs right now, but then again, a chat with a stranger for a few minutes might help break the ice. Smooth things over.

'I can go one better. My brother's up there too. Come for a beer?'

'If you're sure? I'm Matt, by the way.'

'Leo, and my brother is Ben. Come on, we're just up here.'

Scrambling up the bank, Leo snags his hand on a branch and it stings. He sees a touch of blood, and as they arrive at the flat site, he sucks the edge of his hand before reaching into the cooler for a few bottles.

'Ben!' he calls. 'We've got company.'

Ben emerges, looking anything but happy to see Matt, but he quickly smiles and heads out to join them. Leo throws himself down on the ground and looks across the sea at the falling sun.

'You're cycling late,' he says.

Matt takes off his helmet, laying it by his side, and takes a drink. 'Yeah, mate. I got a flat further back, which set me back about half an hour. Not got long to go now. I told my buddies to head off without me. They're waiting at a pub further down the track. We've got some rooms booked for the night. Not roughing it exactly.'

Leo smiles, taking a swallow. He's starting to regret inviting this stranger up to have a drink. Ben is quiet, and he thinks of the things he wants to say. Perversely, he's pleased he's finally told him about his night with Ana. He'd never liked keeping secrets from Ben.

Ben smiles, nodding at the track. 'Nice bike.'

'She's not bad. Check this out,' Matt says, holding out a camera. 'Got some great shots earlier. My new helmet camera: new toy. Here, let me hold your beer.' He hands the camera to Ben, who passes him his beer.

Leo leans in to look. The shots are crystal. 'It's a Garmin?' he asks.

Matt nods. 'Yeah, I looked at GoPro, I think when you're going top of the range there's not much in it.'

Leo tunes out, tired. He finishes his beer quickly, really regretting asking Matt up. There's some discussion of cameras, Matt mentions his mates, his sister. Ben had bought a new fishing knife for the trip, but they've not fished yet. Leo uses it to carve off a hunk of soft white cheese, laying it on a large wooden board, smearing it over some French bread. He tears off more chunks and hands it round.

The sky sits like a dark velvet curtain, suspended above them, and the sea is still. Even the flies are starting to disappear and Leo's at the point when he's about to say he's turning in when Matt stands and offers a thanks. 'Best head off,' he says. 'Thanks for the drink. It was good to rest up for half an hour. I'll be off.'

He moves quickly, lifting his arm and heading down the bank.

Ben rubs his head with his hand, the beginnings of a headache. He reaches into the nearby bag and pulls out a sharing bag of crisps. 'Chips?' he says, smiling and offering the bag to Leo.

It's his piss-take of Leo's Americanisms and Leo smiles. It's a peace offering.

It's not going to be easy. But maybe it will be OK.

65

BEN

The water from the shower falls hard on Ben's head. Even in the shower he sweats, the heat like an oven today. He feels its press, swamping him. He tips his head forward, touching his forehead to the stainless steel, feeling the water on his neck.

He needs to let the police know. The man in the middle of the photo… It's been ticking over in his brain, but it's landed like a plane on fire, zinging.

'Come on, lads. Speed it up.' The guard's shout is loud, but Ben hears a cry at the end of it. A yelp.

'Oi, stop that!' The guard's voice is angry now, has an edge to it. He's scared, Ben thinks. And the room takes on an energy that is familiar. And makes him tremble.

Ben sees the guard take a step backwards. Another stands by the door and they exchange a look. The one by the door speaks into his radio.

A bottle, shampoo perhaps, flies over and smacks the guard full in the face, and then there is banging. The prisoners start banging on the showers, on the metal, hitting it hard with whatever they can lay their hands on. A cacophony of shower gel. Of soap bars.

Ben goes cold. He flattens his back against the side of the shower wall.

No. Not now. Not when he's so close to getting out. To being free.

'Right, you lot want to fight?' The shout of the guard is barely audible. 'Well, fucking fight then!' He retreats.

Ben wants to run after them, to say he's not involved in all this. He's just here by mistake.

The doors lock. He knows two guards aren't enough. They will call for backup, and if it's a riot they send for the lot that are an hour away. Procedure is to lock the doors until they have the numbers.

He's locked in here.

Even the ones who weren't in on it have taken the scent like baying wolves, and he closes his eyes. All he can hope is that by staying here, staying quiet, staying with his head down, he'll remain unscathed. He assumes they're after Tabs.

Tabs is bleeding, over the other side. He's kneeling on the tiles and the blood from his mouth spills into the swirling pools of water that run down the plugholes. The water amplifies the blood. One teaspoon becomes a pint. One pint a bucket. Soon, the ground is soaked like a battlefield.

But they've stopped. The fists were quick. It's not Tabs today.

'Getting out, I hear?' Macca stands at the edge of Ben's shower. His feet planted like trees, his pit-bull snarl smiles at Ben, lip caught just at one edge. His hair shaved down, a faint tattoo on his scalp.

'We thought it would only be fair to send you off with a goodbye party, since you're asking. Wouldn't want you to miss out, like. Eh, Benny boy.'

Ben's heart races, his breath comes in spurts. They've come for him. Not for Tabs. They've come for him.

'Please, I'll pay you. You can have everything on my canteen. Please, anything.'

'Knows how to pay, this one. Don't he.' Macca's breath is hot on his face. Someone kicks him in the lower back. Someone else lands a blow to the back of his ribs. They pull him out of his cubicle. He grabs the steel with his fingers, but they slip, and he sees the trails of his own desperation marked out as his fingernails scratch on the scored walls.

He's horizontal now. His legs kick upwards, his trunk dipping and rising, trying to shake off the hands. But they're clamped. There's no breaking free.

The fear in Tabs's eyes is all for him as he scrambles up and back out of the way. He sees in glimpses Tabs move to the back, and he knows he can do nothing for him, but he still screams his name, through the heat, the water vapour, the smell that stands in the room like a body.

'Tabs!'

'He can't help you, mate. That nonce.' Macca's face is close and Ben can smell tobacco.

'Macca, you want me to do him?'

Ben can't see who speaks but thinks of the tall man with dark hair whose arm Macca broke last year. Who has spent the last few months like a lapdog, head bowed, anxious to avoid trouble, to offer up his fists in exchange for a free pass.

'Nah.' Macca spits, and the globule lands on Ben's cheek, sliding slowly down.

'Got more than fists for you, we have. Something special, innit.'

His mouth is clamped. He struggles back against the hands pressing his shoulders down.

Ben's hands are pulled tight round his back. He's flipped up and over, and he lies flat on the floor; his face chokes on water, on blood. On shampoo bubbles.

There's a knee in his back and someone clamps him in a headlock, his chin straining against someone's forearm, the bent curve of the inner elbow to the right of Ben's jaw.

His back strains, his neck strains. He can hear the alarm sounding. He can hear gathering voices outside. Maybe they've got enough guards together. Maybe they're coming back in.

The metal of the damaged vape is brown at the join. The smoky glass valve, a sure sign of spice, is active. A tiny volcano, about to blow apart his world.

'No,' he tries to say, spitting the water from the floor. His kidneys ache and someone must be sitting on his lower legs. His calves scream.

'Not sure, are we, Benny? You'll love it.'

The hand at the back of his head presses him hard. It forces his head forward and the back of his neck aches He can't open his mouth to shout for help, because it's pointless. There's no one to help.

'It's total zoning out, it's fucking lush!' Kiz says, his voice high in pitch, excited. But Ben can see the fear in his eyes.

'But I tell you what, if he don't want it, I'll take it. Give it to me, I'll take it.' Kiz's eyes find Ben's. Ben's panic is fierce but he knows Kiz is trying, trying to save him.

He holds Kiz's eyes with his own, his head rocking back as far as it will go, his neck pulling tight, as though something will snap.

He kicks his feet, trying to grind his toes into the floor and push back, away from Macca, who lowers his weight and his fat hands; that smell of nicotine, of dope, approaches his face. But the weight on his legs holds him. He doesn't move an inch.

'Oh, he wants it. Look at him. He just doesn't know it yet. You know you want it, Benny boy. Been too good for the likes of us, ain't yer. Well, not any more. You're one of us now. Teach you how to behave in 'ere.' He lowers his head and his words hiss into Ben's ear. 'Think you can fucking snitch on me? When they find you high on this we'll let them know who's been hoarding it in here. I'll put a stash in your pad. Get your sentence extended. I've got five here who'll swear blind you sold it to them.'

'Aw, come on, Macca. You can give it to me. Why waste it on him?' Kiz's voice is in the distance now. Ben can't see anything beyond the metal, which comes closer. Macca's voice a confidant in his ear.

His body tenses; he shakes his head. There's a sound outside. Will they come in? Will they get to him in time? He opens his mouth to shout for help. His chest won't take it. He's still on the antibiotics, he's weak.

'Help me—'

And it's clamped into his mouth, thrust almost at the back of his throat, and he feels himself gagging, trying not to breathe it in. Trying to hold his breath.

But the tightness in his throat, his neck. The pain in his head. He can tell he's going to inhale, and there's nothing he can do to stop it.

'Argh!' he shouts. As loud as he can make it.

The last sight he sees is Kiz's brown eyes, worried, darting back, looking to the door.

Tabs by the door, hammering with his fist, his mouth moving, but Ben can't hear anything.

There's no sound any more.

66

ANA

Hot chocolate, with brandy for the shock, warms her hands; exhaustion makes her drowsy. The adrenaline of earlier has faded and leaves behind it a blankness. Lassitude. The three of them sit, curled on the sofas. The pitter-patter of rain is light outside.

'I don't think I'll be able to sleep,' Maisie says. 'Or eat. My stomach is still in knots. Thank God he's been arrested. It's all over.' She shakes her head. 'I'm done in.'

They'd been told to rest for the night. Statements and final interviews could wait.

Ana, sick that someone has waged such war against her, feels broken. This thing has tried to smother her.

'Any of us think they'll get any sleep tonight?' she says, a laugh stopping in her throat.

'Rain's getting heavier,' her mum says, glancing outside.

They gaze at the darkening window. The tapping of the water louder now.

'Shit! I left the washing out!' Maisie jumps up. 'Haven't had to worry about that for a while. I'll head out and bring it in. You two go on to bed. I'll lock up.'

She hugs Ana on her way out. 'It's almost over. Crap as it is, it's nearly finished.'

It must be well past midnight. She checks her clock: only 10.56 p.m.

She has kicked the sheet off. It lies in a tangle on the floor. Her vest is damp. Her PJ shorts are twisted round her legs.

Rain crashes outside. It must be that which has woken her.

But she's tense. The beating of her heart is fast, racing. She forces herself to take a deep breath. To listen.

No, there's a beep. It's a noise that's woken her, but she's not sure what.

Something is niggling in her brain. There's something wrong. She doesn't know what it is. Like when you might have left the iron on.

Or left the washing out in the rain.

There's another beep. It's a text message. She picks up the phone. There are two of them.

LEO: Not gone yet, Ana.

LEO: Got something you might want back.

She runs down the corridor. She would call out but she still doesn't have control of her breathing, and she's crying. Not tonight. Please, not Maisie. Don't let it be Maisie.

The door to Maisie's room cracks ajar, but the curtains remain open. The bed lies made.

There's no Maisie.

There's no one at all.

67

Friday 29th June

MAARTEN

'Katie, can I ask you about Katie? Aggie, who is Katie?'

He sees her pupils shrink as she opens her eyes to the light. His hand is on her arm, but gently. It's never entirely dark in the hospital, even at 11 p.m.; it had taken a while to be allowed to wake her.

Pale, almost translucent, the blue is watery as her lids lift a crack.

'Is it morning? Already? Did I sleep?'

'Aggie, this is Maarten, the policeman. I'm Liv's husband. She went home this morning, do you remember? You called her Katie?'

The pale face is soft around the cracks that line her skin like ruts in the earth. They fill with tears. The rain has started outside. He can hear a clang, the ring of water on the glass panes.

'Katie.' She cries, her sobs come, and she gulps them back. She grabs his hand quickly, squeezing it tight, pulling him in. 'I didn't say,' she whispers. 'I promised I wouldn't tell and I didn't. Even when...'

The sobs overtake her and the nurse steps forward.

'Look, I'm sorry, she's getting upset. You can't carry on,' she says.

'One more try?' he asks. 'Please?'

Nodding, reluctant, stepping back, the nurse is nervous; glances at the door.

He doesn't have long.

'Aggie, you didn't tell about what? What was it that Katie asked you not to tell?'

'I didn't, I didn't say a word. Not a word. Not even when I heard her mum was frail, and came back, asking round, asking everyone if they knew why she'd done it. I never said.'

'What did Katie do, Aggie?'

'Well, killed herself, of course!' Aggie's tone is now cross. She pushes Maarten's hand away. 'Be off with you! Pretending you don't know she hung herself up in them woods. And all because of that baby. That little baby. Barely anything it was. Just a tiny heartbeat. A tiny beat. Then it was gone. It was all she wanted. Her dad had left them, her mother was never around. That baby was the brightest thing to happen to her. When she lost it, I saw her... broken. They talk about miscarriage like it's nothing. When she bled, when she lost it, she grieved like she'd lost the breathing baby. And she thought he'd killed it – payback for what he did.'

'What happened to the baby? Did someone hurt it?'

'Don't be so stupid! It was nature, taking its course. You can't hurt it. Not like that. Only weeks it had been growing. Stupid, don't be stupid.' Aggie's eyelids are falling and her head tips back down. He can see white hairs sticking up at angles from the chin, catching the shine of the strip light. The crevasses in her face, empty of water, relax out.

'Katie killed herself? She hanged herself? Because she lost her baby?'

'Barely eight weeks, it was, I'd guess. Barely anything at all. That baby was all the love she was missing. And she never even told the dad. She said she'd tried to tell her boyfriend but he'd run off. The dad was from school, she said. It broke her mum, her dying like that. Cried that she should have listened more, that she should have been there. They moved away, didn't they. But I never said. I never said a word. It's a sin, suicide, isn't it. But I never said. She just needed someone to talk to. I know she'd have changed her mind, once it was too late.'

The nurse steps forward again, and this time it's clear she means it. 'That's enough now. We need to let her sleep.'

Outside the hospital, Maarten stands under the covered entrance, next to a patient in a white gown, smoking a cigarette and holding their IV unit, wheeled out alongside them.

The rain falls on the flat roof above them and it's hard to hear Adrika's voice as she answers her phone.

He doesn't want to shout, to pass it on to everyone. But he needs to be heard. 'Katie is the one who hanged herself. She must be Caitlin, it must be the same girl. And she had been pregnant. Only just, but she lost the baby very early. It's got to be that. It must be.'

Adrika's voice crackles down. The rain soaking everything. Even the signal sounds waterlogged. 'It says in the report she was found by her brother, an A. Miller. It's him again.'

Maarten looks up. The rain is biblical. Cigarette smoke curls back under the entrance, blown by the weight of the water cascading; torrents from the sky. It all started at the graveyard.

'Something is niggling. Meet me in Ayot. I'm leaving now. We need to check the graveyard one more time. I know it's late – shouldn't be long,' he says, and he pockets his phone then runs to the car.

The smell of antiseptic and ash merges with the perfume of the newly soaked flowers. Nature bends under the downpour they have waited for, the earth has been thirsty for.

It falls like a flood.

68

LEO

It's dark. The wind is howling and Leo hears a noise. Listening in the black of night, he feels scared. It's an uncomfortable sensation – he has no idea why he feels the fright. There's nothing to fear out here. He's camped in Canada, near the bears – there it makes sense to be on red alert. And in the Australian outback. There they have snakes.

'Ben,' he hisses. He shakes his brother but he's dead to the world. 'Ben,' he says again, but nothing. He's out for the count.

Cursing, he unzips the tent and looks outside.

In a second, he feels his head in a lock. He shouts, but there's nothing, the hold just tightens. In the panic of the instant, he wonders if it's an animal... but of course it isn't. He's being attacked.

'My wallet's inside,' he stutters out. The air is cold and he can see the sea in the moonlight – black and purple.

Something sharp pokes at his chest. He's sure it's a knife. He starts to panic, shifting left and right, but the hold round his neck is tight.

A voice whispers in his ear. 'Leo Fenton. Remember me?'

Leo can't see who it is, doesn't recognise the voice. The sharp point at his chest presses hard. He's wearing an old Springsteen T-shirt; he thinks of the grey soaking to black.

'Who are you?' he manages. Talking is difficult. His throat is tight. Panic makes his breath shallow.

'Don't worry so much about who I am as who my sister is. Is there anyone to whom you should be saying sorry, Leo Fenton? Anyone in this world?'

There's something about a wished-for penance, Leo thinks, in what is almost his last thought. You wish for it, but when it arrives, as this has arrived, all he can think about is the value of life. Of life bold and bright. The dark of the sea, of the night sky. This is his last vision. He soaks it up, desperately hoping Ben will wake. He starts to struggle – really struggle. He is strong, but these hands are stronger.

'You're Andy Miller,' he manages. Tears fall down his face and he thinks of what he did. Has he always expected some kind of payback?

'You're Andy Miller,' he says again, and the hold slackens off round his neck. The knife is still sharp, and he knows that to struggle too much will be deadly.

'What are you going to do?' Leo asks, although he knows. He hears the accent twang, recognises the voice. 'You're the cyclist from earlier,' he says. 'But the accent?'

Leo thinks of Katie's elder brother. He had been an indie muso, with longish brown hair. Brown eyes. Girls had fancied him. He hadn't recognised him at all.

"Accents can be adopted, Leo. And I broke my nose surfing. Getting it fixed changed my face – that's when I changed my name. Gave me a new start, for a while. But you think it's easy holding on after your sister goes, just like that?' His voice is soft, it creeps into Leo's ear, like a serpent. Whatever accent he'd been affecting he drops now, as easily as he'd picked it up. 'Let's see how your brother handles it. Handles losing you. You fucking abandoned her. I found her. Hanging. Imagine that? You were her boyfriend. You should have been there. You deserve to pay.'

Leo shouts. His own voice echoes back at him. He screams for Ben.

'No point, mate. Popped some stuff in his beer.'

The velvet sea, the midnight-blue sky. A full moon.

He thinks of Fleeta, of Katie. He thinks of Ana.

He thinks of Ben.

69

Saturday 30th June

ANA

'Maisie!' The rain falls vertically, in lines of black rope that come from the sky and lie precisely perpendicular to the earth, like arrow rods. It lashes, throwing itself down, a beast. Plunging, bouncing back upwards, the drops hit the ground with rebound.

Ana searches left and right, running. Screaming.

'Maisie!'

Running up the road, she is wearing only flip-flops, and her feet betray her, slipping sideways, tipping her. She kicks them off, running. The air is tight in her lungs and she sprints faster.

'Maisie!'

There are lights across the field. They are flashing. Ana grabs the wooden fence, straining to see. They flash again.

Holding the top of the fence, she vaults over, spinning her legs and landing with her knees bent, in a crouch, and then sprinting up again. The grass is slippery;

stems broken off when the grass was brittle are sharp underfoot. They spear her feet like needles.

She runs.

'Maisie!'

Her fists are clenched. Her eyes strain to see, strain to find her.

'Maisie!'

There. There she is. She is bent forward, holding her knees, leaning like she's having trouble breathing. And the rain has drenched her. Her hair lies flat on her head, plastered, slicked.

'Oh God, Maisie. Are you...' But Ana can see Maisie is struggling to stand. She's not bent to help herself catch her breath, she's bent because there's weight on her neck. There's weight pushing her down.

They stand at the edge of the graveyard. They stand on earth that has been dry for months and is now so hard the rainwater isn't soaking away, but pools around her feet, splashes as she steps forward, one arm outstretched.

This time it's a whisper, and she can barely hear it herself; it floats from her mouth, but is weighted and drowned by the rain.

'Maisie...'

'You think you can have her back?' Sharp steel cutting through the night, his voice comes sailing through the rain, keeling, tacking. She recognises the voice, but the words don't make any sense. 'You think, after everything I lost, *you* can have *her* back?' He shakes his head. His blond hair, bright with wet, even in the black night, flashes like a lighthouse each time the torchlight catches it. It is Leith Kirwan. Her boss. Why is he here? Her brain feels slow, sluggish.

'I can never get Katie back. And you took her. You took her from me. And her baby. You took it all.' He shakes his head, and the hand that holds Maisie's body pushes forward, and Maisie stumbles. Kneeling down now, she crashes forward with no sound.

'Maisie…'

'All the lives she could have lived. All of them, ripped from her…'

It's only now, as Maisie tips even closer to the earth – this once scorched earth, now swamped with rain it can't absorb – that Ana looks at him. Stares him in the eye. Shakes her head.

'Leith, I don't know what you're talking about. This is Maisie – she's my sister. What are you doing? Have you gone mad? She's not here to hurt me.'

Who is this man? Who is he to turn from protector to aggressor? Who is he to grab her sister by the scruff of the neck in the dead of night and bring her here?

'What are you doing?' she screams.

'Do you remember *my* sister? Little Katie Miller. Caitlin Miller. You remember her? Only sixteen years old when she died? When she hanged herself?'

Like gunfire, the rain slams hard against the pools on

the earth. The swell rises quickly, water pours from the roof of the church.

'What are you talking about? I didn't kill your sister! I didn't even know her!'

'It was you! It was you who lied to her – told her...' His face, black with the night, with his rage. Twisted in frenzy. Grief. Tight and unrepentant. Terrifying.

'You told her... You told her I'd *raped* you.' The words land as a spit. They merge with the water on the ground, but don't dissolve. They lie like spilled oil. A pollutant.

'Andy Miller. You are Andy Miller.' Reeling in shock, Ana stumbles. The wooden fence slippery beneath her fingers as she reaches back for support. 'But you have blond hair? Blue eyes?'

'Dyed my hair, and I wear blue contacts. I went to Australia in the end. After you took everything from me.'

The feeling of the pain, as it shot up from inside her. Pain she's never shaken off. As she tried to make herself ready, unsure, drunk. She hadn't said it loud enough. She hadn't wanted it. The feeling of the weight of him, the noise of him...

'But you did rape me. Sex needs consent. And I said no.' Saying it aloud, for the very first time – the release of the words. She's kept them back. Because she's never been exactly sure. Alice Sheppard's words have embedded themselves in her brain, like an advert ditty you never forget: 'It's not rape if you've already started.

What if he didn't hear you say no?' Even though people have said, and she knows now, still, there had been *shame*. She's never really been sure she'd said no *loud enough*. To be sure now, she screams it. Out into the night. She screams it at Andy Leith Miller Kirwan, she screams it so the dead can hear.

'You raped me! I said no!'

The rain falls. No one speaks. Leith shakes his head. She's not sure if he's disagreeing or unsure.

'She asked you. She said she'd been in the loo when you'd told Alice Sheppard, and she'd heard. She heard you say you hadn't wanted it. She asked you if it was rape, but you'd been sick. You'd thrown up in the sink, for fuck's sake. How can you even remember what you said? You were drunk. How can you even remember what I did? You went along with it all.'

Ana can feel her hands shaking. It's not the cold. Despite the rain, the temperature is still hot, humid. Her head is shaking too. The water flies from the ends of her hair, which has come loose in the run. She feels it whip her neck.

Is it the smell, most of all? The smell that has stayed with her? Of crisps, beer, of chewing gum and the flowers that had grown near the ground where she had lain. It had hurt, but he hadn't hit her. What had she done? She'd kissed him. Danced with him. Gone outside with him.

But she had been sixteen and she hadn't wanted sex.

'It was rape, Leith,' she says. She lifts her arms, gesturing to the sky. 'That's it. That's all of it.'

'No. I told her it was bullshit. I said you'd kissed me back. You'd come outside. *We'd* had sex. Not just me. And she screamed at me! Fuck.' He shakes his head. His hand is still on Maisie. She's still bent, leaning. Prostrate.

'Even so, killing herself? How is that—'

'She was pregnant. She was pregnant. We rowed, and I turned and walked away from her – I was so angry... and she followed me. I ran down the steps and she came after me. She put out her hand and I pulled away... She fell. I went to her. I ran! But she was curled at the bottom. When I lifted her, sat her down... There was already blood.' His eyes close and Ana shakes her head, thinking of Caitlin Miller. Of a wound.

'I will never, never forget the look on her face.'

He lets go of Maisie and she falls to the ground in a heap. Ana can see she's not badly hurt. But struggling. She lifts herself on her forearms, taking gasps of air, lifting herself out of the pools that now swell around the graves.

'A midwife helped Katie that night. But the baby had already gone. The miscarriage tore her apart. It left her half dead – she looked... I should have told someone – the doctor – mum. She wasn't herself. But she wouldn't look at me. Wouldn't look at a rapist! I'm no fucking rapist!'

Ana wonders if Maisie can run with her, if she grabs

her hand, can she run with her? But Maisie is coughing, head forward.

'She told me the next day she wondered if it was doled out because of what I did. Because of what *we* did. Because of what *you* told her. That there is equal measure in all things. That if I hadn't...' He is crying now. Ana can hear the crack in his voice but she can't make out tears on his face.

They are all drenched.

'And then that night she walked into the woods and hanged herself.' He takes a step towards Ana and his voice is louder now. 'And I found her! I found her hanging in the woods. Can you imagine what that's like? We moved away. Mum was a mess. She started drinking, then she got sick, and wouldn't fight it. Wouldn't eat the right things, just drank. Then I lost mum too.'

A gasp from Maisie attracts Ana's attention. She has turned her head towards Leith. Her voice is loud when she speaks, still gasping, still sore, but loud.

'Who was the father?'

Leith shakes his head. And then he smiles. In flashing drops of rain that catch his torch, veil his face, like a waterfall.

Maisie screams, banging the earth with the flat of her hand. 'Who was the father?'

Leith turns his smile to Ana. 'Leo fucking Fenton.'

70

Saturday 30th June

MAARTEN

There's the smell of burning. The rain has come just in time. A barn is ablaze on the edge of a field, and had it not been raining, the whole field would have caught alight. The fire is real, rising high in the sky like a twisting snake, but rain powers down.

The smoke makes him heady. It mingles with the rain and the already dark night becomes opaque.

He coughs as he climbs out of the car. He can see Adrika parking further up in the road.

Fay Seabrook appears to his left, like an apparition. She's standing at the edge of the road, just out beyond the pub. She wears a raincoat over her nightclothes.

'They're gone!' she screams.

'Get back inside!' he shouts. He'd been waiting for something, he just didn't know what. 'I'll get them. The graveyard,' he calls to Adrika.

Running through the fields, he throws his jacket off despite the rain, hooking it over his arm as he sees the church. The night is close. His feet slip in the wet, and it's hard to see with his glasses. The water blurs them. He pulls them off, running faster.

The track they follow takes them under a copse of trees and out the other side. Here, the temple lies white against the black of the sky. It's visible only in blinks, as his eyes work to keep out the rain. Adrika coughs next to him.

Searching the scene for a tell as they approach, he first sees someone tall. Blond hair, even in the dark.

Slotting together, like a puzzle, he fits the blond hair to the photo Sunny had shown Ben. The blond man had been standing next to Jack Thurbridge. Fenton had identified the man in the centre as the cyclist. Had Sunny never been more specific than that? Why the fuck? Maarten curses himself for not checking. He is softening. He needs to firm back up, tighten up.

Who had it been? He thinks of Sunny's words: Leith Kirwan, Ana's boss. He's standing tall, holding a gun in his hand.

And she'd had the affair with Leo in New York on a work conference. Kirwan would have been in the bar at some point too. He must have seen. He has all the clues to work with. Thoughts fall into place like dominoes.

Adrika is calling for backup as Maarten searches for the two women. He sees one, flat on the ground. And he hopes she is still alive, that they are not too late.

Searching again, he sees the other. Her figure is obscured by the wet, but he sees she is bending and rising, bending and rising.

He feels sick. 'Adrika, how long will backup be?'

'Don't know – ten minutes? Shall I go round the back of them?'

'Leith Kirwan is there with both women, and he's got a gun.' More than that, what he doesn't need to say, is while one is lying flat on the ground, the other is digging.

Digging in a graveyard.

'*Kak*,' Maarten mutters.

Leith Kirwan holds a gun, and it is pointed at the back of Maisie Seabrook's head, who lies on the ground.

'Shall I? Go round the back?' Adrika repeats.

'No,' he says. 'Or rather yes, but listen, stay hidden. We've got no protection and this man is dangerous. Do not come out unless I can disarm him, or he puts the gun down.' His whispers are fierce. 'I mean it, Adrika. You're there to assist once the shooter is disarmed. You are not to show yourself.'

'Right.'

Her hair plastered to her head, Adrika nods. He can see she's scared. He's terrified. She turns and runs down the field. She is a fading figure in the dark, washed away by the rain, and he is gripped by fear: that this is the last time he will see her. He almost calls her back, shouts her name.

Is it the heat that has loosened his sensibilities? Turned him into someone fearful? Made him aware of mortality? Or is it this graveyard, with its dark, its twinned sense of eternity and fleeting life?

He walks towards the tall pillars of the temple. The rain powers down on them and spills from the roof in floods. The ground is awash. The heavens have answered the long-standing call for rain. It will take the earth a moment to adjust.

'Leith,' he says. His voice reaches out into the dark, through the wetness.

There is no response. The gun remains pointed down; Ana Seabrook carries on digging a grave.

'Leith!' This time he is louder, and Leith's head turns quickly, responding to the shout like a gun has been fired.

'Who's that?' The gun lifts and points at Maarten. Again, that sense of death searching for where to land shifts and Maarten lifts both hands, stepping sideways to the tree that stands by the fence.

'It's DCI Jansen. It's the police. Please, don't do anything rash. Backup are on their way. It's over now. It's time to put down your weapon.'

'It's not over!' The scream flies through the wet night.

Maarten ducks behind the tree, panting. He takes a breath. His body lies flat up against the damp bark. The tree grounds him, offers him some protection.

It is clear Leith Kirwan has passed the point of talk-down. His anger is vivid in the dark, like a bonfire. There is no dampening it.

'Leith, please. You can't get away from this. But you can let the women go. You will help yourself in the long run if you can halt this now!'

'Please!' It's Ana Seabrook. 'Please help us! Maisie is…'

The sudden silence is swift, as Leith Kirwan lifts the gun and with one swing slams the butt into Ana's head. She falls sideways, landing on the earth that she has been digging.

Maarten drops to his knees and peers from behind the tree. Ana is lying, moaning, on the earth. She lifts herself, starting to crawl to Maisie, and Leith kicks her. Her body lifts and falls like a rag doll. But she lifts herself again and this time Leith points the gun. He's screaming at her as she tries to stand.

'Ever since you walked into that firm, looking like you had the world at your feet, I swore you would feel how I felt. You stole my life from me, Ana. You and Leo. You stole my sister and you stole my mother. All I have wanted, since you perched on that chair and looked so complete, so fucking happy, was to steal everything from you in return.'

Ana raises her head from the dirt. Her voice is hoarse. 'It was you. Wearing Leo's cap, following me, terrifying me.'

Leith is still. 'As terrified as my sister was when she walked in the woods? I don't think so. I thought it would be over, once Leo was dead. But it wasn't. And then they put that house up for sale. It was a calling card. He needed to lie near her. Near you. And near her. She needed to know I'd done it. Done it for her.'

Ana's voice gains strength. 'You think you're dispensing justice? You're not. You are a stalker, a rapist and a murderer!'

The gun wavers. Maarten stands. There's no time. This finger of fate, moving quickly in the night, is about to land. He can't waste any more time. He walks towards the graveyard. He can hear sirens in the background. But they will be too late. The armed units will not arrive soon enough. He cannot allow this man to kill these women.

'You ripped everything from me,' Leith says.

Ana Seabrook is kneeling in the dirt. She has made it to her sister, and she kneels over her body. The sound of the sobbing mixes with the falling rain, and the night is awash with dissolution. Disintegration.

'Leith, no!' Maarten speeds up as the gun lifts slightly.

Leith changes his stance, holds the gun more firmly and steadies his wrist with his other hand, preparing for the kickback.

'Don't shoot!' It's Adrika. She appears from the other side of the graveyard and he is surrounded.

It's like trying to cage a tiger with bare hands,

Maarten thinks. They cannot contain this rage. The gun will go off and someone will be shot.

He sees Adrika begin to run and he curses, running too.

The gun is wet and slick in the shadowy night; he whispers a message of love to Liv.

'Tell Ben I'm sorry,' Ana Seabrook calls, through sobs that fill the night. 'Tell him I'm sorry for all of this.'

And there's another voice too. 'Stay back, Adrika!' Harper Carroll appears, bent forward and sprinting.

A crash of thunder sounds, and they all race towards the gun.

Someone screams, someone cries.

The gun fires. And fires again.

They all fall. Sprawling, collapsing on the softening earth.

71

Saturday 30ᵗʰ June

MAARTEN

He's back in the hospital. This time it's his arm that's bleeding, and Liv sits holding his hand as he fades back into consciousness.

'Maart, how are you feeling?'

His view is fuzzy. The room is hot, but he can hear the rain outside. It's bright, but with the blue light of a predawn morning.

'What... what happened? Are they—?'

'They're all here.' Liv squeezes his hand. 'Adrika's fine. The two girls are OK. The man, Leith? He's in custody. Sunny took him in and he's waiting for you before he does anything. There's no panic for you to move. The doctors have said you're OK to go home once you've woken. They had to stitch you up. They gave you a local last night, but you were out of it. I think you'd banged your head. They said you might not remember.'

He can remember someone saying 'Sharp sting';

someone else had said 'Sit still'. He'd been sick. His head aches.

The memory of the dark, of the thundering rain, comes back to him. Makes him lie his head back on the pillow. And the sound of the shot. His arm hadn't hurt right away.

'It seems you were grazed by a bullet. One of the girls – Ana – said you ran towards it.' Liv's voice catches, and she stops for a second, strokes his hand. 'Maart...'

All he can remember is the rain, the feeling of being drenched, of even his feet soaking in his shoes. And when he'd seen the gun, and Harper, he'd run. Then lying on the ground as the rain fell into his eyes, his mouth, his nostrils. And his arm had stung then. He'd slipped away, into nothing.

'You fell and hit a stone on the way down. They panicked because you threw up, but it was just the once. You've been here for six hours, so they said as long as you take it easy you can leave. I knew you'd want to. I've brought you some clothes, and there's a shower just down the hall. You can't get your arm wet for ten days, so I've brought some cling film for you to wrap round it.'

He lies back, opens his eyes and holds her hand. The dark, the night. The rain. The gunshot. It won't leave his head. He sits upright. 'Did anyone get hit? Leith Kirwan, he shot the gun.'

'He shot three times,' Liv says. She covers his hand with hers and her face is wet with silent tears, like the quietening rain. 'One of the bullets cut into your arm, but it was a glancing shot. You'll be fine. We just need to watch out for infection. The second one...'

'Liv,' he says.

'It hit the other DI. Adrika is fine, but Harper, she's taken a bullet in the chest. She flung herself in front of it. Adrika's with her now.'

'But... how is she?'

Liv shakes her head. 'They don't know. She's not awake. She was in theatre for four hours, so it's early. They've taken the bullet out, and they've done everything they can. If she wakes up, they'll be able to assess a bit more. She lost a lot of blood.'

'You said three times. You said he shot the gun three times.'

'Maart, he turned the last one on himself. He held it to his head and pulled the trigger.'

A flash, a bang. Maarten feels the rain on his arms. The smell of the graveyard, wet and thick in the air – earth beginning to slip in his fingers as his hands flail outwards, grasping at something to hold him steady.

And the last bang. He couldn't see anything, but he imagines Leith turning the gun on himself. Everyone else flat to the floor. Falling on his sword. Trying for a very tragic death, revenge and pathos.

'But he survived?'

'Yes, but not for long. A lot of blood. Sunny has him under custody in the hospital but he won't survive.'

'Will she live? Will Harper live?'

Liv smiles at him; her tears increase. There's a tiny shake of her head. She strokes his hand. Her voice cracks as it whispers, 'I don't think so, Maart. They don't think so.'

'I need to go to Adrika. I need to go to them.'

The room is losing its dark as Maarten, dressed and showered, enters. Adrika sits at the edge of Harper's bed, holding her hand. The red hair is darker against the pillow, and there are tubes, the same sort Liv had when she was sleeping, waiting to wake.

He sits by Adrika.

She looks at him; her eyes glisten. There is dirt on her face. And blood. The ravages of the night are marked in black, red and grey. Her bare legs are muddied. She shivers slightly, but the heat is building in the room, after the break of the storm.

He pours a glass of water and gives it to her. Her hands tremble as she takes it.

Outside, the sun is rising. The birds are singing. There are doors slamming as cars pull up.

There is a peace in the room. He lays his hand over hers.

They sit.

72

Saturday 30th June

ANA

'Maisie, can you hear me?' Ana leans. Her sister's cheeks are blanched, and her eyelashes lie against them, dark, long.

'Mais?' Ana tries again, but her sister sleeps. Lies with her head tilted to the right and her mouth partly open.

'Is she awake?' Her mum slips in and sits next to Ana, placing one hand on Maisie's blanket, and the other takes Ana's hand, squeezes it tight.

'Not yet. They gave her something and it hasn't worn off. They put her in the MRI, but she was disorientated, distressed. Whatever they gave her they said would take a while to leave her system. It's all clear. She should be OK. She should be as right as rain when she wakes up.'

'And how are you, Ana? Are you OK?'

Nodding, Ana leans and puts her head on her mother's shoulder, starting to cry. 'Mum, it was horrible! I thought he was going to kill her. He *was* going to kill her. And it was all because of me.'

'Shhh,' says her mum. Slowly, she strokes her hair, smoothing down the mess, the dried knots, tangled by the rain, the running. 'Ana, love, they told me what he said. It was nothing to do with you. My poor Ana. When I heard what he'd done to you, all those years ago.'

Ana sobs. Her mind is sticky with the words from last night, the image of Maisie bent forward in the drowning earth. The sound of the gun. And the memory of years ago, of the sudden pain, as she had tried to make herself ready for something she couldn't stop.

'My Ana. All you have had to put up with. To deal with.'

The sunlight is creeping through the blinds as Ana lifts her head. It's a gentle yellow. She can't hear the rain. It must have stopped. It will feel fresh outside.

'The other policewoman. Have you heard how she is?'

Fay Seabrook shakes her head. Her blue eyes are watery, her cheeks pale with tiny roses. 'She had quite serious surgery, I think. They're just waiting.'

Again, Maisie tipping forward, the rain lashing down, bouncing on her head, her arms. The flash of the gun in the glancing torchlight, the ricochet. Like spinning on the waltzers, images flashing up, spinning round.

'Have you heard about Ben?' her mum says, and Ana shakes her head.

She just can't think about him. He had shut her out. Maisie has to come first.

'Ana, he was attacked. He's in hospital. I don't know any details. One of the police officers mentioned it. I'll find out more for you.'

Still she can't think of him. Maisie lies here, the DI unconscious. She is at the heart of all of this and she can't pull it all together.

'Look, they're bound to release him now. He won't go back to the prison. Once we know a bit more, shall I ask that he's brought to the pub? He could come and stay with us?' her mum says, smiling, her hand still stroking her hair, smoothing out the worry. 'We have room. You wouldn't have to decide anything straight away.'

'Mum.' Her voice is a whisper. 'I can't think right now. It's Ben. Of course he must come to us. But I feel…' It's too much. She will go to Ben once she's sure about Maisie.

Next to them, in the first light of the morning, Maisie opens her eyes. 'Have they got him?' she asks. Her hand reaches out and holds Ana's. 'Is he gone?'

Ana nods, leaning and kissing her sister's cheek.

'Yes,' she says. 'All gone.'

The sunlight is warm, and Maisie's cheeks have some pink in them now, like a pale rose, or marshmallows.

'And he's not coming back,' she whispers.

73

Sunday 1st July

BEN

The first thing that hurts is his throat. It's swollen, and when he tries to swallow, he gags. His eyes fly open and something starts beeping. He tries to lift his arms, to release his hands and claw at his face, instinct driving them before his mind realises that he's choking to death. But his arms won't move – they're heavy too.

His eyes fly open; the whiteness is blinding. But there's no air.

No air to even mouth the word 'Help.'

And then the face of someone he doesn't recognise appears, and the room spins, and he fades.

When he wakes next, his throat is dry, still swollen, but there's no blockage.

And there she is. She stands at the door. She is crying and there is a cut on her face, and her hand has a bandage wrapped around it.

Ana.

He opens his mouth but it's still impossible to make a sound. Like a fish, he opens it, closes it.

Still there; time hangs like a picture frame around her face, and he closes his mouth. Using his eyes to speak to her.

He worries she won't move. That she'll just stay there and watch him. He's felt like nothing for such a long time. A pack animal. A hound. He's been herded. Locked up. Mealtimes, exercise times, shower times. It's all been about reduction, like boiling a sauce down so it's thick and turgid. He's congealed.

And then she comes.

Ana.

Her arms as warm as he's remembered.

Ana.

74

ANA

'Is he OK?' Ana means it. She's not just being polite. Jack had done nothing wrong. He'd pulled her off the tracks, been arrested for becoming involved. She imagines he's angry.

'Yeah, he's fine. He's back at work. The press around the shooting has been everywhere – he was arrested but everyone knows he's innocent now. He's enjoying a brief flirtation with fame. If anything, he's a sympathetic figure. Gets to bask in reflected horror.' Fran rolls her eyes, moving her hands as she speaks, pulling her chair in. She leans in close, her long hair brushing Ana's hand as she hugs her gently.

'But it wasn't him it happened to,' Fran continues, whispering the next three words, 'it was you. And there's nothing for you to bask in except nightmares. So really, it's all about you. Don't you start worrying about how anyone else is coping with this.'

Shaking her head quickly, trying to brush it off, but

her eyes sting again. At some point these tears must stop. She can't drink water fast enough to replenish them.

'I heard he was framed by coincidence. The Leith thought something was going on between you two, that it made him an easy target. And he knew Leo worked in pharmaceuticals abroad... I don't think even Leith knew about the university thing. But following you on the platform, pushing Jack. And apparently he paid that motorcyclist to scare you, part of his whole tactics. The Leith. Who would have known?'

'It's OK. I get Ben back. I wouldn't have otherwise. It's been horrible, horrible, horrible. But it's over. And Ben's coming out. I saw him today. He's OK.'

'Are you OK together?' Fran asks, reaching for the chocolates she had brought, opening them and eating one, gesturing to Ana to eat one too. Her fingers deft with the box, her hands sweeping quickly.

'Yes. Baby steps. But yes.' She hadn't told him about sleeping with Leo, but she's decided she will. 'He told me he loves me. I know he loves me. It will be OK.'

'Must be a bit weird. Not having seen him for almost two years.'

There's a movement outside. Ana sees Jansen climb out of his car. The sun is back. The light bounces off the bonnet and Jansen's face looks older, tired, in the glare.

'One step at a time, I think. Just knowing he's safe is good for today. I've dreamed about him, longed for him. But I think at some point he became an idea... he was like a fragment of a memory. Not a living thing. He chose to do this bit on his own. Part of that is rejection.' She ducks her head, her eyes dry, but she's suddenly tired. An ache begins quickly in her head and she knows Jansen's come to update her. It makes her shake, thinking about that night. She's not sure when the nightmares will finish.

She reaches for a chocolate so she has something to do and Fran kisses both her cheeks, stands, collecting her bag. The energy that is Fran moves backwards, nodding a goodbye, and she's almost gone.

'So, are you seeing Jack again? Like on a date?' Ana says, remembering she has forgotten to ask.

'Jack812? That dreamboat?' Fran winks and makes a clicking noise with her tongue, clapping her hands quickly. Laughing. 'You betcha!'

Jess enters quietly, her walk slow. Her hair, Ana sees, has green streaks at the end that pick up the colour of her eyes, which fill as she sits before Ana.

Reaching out, Ana takes her hand. 'Jess, what is it?'

She shakes her head. 'I'm so sorry,' she whispers. 'Aggie's finally in a home now, and I went to clear out her stuff. Me and Charlie did it together. A whole life, now in a few bin bags.' She shakes her head again. She is crying now, and her voice breaks as she pushes a book into Ana's hands. It has 'Diary' written on the front, and Jess has it open at a page with a bookmark.

'I found these diaries. She'd kept them for years. I sat down and read them all. Every single one. I started reading them just for me. But all the babies she's brought into the world – there are some stories in there. And then I found this. All what you've been through.' She smooths the page out on Ana's lap.

'It should make sense,' Jess says. 'I'll go and make us a cup of tea, and leave you to read it in peace.'

Starting at the top, Ana sees the date: June 2010. The handwriting a spider's scrawl; it takes her a moment to make it out. It's when she sees the name 'Katie' that she catches her breath, reading quickly, then rereading. There's one sentence:

... Katie said her boyfriend knows. He found her being sick after school and she'd only just done a test. Later he sent her a text saying he can't see her for a few days, that he needs more time. What is it with these boys? This girl is no one's toy to be chucked to the side. She owes him nothing – but she's still feeling guilty. He didn't even stick around long enough to hear that he wasn't the father. She told me they only slept together a few weeks ago, and that girl wouldn't even know yet if it was his. She's at least eight weeks gone.

I finally pulled it out of her – David Tabbard is the father. That young teacher at the school – they all race after him like puppies. She said he'd been helping her with a science project, and she'd wanted to enter a competition. Bet he thought all his Christmases had come at once, having her on his own. Beautiful little thing she is, and she don't even know it. It happened quickly, she said – she doesn't regret it. But it was only afterwards he said it was to be just the once. That he was leaving the school. She knew she'd been dropped like a hot potato. That teacher needs locking up!

I wanted to go to the police about him, but she didn't let me. Says she's happy just as she is – she doesn't care about any of them any more. Just the baby. She holds her stomach like she's cradling silver. She gleams, that one. No looking back. There's no regret.

Ana lets the diary fall to her knee and she grips the arm of the chair for support. So it had never been Leo. His guilt, Ben's guilt – Andy Miller's anger. It had never been him.

Jess appears in the doorway, holding two mugs of tea. 'I'm so sorry,' she whispers.

Epilogue

'She was going to be all mine.

I want to just say now that it's the right decision. Whatever anyone says. It's the right decision. I've just cried and cried. So if anyone reads this – I'm doing the right thing. I just can't carry on. I can't carry on like this.

I look at things. Everyday things – my toothbrush, the mug, the kettle when it boils. My phone. My pen at school. I hold it in my hand but I can't use it. School is so pointless! It makes me want to scream. I locked the door in the toilets at break today. I could hear some girls smoking and I sat quiet. I don't belong here any more. I don't feel, really, not any more. It's like I'm numb. It's like it's me who died.

I want to be dead.

Maybe, maybe I could find her. Maybe she's waiting for me. And I could get to hold her?

I know I've done something wrong. I should have spoken up when I heard the girl crying and being sick. I could have helped her. It makes me feel sick, to think of her and now here I am. We both let her down.

I'm so sorry. I really love you Mum and Andy. I really do.'

Maarten reads this goodbye letter. He thinks of the smell of the summer, of the trees in the woods.

The letter had been found in Leith Kirwan's apartment. It had been in his bedside table. Its edges worn and faded. Read. Reread.

It was evidence, clear-cut. It was laid out. A young girl consumed by grief.

Her brother had left school, started a new life. But as he had told Ana, sitting in the London office, seeing her arrive for an interview, successful, in love... He had asked her about Ben in the interview, and she had even mentioned Leo.

After that, it had been planning. Just casual interest, from a distance. Hearing of the trip. Scoping it out. Renting the shed. He could keep the body there, under lock and key. Never quite getting rid of it.

But the house had been put up for sale – his hand was forced. And what better way to finish it all than by setting up Ana as an accomplice? First to suggest she had killed Leo, and then, when that didn't work, to suggest Leo was never dead at all. To seed the idea in the mind of the police that Leo and Ana had faked Leo's death. The photos he'd found on Leo's phone suggesting an affair provided a motive.

Insane with grief. Insane. He wasn't the first.

Maarten thinks of his own reaction. To zip himself up. To hold it in. He had always been anxious to move on. He had always struggled with cars. When he drove, he drove against himself. There had been an incident in Rotterdam, and then St Albans.

The haziness of death that has hung over him since Liv's car crash – since he has grasped hold of the memory of hearing the news of his parents. All that loss.

He'd known something was wrong, started to weep silently as the *politieagent* came into the house and his grandparents sat him down.

Liv had suggested that instead of a beach holiday, they go to Rotterdam. That they show the kids the graves. That Maarten visit the graves. Something had come full circle. Dots were merging into a solid line.

He thinks of Katie Miller, feeling that everything she had in the world had vanished. That the grief she held in her heart was too big to carry. Much too heavy a load. A father who'd left them, a teacher who'd abused his position and abandoned her, miscarriage and only sixteen.

His own heart, ripped down the centre and, even now, scarred over. His parents' car had veered and plunged off the road: 'sudden impact', 'fatal injuries'. He had sat upright on the edge of the sofa at his grandparents' house. His *opa* had held his hand and his *oma* had wept.

It hadn't seemed real. He'd tried to imagine their last thoughts, as he tried to imagine Katie Miller's now. He wonders if his parents' last thoughts had been of him, as Katie's had been of the baby she'd lost.

Maarten had chased down the father, the teacher – he

was already serving time in the same prison Ben Fenton had been in.

He thinks of how she must have walked into the forest once the sun had sunk and the moon had risen. She had found a branch she could reach. The report said that there had been a tree stump nearby. That she must have climbed on the tree stump and jumped.

The smell of the forest in the dark of a summer's night. The sound of the chorus of creatures. The clicking, the creaking. The humming alive all around her.

The funeral of his parents, stark in his head, with blankets of mist lying across the flat land of Holland. They had gone back to his family home in Rotterdam afterwards. There had been dishes still in the drying rack that hung above the sink. Clothes sat in the basket at the foot of the stairs to be taken up and placed in drawers. And they had packed up his things to move to his grandparents' farm.

The dry voice of the priest echoing in the church. The sobs of his *oma*. His own throat aching.

And then Andy Miller, running to the forest, searching for his sister. Finding her.

So much death. So much loss.

He closes the letter. It had been much read. It had been treasured, as it should. Andy Miller had sought vengeance where he should not. He had allowed his grief to twist him. But he had remembered his sister. He had kept her alive.

He sometimes wonders if in trying to close the wound of his parents' death, he had closed off a part of himself. Maybe Liv's crash had opened the part he'd kept locked for years.

The sun is back in the sky as he glances outside. The street, the trees, the tips of the park he can see in the distance – it all blurs.

Blurs beneath the tears that fall for all of them.

About the Author

RACHAEL BLOK grew up in Durham and studied Literature at Warwick University. She taught English at a London Comprehensive and is now a full-time writer living in Hertfordshire with her husband and children. Her first novel, *Under The Ice* was published in 2018 by Head of Zeus.

Acknowledgments

Huge thanks are owed to people without whom the book would not exist. Firstly, to Eve White, my brilliant agent, and her assistant Ludo Cinelli. They're the perfect team and I'd be nowhere without them. Also, to all those at Head of Zeus, in particular to Laura Palmer, the best editor in town, and Chrissy Ryan, Florence Hare, Christian Duck, Nikky Ward, Victoria Joss, Leah Jacobs-Gordon and Jenni Davis.

Many people have generously donated their time and professional expertise, including Rachel Barnes, of Three Raymond Buildings, and David Bently QC, who provided the legal advice which allowed me the necessary scope for the plot. Ben's storyline could not have been written without Supervising Officer Kevin James' invaluable tour of a prison in County Durham. Thanks to him also for the coffee, and the chat with Christine Foster, the inspiring librarian at the prison.

Emma Game's expertise in medical trials is enormously appreciated, as is Cathy Leahy's insight into the soil map research. Also, thanks to Matthew Quinney for his insider knowledge of New York bars.

Also, a huge thanks to Richard Johnson, an officer in the Hertfordshire police service, for his time; I am indebted to him. And not forgetting Pieter Blok, for all his support and photographic services.

For all of this advice, I may have twisted procedure and the information received a little at times for the sake of the novel, but this is all me.

I could not write a single word without the support of the best of friends, including Rachael Mason, Imogen Pitt, Rima Nixon, Zoe Latimer, Rachel Mason, Lucy Higgs, Simone Isaacs, Ben Jones, Matthew and Jane Beniston, Helen and Liam O'Connor, Victoria Quinney, Marielle Sutherland, Emma Leahy, Rachael Oomen, Louise Batty, Tara Abelaira, Shelagh O'Connell, Aine Magee, Hilary McKie, Nicola James, Vicki Atkinson, Pamela Flowers, Geraldine Gardener, Anna Davies, Rebecca Fox, Emma Betteridge, Serena Pattison, Hannah Hope and Megan Foxcroft.

Always thanks to the inspiring Curtis Brown Creative course, and all I learnt from Louise Wener and Anna Davis, as well as a hugely supportive writing community, including Erin Kelly, Angela Clarke, Roz Watkins, Clare Empson, Victoria Selman, Melanie Golding, Alex Dahl, J.S. Monroe, Lesley Thomson, Tania Steere, Ella Berman, Louise McCreesh, Jodie Chapman, Ailsa Caine, Claire McVey, Neil Canetty-Clarke and Christine Evans. Also, thanks to my Bookclub who choose books I'd never think of and I'm all the better for reading: Kelly Irwin, George Cooper, Naomi Love, Sarah Milton, Clare Sayce, Sarah Shaw, Fay McNaught, Kathryn Crowdell.

DCI Jansen wouldn't be the same without the stunning locations of St Albans and Blakeney, both the real and the slightly blurred that appear in the novel. And whilst I have blended the villages of Ayot and their geography a touch, I have in no way exaggerated the beauty of the Palladian Church in Ayot St Lawrence, the background to novel.

And finally, my family. The best of parents, my sister Dawnie, and my first reader, Rob, who listens to all my ideas even when he's far too tired. And my two children, who are unfailingly the best parts of my day.

A letter from the publisher

We hope you enjoyed this book. We are an independent publisher dedicated to discovering brilliant books, new authors and great storytelling. If you want to hear more, why not join our community of book-lovers at:

www.headofzeus.com

We'll keep you up-to-date with our latest books, author blogs, tempting offers, chances to win signed editions, events across the UK and much more.

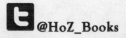 @HoZ_Books

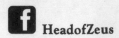 HeadofZeus

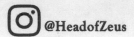 @HeadofZeus